A KILLING

AT

EARLY DAWN

ALSO BY

FICTION

A Killing at Early Dawn

Redemption By Default

SinSation

Dinner With Lexie (A short story)

The Silent Syringe (A short story)

The Queen's Quest (A short story)

ALL-IN (A short story)

The Good Daughter (A short story)

Free Psychological Thriller Novella: I Was Not Innocent

You can pre-order ***Sin of the Priest*** on Amazon by CLICKING HERE

———◆———

NONFICTION

Letting Him Go When He Cheats

The Treasured Coloring Book Collection For Toddlers

A KILLING
AT
EARLY DAWN

KATHRYN McGRADY

For my amazing sons:
Chris Carter and Dr. Daw-Nay N.R. Evans Jr.
Thank you for believing in me.

———— ◆○◆ ————

For my husband Kenneth N. McGrady, my Scrabble King,
who has shown me that the only voice I need to trust is my own.

PROLOGUE

H igh above the Grant's home, in the celestial realm, a table, scarred by eternity, cradled a Cosmic Chessboard forged from the marrow of creation.

Two forces met across the board—one, an ocean of serenity, the other, a tempest of shadow and defiance.

The Devil's voice, smooth and venomous, curled through the void. "Shall we play, Creator? Or has the weight of eternity made You... cautious?"

God regarded the Devil, he knew him well. "You only summon the board, Fallen Angel, when You crave destruction."

On earth, in a quiet neighborhood called Cypress Lane, Lexie Grant turned in her bed and woke with a sudden, inexplicable ache—like something precious was about to be taken from her... and she wouldn't know how to stop it.

Lexie didn't believe in God.
He never touched her life—until now.

WILLIAM & LEXIE

The room shimmered in candlelight, golden flickers dancing across silk sheets and tracing delicate patterns along the walls. A breeze slipped through the open window, carrying jasmine—sweet enough to convince Lexie for a second, that everything was still safe. But she knew better, something had shifted, something she couldn't name or identify.

Candlelight meant romance. Jasmine meant comfort. A familiar song meant the night would end the way it always did—William charming, Lexie melting, both of them pretending the cracks didn't exist.

But the space beside her stayed cold—and lately, cold felt like a warning.

She lay on her side, fingers grazing the sheet where his body should have been and listened. The house held its breath. No keys. No footsteps. No quiet laugh drifting down the hall.

The phone on the nightstand lit up. One new notification. Not from William.

Her stomach tightened, and she hated herself for it—hated how her mind went to the same place it always went now. Who is he with? What excuse will it be tonight?

She reached over and turned on her Bose speaker, forcing the room to fill with the smooth voice of Luther Vandross. A voice that promised devotion even when real life didn't.

Lexie adjusted the strap of her lacy lingerie, not for vanity—never for vanity—but because she needed to feel like the woman William still reached for. The woman he swore he loved. The woman who didn't ask for more than he could give. But her natural elegance carried an underlying vulnerability that showed through. A vulnerability that made her more like the woman she'd always longed to be in private.

Scrolling through her phone, she paused on pictures of carved wooden cribs, tiny baby clothes, and colorful onesies. This life—the one she dreamed of— defined her deepest craving. A warmth tugged at her heart as she lingered on images of pregnant bellies and newborn babies. Without that future, the future she had imagined, one she had tried to will into existence, remained difficult, and the hunger sharp, like grief.

This life, the one she'd pictured since she was a little girl, was becoming a deadline.

William didn't want children; he had made that clear. But she did, and a small regret lingered.

I should have been clear about my need to have a baby... before we got married. I should have explained to him that not becoming a mother wasn't an option.

She had forgiven him for that indiscretion years ago, but she hadn't forgotten and the trust, once solid, had shattered into a million broken pieces. She continued strolling, her mind restless. There were other things she had forgiven, too. Not forgotten but filed away the way a careful woman files away evidence. The way a wife does when she loves a man she doesn't trust.

I've been the loving, forgiving wife, it's my turn to have my needs fulfilled. I love William, but the clock is ticking and if I don't get pregnant soon... I never will. How do I—

"Ahem. Ahem." William's voice cut through the room, warm and teasing.

Lexie glanced up, her lips curving into a loving smile as her husband stood there, framed in the soft light spilling from the hall. His tall figure, draped in black silk pajamas, with the top button unfastened, exposed a smooth, solid chest that glistened in the low light of the lamp. Truly a vision of seduction, William shifted through a series of poses, each one eliciting a laugh from her.

Her eyes took him in the way they always did, like hunger, like history, and still that small hard knot inside her didn't loosen.

"May I have this dance?" He extended his hand in a grand gesture, his eyes sparkling with mischief.

Lexie couldn't conceal the smile that spread across her face. She placed her cell phone on the nightstand as if setting down a weapon. She reached out, her fingers sliding into his fingers. Rising from bed she studied William. *How does he do it? How does he make me love him so much that my heart pounds so hard it may burst? Yet, a little part of me dies a slow death every day. That's not a good thing.*

His arm slipped around her waist drawing her close and guiding her into a slow swaying rhythm. They moved together into a sensual dance, romantic music filling the entire room. His warm hand rested on the small side of her back, fingers grazing her spine while his other held hers, their fingers interlaced. His eyes lingered on her.

William's thumb traced a line along her back, sending soft intense shivers through her.

"You're beautiful," he whispered, his voice low, like someone sharing a secret.

Her insecurities flared, almost interrupting the moment as her cheeks turned pink. But his hand on her back tightened, reassuring her with a gentle squeeze. She pulled back, admiring his face, and he smiled at her with such soft tenderness that it quieted every anxious thought in her mind.

"You are everything to me," William continued. "Everything I could ever want, I find in you."

Lexie held the smile. And still something didn't fit.

Their bodies pressed together, breaths mingling as the dance slowed, each step heavier with emotion. He leaned in, his forehead brushing hers, his breath a warm caress on her cheek. She slid her hands up to his chest, the pulse beneath her palm beating in time with the music—and maybe something more.

They talked, murmuring soft words about the memories they shared. Their closeness communicated in the way they held each other in those dark moments. She laughed as he recalled a story from years ago, their marriage young, their lives simpler and their dreams were like untouched snow. She peered into his eyes, seeing a love and desire that had strengthened over the years.

William made a quick move in the dance and Lexie stumbled. They both fell in a heap on the bed. Their breath came in short gasps as they suppressed their giggles. She propped herself up on one elbow as she glanced down at her husband, who peered back at her as if she were the only woman on earth. She swam in those eyes and couldn't help but admire and adore him—for the most part.

The silence, like a warm fuzzy blanket, covered them in a special warmth. Lexie reached up and brushed a strand of hair back from his forehead. Her fingers lingered over the small creases across his forehead, trying to erase the worries and burdens he carried. She leaned over and kissed it.

Lexie continued with small kisses on his collarbone and across his chest. Her breath grazed over his left nipple as she explored every inch of the body that belonged to her. Her hand moved further down the familiar trail, and she caught a glimpse of his face. The huge confirmation that he appreciated the attention delighted her.

William smiled. His eyes closed for a moment, savoring the closeness. His hand, with a mind of its own, slid around her waist. He grabbed her and their bodies were grounded at that moment, a fluid connection that bonded their minds as well as their bodies. They lay in that embrace, their eyes locked, their souls healing. A fragile cocoon held them in that space of shared memories and whispered promises of a shared future.

Their movements took on a deep meaning; their breathing, their fingers tracing little patterns along each other's bodies. Lexie's worries faded away and she relaxed in his arms. His hands made tiny circles on her back, and the warmth calmed her. His presence offered her a soothing certainty that lingered in the air, like an unspoken promise.

A timeless understanding existed between them and neither one of them needed to speak. This understanding had been built over countless moments—thousands upon thousands of gestures and silent looks. A natural language, created over time. Neither of them needed to define or manipulate a language they both understood. Their sweet language of love. Sometimes words were spoken, but other times, complete silence, and the complete awareness that their love could either build a grand life or create a living nightmare. A choice of which they were aware. And that choice happened with each conversation and with each touch.

Nothing else existed in that wordless intimacy except knowing with certainty that they belonged to each other.

Lexie caught an obvious display of love and joy resting in his eyes. A visual respite from all the worries and frustrations of her day. During these times she believed everything would be as it should be.

Their breaths blended into a harmonious rhythm, a melody theirs alone in the darkness as they held each other. In his arms, she found a profound sense of peace, her sole protector. No matter what challenges she faced, he would take care of it, as he always did. She could always lean on him for comfort and support. But a raging fire burned within her and nothing would be the same again.

A gentle glow of moonlight filtered through the blinds, casting soft shadows across the bed where Lexie lay nestled close to William. A lingering intimacy spread a warmth through their entwined bodies and that special bond surfaced in the dark hours as they lie side by side. During those moments, the world didn't matter. Her heart raced as her breath slowed, savoring the soft steady rhythm of his breathing next to her. *I'm glad you're in my life; I love you so much.*

She draped an arm around the familiar waist, enjoying the reassuring solidity under her hand. These were special moments where they lay wrapped in the soft fabric of the sheets, which made her bold and adventurous. Her hand traced gentle patterns along his side, pressing her cheek against his shoulder. *Dare I ask?*

"Let's do it again," she whispered.

Amused, he laughed and brushed a stray strand of hair from her face. He admires her naked body.

"Not possible," he teased. "Woman, you're insatiable. Beautiful, but truly insatiable." He planted a kiss on her forehead.

Lexie raised an eyebrow, a small grin tugged at her lips. "Can't get it up?" she challenged.

"That kindergarten psychology doesn't work on me," he replied, his voice full of humor.

"Oh?" She leaned in, pressing her lips to the side of his neck. She dared him with small, tender caresses. Despite his feeble attempts to hide it, his body responded. She smiled.

"Mm-hmm," he groaned, straining to resist. "Is that the best you can do woman? You need to bring your A game with me, Lex."

"I will if you will." She laughed.

"Grasshopper, do you question my skills?" William teased.

Lexie enjoyed playing with him, and he enjoyed playing with her. One of many reasons she loved him. Their relationship flowed with ease and humor.

She planted little kisses along his collarbone, and down his chest. She paused to pay equal attention to each nipple, her tongue inching to a forbidden area much further down.

He closed his eyes and gasped.

"You sure?" she teased.

His resistance collapsed. He didn't need further prompting. He kissed her back with equal intensity. "Insatiable," he whispered again. He leaned in and brushed her lips in another long lingering kiss.

Their lovemaking wrapped them in a private cocoon not touched or entered by anything or anyone. In the afterglow, they lay together with her head resting on his chest.

Her hand drifted over his chest, her fingertips traced the faint outline of a scar near his collarbone, an old wound, a relic from a time before they met, when his father would beat him for no good reason. He never talked about it much, but it weighed on him. It would have a profound effect on anyone. He wouldn't welcome her questions, but the scar fascinated her. She loved how it told a story of resilience, of survival.

"Does it ever ache?" she whispered.

His hand paused in her hair, and he glanced at her, his eyes warm but puzzled. "The scar?"

She nodded, her fingers lingering over the faint ridge of raised skin.

"Not anymore," he said, his voice low and steady. "It used to when the weather turned. But now it's a part of me. Like you."

Lexie tilted her head up. Her lips were curved into a small smile. "I'm a scar now, am I?"

"No, not a scar," he chuckled. "You're more like a tattoo—something I chose. Something beautiful and permanent."

The corners of her eyes crinkled as she laughed, pressing a kiss to his chest. "You know, I could be mistaken, but I believe that might be the most romantic thing you've ever said to me."

His hand resumed its gentle stroking of her hair, his fingers threading through the soft strands. "It's the truth, Lex. You are a part of me in a way nothing else ever has been or ever could be."

Her smile faded as she rested her head back on his chest. *All the moments that had brought them here, the mistrust, the miscommunications, the good times, and the bad times. Yes... even after William's affair, they had made it work. They had always found their way back to each other.*

"I don't say it enough—"

'Say what?" he asked, his hand pausing mid-stroke.

"How much I love you. How much you mean to me."

Staring at Lexie, He leaned down and pressed a kiss at the top of her head.

"You don't have to say it, I feel it every day."

She closed her eyes, letting his words sink in. The warmth of his embrace and the strength in his voice made her whole.

As his breathing deepened and his hand fell still in her hair, she stayed awake a little longer, savoring the moment.

Okay, later today, I will tell him.

With the thrill of the morning lingering, she closed her eyes and fell asleep, a satisfied smile on her face.

BOOM! BOOM!

The floor beneath the bed began to vibrate.

Her eyes flew open. She shook William.

"Wake up. Wake up."

He turned to her groggily.

"Lexie."

BOOM!

Another jarring boom reverberated and echoed throughout the room. The walls shook as if responding to an unseen force.

They glanced around the room. Nothing.

She grabbed William, but he pulled away and sprung out of bed.

He rushed to the front door. She followed, her pulse quickening.

When William opened the door, cold brutal air rushed in. Nothing visual, but he heard the sharp barking of his neighbor's dog, it stopped abruptly.

He slammed the door shut, his expression unreadable.

"What was that?" she asked.

"Let's go back to bed; it could have been anything, maybe some early morning construction work nearby," William replied.

"I guess," she said, resigned.

⚫

From the celestial realm, God reprimands the Devil.

"Fallen Angel, you must play by the rules. Unless I decide otherwise, they shall hear nothing, they shall see nothing. If you can't abide by my command, this game ends." God lounged back in His chair, waiting for the Devil's response. "I wanted to shake them up a little bit. You know, have a little fun. It won't happen again, Holy One." The Devil sneered. "But we both know I should be given a head start. You are, after all, the holy one."

God, in His wisdom, allowed the Devil to whisper and tempt William and Lexie.

The Devil whispered, exuding a thick dark smoke that surrounded her ear as every word floated to her brain.

"Lexie, hear me; you've sacrificed enough while he dismisses your pain and your dreams. He will never change. You deserve this. It isn't a betrayal, Lexie; it's your destiny. You are meant to be a mother. Think about it, didn't he betray you first? Lie beneath another man and the seed you seek will be yours within a fortnight. Take what's yours; William will never know. Every evil deed, every bad word to William, is my work! Behold, I am the Devil," said the Devil.

The dark smoke floated to William, circling him like prey. A cold whisper reached the inner lobes of William's ear oozing from the Devil's mouth.

"It's too late, William, You've already lost her. No matter what you do, she's slipping away. You are not enough, you never were. She needed a man who could give her what she wanted. And you failed her. Now, she resents you. Every time she looks at you, she sees the man who robbed her of motherhood and denied her dreams. She's already pulling away—she's looking elsewhere, and she will betray you. You're pathetic, and deep down, you know it. Every evil deed, every bad word to Lexie, is my work! Behold, I am the Devil," said the Devil.

"Your whispers are futile, for My children hear My voice within their hearts, needing no intermediary," God said. "Fallen Angel, I've given you an advantage I did not have to give. Now we must leave and get back to the Cosmic Chessboard. Let them sleep, they have much ahead of them, they will need their strength."

An evil, dark thunderous laugh erupted from the devil.

ONE DAY EARLIER – A QUIET STORM

D awn crept across the sky with vivid sparkling shades of cobalt blue and bright orange that painted the clouds with a gentle blush that resembled cotton candy. Not a rainbow but a colorful sight to behold. The tranquility of the morning spread throughout the neighborhood, it filled the trees and touched every single blade of grass. This dawn promised a quiet, uneventful day—perfect, serene, nothing strange or surreal. The Grant's home sat on Cypress Lane, calm and undisturbed, wrapped in a cocoon of peace. However...

The Cosmic Chessboard game continued.

The Devil's grin flared. "Destruction? I offer freedom. Choice. And I have selected our pawns. They are... exquisite."

A gesture from His hand, and the air fractured. Images emerged: Lexie Grant, a successful, insecure executive, her eyes ablaze with sorrow and defiance; William Grant, an unemployed architect, his heart a fortress cracking under unseen weight.

God's voice, gentle and thunderous, replied, "They are not yours."

The Devil's smile deepened. "But they are already in motion. Lexie has a burning desire to have a baby. But she's also insecure and distrustful. William's recent unemployment has destroyed his pride and left him with a need for control. They are perfect for this game. Shall we see whose hand guides their final step?"

God's fingers grazed the board. "The rules remain. No mortal can witness the storm we cast, No mortal can witness the Cosmic Chessboard, and I will illuminate the path, but they must walk it."

The Devil's laughter, rich with malice, reverberated. "And I... I will show them what the abyss holds. You promise grace—I promise truth." Shadows spilled from His form, seeping into the board, dark veins through marble. "Pain is clarity. And clarity... never lies."

God's reply came firm, woven with eternity. "Yet grace shines even in ruin."

The Devil's eyes flashed. "But ruin... always keeps its promises. Shall we play then? Or will You surrender them to me now?" The void braced, the fabric of existence stretched taut between them.

The Devil, His voice low and tempting, whispered, "Lexie will break and wonder if You ever truly listened. William will confront himself and in his reflection, he may choose me."

God's voice, soft as dawn, answered, "Yet within their breaking, they may find their strength. Hearts, Fallen Angel, are never easily claimed."

The Devil's grin sharpened. "Then let's see who claims them."

The shards of creation burned through the sky, scattering destiny upon the earth.

With an inevitability older than time—

God moved the first piece... and within seconds the sky turned black.

Lightning flashed across the sky as a dark dense cloud shattered the dawn, blanketing the sky as if the earth itself were under a terrible siege. Boisterous thunder followed the white lightning that stabbed its way through the terrestrial darkness, breaking through the once silent and peaceful neighborhood.

A strong and fierce unrelenting wind swayed trees, and tore leaves from the branches, sending them tumbling across the Grant's lawn in brown spirals. It sent debris flying, threatening to harm anyone in its path.

Among the chaos, a bright blazing object plummeted from the darkened sky, hurtling earthward, fierce, and undeniable in its destination. A meteoroid? Not likely. A comet? No, this carried a far more sinister and deliberate intent.

A gigantic black and white chessboard engulfed in huge flames *slammed* onto Grant's lawn with a *thud* that shook the earth. The house shuddered, the grass singing and curling from the searing heat.

A monstrous black serpent, dark as night, twisted around the burning Cosmic Chessboard, its thick coils gleaming and glistening in the flames, its hard scales reflecting a strange and evil sheen that forbade and deterred any mortal who dared to approach it.

Scorched earth and burning leaves filled the air. A vicious and evil laugh vibrated through the air, breaking through the crackle of flames and the howling wind. It grew louder and bolder. The stark menace pressed down on the trembling house on Cypress Lane as each wave of laughter shook the foundation of the home, straining it, the home cracking from the pressure.

A darkness settled around the house like a blanket as the laughter faded and a thick oppressive silence followed.

In the realm beyond time, where light and shadows danced an eternal waltz, God and the Devil sat across from each other, the polished black and white Cosmic Chessboard their battlefield.

The Devil lounged with a sly, confident smirk, His movements sharp and purposeful, every gesture calculating and cunning. His presence embodied contrast—elegant yet chaotic, as if He carried the raw energy of a storm held in restraint. The black king in His hand gleamed like obsidian, its sharp edges catching the dim light of the room. "Your move," He murmured, His voice smooth as silk, yet laced with an edge that hinted at hidden schemes. This game stood beyond mere pastime; it unfolded as a battle of influence, their pieces more than pawns but lives—Lexie and William among them, ensnared in this cosmic contest.

Across the board, God maintained a serene expression, His hands rested on the edge of the board, fingers poised to guide the pieces with measured precision. Every move carried deliberate intent, embodying patience that stretched through the ages. A faint glow surrounded Him, warm and inviting, a soft golden radiance that spoke of endless wisdom and unyielding hope. Yet, a weight lingered in His eyes, a sorrow born of witnessing countless struggles between good and evil, each choice on the board reflecting the fragile balance between grace and free will.

The Devil leaned forward, His black queen poised for an aggressive opening. He slid the piece across the board with a sharp, deliberate motion, a grin curling His lips. "Every heart has a dark shadow, and I intend to make them swallow in it," He said, His voice like the hiss of an evil snake.

God, calm and steady, touched a white pawn, guiding it forward. "This is not just a game, but a test of their will, their love, and their faith," He replied, comfortable and serene as He surveyed the board. "Even in darkness, my light will find its way to them."

The Devil's fingers drummed against the table's edge as He studied God's move. "Light is fragile, old friend. It flickers with every secret. And these two? They have many." He advanced His knight, its sleek black form looming like a predator stalking its prey. "I'll expose their weaknesses one by one."

God's *White-Gloved Hand* hovered over His rook, His expression unwavering. "You may plot chaos, but even in darkness, I will guide them back to the path." His fingers settled on the piece, pushing it forward with a still and gentle strength. "Your traps will teach them, Your storms will refine them."

The Devil chuckled, leaning back in His chair. "Then let's see if they can survive the refining fire. Your faith is bold, but so is my cunning."

God smiled. "The game isn't won by force, but by faith." The pieces stood poised between them, the board a dangerous battlefield of hope and despair, the fates of Lexie and William resting on every calculated move.

God's *White-Gloved Hand* moved *a white pawn*. In response, a *Red-Gloved Hand* appeared from the flames, dark and poised. With fingers curved around a *black pawn*, the hand wavered, then descended, setting it down with a forceful *thud*.

The *loud boom* echoes as the piece hits the board with the Devil's laughter rippling across the Grant's lawn.

The bright red flames surged higher, the gigantic Cosmic Chessboard shook; it radiated an eerie glow on the black serpent's shimmering scales. The game, whatever this game is, had begun.

QUESTIONS?

Lexie Grant strolled to the front door with a fine-tuned display of composure with every step. Dressed in a luxurious purple silk robe, she smoothed the collar and pulled the sash tight, tying it into an intricate knot suggesting elegance and control. Her polished nails gleamed in the morning light as she lingered on the sash and the knot. Perfect. Perfection easy, but trust? In Lexie's immaculate life, trust didn't exist. She opened the door.

Jane Spencer, an older woman around seventy, her neighbor from across the street stood there leaning on her cane. A green band pulled her hair back in a neat bun.

Lexie didn't like being rudely awakened so early in the morning, but she kept her voice sweet. "Good Morning Jane, it's a little early."

"Forgive me for interrupting your morning." The tremor in Jane's faint voice betrayed something beyond morning cheer. Her eyes peeked over Lexie's shoulder into the house. She glanced from corner to corner, holding a small cup between her hands, the light reflecting the fine lines in her wrinkled skin.

"I hate to intrude, but if you don't mind, I'm fixing breakfast and I'm out of sugar. Can you spare a cup?"

Lexie smiled, a smile that showed neither pity nor annoyance.

"Come in. I got you."

Jane hesitated for a moment. But Lexie pulled her arm, compelling her inside. Her steps clacked on the polished floors of the foyer.

As Jane slid across the expansive entryway, her eyes roamed the nineteenth-century paintings and the high vaulted ceilings like a hawk searching for something or someone. Lexie glared as she became aware of Jane's nosiness, though she kept her demeanor light.

"I hope I'm not bothering you," Jane said as she peeked up the winding staircase that curved from the foyer to the upper floor.

Lexie remained relaxed and curious. "It's no bother," she replied, her eyes still tracing Jane's upward glance. "You seem curious this morning. Can I help with anything else?"

Jane shifted as she turned away, her cheeks flushed pink. She picked up an unusual vase from the hall table, turning it and admiring its artistic beauty. Seconds later, she placed it back on the table. Gathering her nerve, she turned to Lexie. "Ah... is your husband home?"

"Yes, he's here, in the bathroom," she replied, keeping her tone light.

"Did you need to speak with him?"

"Oh no. No, no." Jane's body trembled as she shook her head. Her eyes darted around the room once more, searching and probing.

"Alright." Lexie's voice softened; she pitied the old lady. She didn't have a life. "One second."

Lexie glided across the polished floor to the kitchen cabinet. From the cupboard, she pulled out a bag of sugar and filled Jane's cup.

When Lexie returned, she sensed the apparent scrutiny. Jane didn't want sugar to make breakfast. No, there's somthing else going on. But she kept her thoughts to herself, letting the unknown quest swell between them.

Lexie handed the cup of sugar to Jane. "Don't bother returning it. Just enjoy your breakfast."

Jane reached out and took the cup. "Thank you, dear. You're an angel." Her eyes betrayed the politeness of her voice. Lexie sensed curiosity and unease as if what she wanted to say might offend her.

Jane's eyes were full of questions. She took a step closer to Lexie and whispered. "Lexie... I think you should know something, uh, something I've been seeing—daily."

"You've been watching my house—daily?" Lexie became impatient. "What is it? What do you want to tell me?"

Jane glanced down for a moment, then back at Lexie.

"Let it out, Jane; what is this about?" Lexie asked. Jane's reluctance causes Lexie to panic. What could this woman have to say? And the audacity to watch her house?

Jane leaned over and whispered in Lexie's ear. "A woman visits while you're at work. I've seen her parked in your driveway for hours at a time."

Lexie winced, and her cheeks flushed. *Be calm.* Seconds passed as her mind raced to think of an appropriate response to her nosy neighbor's accusations. *How dare she even have the audacity to approach her like this? Jane had always been too curious, too involved in things that didn't concern her. But this crossed the line.*

Lexie's breath caught in her chest, and she forced herself to maintain a calm expression. Her stomach tightened, the knot of anxiety already forming. Jane's implications, dark and unwanted settled over Lexie. She had to be mistaken. But the unease in her voice, the look of concern on her face, made Lexie's pulse quicken.

"Oh, but of course, I know all about it." She smiled, the tightness in her jaw betraying the calmness she wanted to project.

"You...you know?" Jane asked, stunned.

"Yes, I know," Lexie lied. "She's a friend of mine. I asked her to assist my husband on a project he's working on." *Good answer!*

Jane's inquisitive and suspicious questions challenged Lexie. Did Jane suspect something nefarious?

"Oh, really?" she asked, her tone laced with incredulity. "I've never seen her with you."

Lexie's heart skipped a beat. She couldn't give Jane any more fuel for her nosy little fire. Jane's prying had made Lexie's skin crawl. She kept her tone casual, masking the unease with forced nonchalance.

"Yes," Lexie replied, her voice steady despite the storm brewing inside her. "It's just a friend. Someone I've known for years. No big deal." She forced another smile, this one even more calculated than the first.

"Funny, I don't remember you mentioning her, does she live here in the city?" Jane asked.

The heat in Lexie's chest spread to her face, but she masked it, shifting the conversation away from uncomfortable territory.

"I'm sure she's helping my husband as much as she can, and that's nothing for you to worry about. We are colleagues and haven't had time to catch up. You know how it goes." She let out a small laugh, pretending to brush off the question as if it were no more than a harmless curiosity.

But Jane continued. Her voice lowered even further, as though the conversation was a secret they were sharing.

"I'm just worried, you're always so private, and this woman visited for hours on various days—well, I just wanted you to know," Jane said, waiting and listening for my answer.

A tense silence stretched between them. The weight of Jane's words pressed down on her, each syllable a reminder that a simple and easy life never existed for Lexie and she couldn't explain that without being vulnerable. *And to Jane?*

The walls closed in on Lexie, the world outside her little bubble slipped further away. She had kept her private life private and now Jane was intruding on that privacy. *Who visited her home while she worked and what part does William play in all this?*

Lexie took a step back, trying to put some space between herself and Jane. "Thanks for your concern, though. I'll be sure to keep you posted if anything unusual happens."

Jane didn't seem satisfied, but she nodded, her eyes narrowing with suspicion. "I'd appreciate that," she said, a hint of doubt in her voice. She turned to leave, casting one last lingering look over her shoulder. She asked again.

"A friend?" Jane asked, her voice rising in disbelief. "But—"

"I must dress for work. I have an early morning meeting."

Jane took one more questioning look at Lexie. Unphased, Lexie led her to the front door.

"I... yes. Of course. Thank you for the sugar."

"Sure, anytime," Lexie responded, closing the door in Jane's face.

Lexie let out a long, shaky breath. She pressed her hand against her chest, hoping to still the rapid thump of her heart. *What was she going to do? Is William having an affair?*

For now, all she could do involved hoping Jane took her words at face value— that the nosy neighbor might forget about the woman she'd seen. If her husband had strayed, it remained none of Jane's business. Jane's curiosity thrived on mystery, so she braced for a storm that hadn't passed.

Lexie took a deep breath and stood with her back at the door, her hand resting on the knob. The weight of the uneasiness settled around her, almost suffocating in its thickness. She glanced up at the winding stairway. *What secret is William hiding from her? Who is this woman? Who visited her home?*

Jane's curiosity about what unfolded inside her own home hung in the air like smoke. *You'd think she might mind her own business, stay in her own lane—but no, she stand here stooping into my world, trying to destroy my life through doubt and suspicion. Just a hater.*

As she turned toward the stairs, she vowed that no one would disrupt the peace within her home, and nor would they ever come close to destroying the bond that she and William had built over the years. She would do whatever it took to keep their lives as they are now. She would not allow herself to question William's love or his attention. *He wouldn't cheat on her again. Would he?*

Jane's a nosy neighbor with no life, who cares what she thinks.

———— ◆ ————

The Devil moved his knight with a flourish, blocking one of God's advancing pawns. "Ah, the fragile facade of peace," he mused, his tone laced with mockery. "So easy to defend with words, yet so vulnerable to doubt. All it takes is one crack, and the whole foundation crumbles. Jane's curiosity is just the beginning."

God slid his bishop across the board, a serene determination in his movements. "Vows made in earnest are not so easily broken. Even under the weight of doubt, love can endure."

The Devil laughed, leaning back with a smirk. "Love? Is that what you see here? No, my friend, this is desperation dressed as loyalty. The bond she clings to is as fragile as a spider's web. I only need to tug."

"And yet, even a web, fragile as it may seem, can withstand the strongest winds if the will to hold remains steadfast. Observe Fallen Angel, for her strength may surprise even you," God said as he remained steady and calm.

ASK JOYCE

Lexie grabbed the laundry basket from the bathroom closet and carried it to the laundry room. The chores were done on autopilot. Mundane and nothing unusual, but her mind returned to the baby she craved, the longing now entangled with the devastating thought that William might be cheating on her. *How could she have a baby with him if he's cheating?*

She picked up a pair of William's pants and went through the pockets, as she would always check for change or tissues prior to loading the washer. A piece of paper fell to the floor. She picked it up. *Zisner's?* A receipt from a local restaurant. *We haven't been to Zisner's in months.*

———◆———

Lexie paced the bedroom, the soles of her feet sinking deep into the plush carpet. That weight on her chest pressed down, a gnawing that had stolen sleep the night before. She walked across the room, stopped at the nightstand, and picked up her phone. Her hands trembled a bit as she scrolled through her contacts to Joyce's number and pressed the call button. On the first ring her friend's familiar, warm voice answered.

"Joyce, you got a minute?" she asked, her voice tight.

"What's up?" Joyce said, with concern in her voice.

"I think... William is having an affair."

A slight pause at the other end, within seconds, Joyce's voice came through, calm, almost teasing. "Why?"

Lexie squeezed her eyes closed and willed the questions that clouded her mind. "Jane, the next-door neighbor observed a woman coming here while I'm at work," she continued, "William spoke to someone on the phone, it could have been a woman—and I found a restaurant bill in his pants. He went to Zisner's."

Joyce laughed — a knowing, dry laugh. "A restaurant receipt? Really? You know he could have seen anyone. Hell, it could have been an interview lunch. And you can't believe the neighbors."

Her thoughts drifted back to the previous night, his hushed voice, the odd phrasing, the familiar sound of restraint in his voice. Lexie whispered, "What about the phone call. William told someone 'it won't always be like this.' What does that say to you?"

"It says, 'It won't always be like this,'" Joyce replied with a laugh. "It does not say 'I'll be over to fuck you soon.'"

"Joyce."

"Relax," Joyce continued. "You're making a big deal over this, and you really shouldn't. William's a good man."

"He's different, Joyce, he's been acting a little strange. At times I don't recognize him. Something is going on with him."

"Acting strange doesn't mean he's being unfaithful," Joyce said, her voice always full of practical wisdom, and sometimes she resents it.

"Maybe not," Lexie said, knowing she disagreed.

"You're thinking about the past and how he betrayed you. It would be smart to let that go."

Lexie clenched the phone. Could there be any truth in what Joyce said? She must be imagining things, creating scenarios in her mind. *Yes, William had cheated on her and now she's afraid it might happen again.*

"I don't know how to get past it, I can't trust him, even though I want to—it's very hard." She sighed.

"Trust the life you have built with him, you'll find a way to trust him again, it takes a lot of time and commitment."

"He has become someone I don't even know anymore. He's changed. That might explain his recent behavior."

"You know you don't mean that. You know as well as I do that William adores you, he wouldn't cheat on you again with another woman, and the sooner you accept that fact, the better—for you and for William."

Lexie inhaled as she gripped the phone tighter. "In my soul I know you're right, he would never cheat on me again," she said.

She envisioned Joyce nodding her head in agreement.

"Have you questioned him about any of this?"

"No, I haven't had a chance."

"You really shouldn't. But if you do, try to listen to what he has to say," Joyce suggested.

"Just what are you implying?" Lexie asked with an edge to her voice.

"You have a tendency to be rather harsh and insensitive."

"I just tell it like it is."

"Sometimes that can backfire, if you're not careful," Joyce said.

The words hit Lexie like a ton of bricks.

"Maybe," she conceded. "But I know he's up to something, something sinister, I can feel it. I need to find out what it is."

Joyce sighed. "You sound like you want him to have an affair."

"I don't want to be caught off guard." Lexie's stomach tightened. "If he's cheating, I want to know now."

"You shouldn't believe your nosy neighbor," Joyce replied, her voice low.

The silence stretched out between them and the words lingered in the air. She didn't want to question Joyce or herself. She wanted to question William.

"Okay, I think I've had enough of your abuse for one day," Lexie said, forcing a playful tone. "You can hang up now!"

Joyce laughed. "Just remember to be careful with your words, they can sting. And maybe—just maybe—you're wrong about this. It could be quite innocent."

Footsteps echoed from the hallway. The sound made her pulse spike. The muscles in her body were tense. She glanced toward the door, trying hard to make out any familiar shape that might signal William's approach. Her heartbeat pounded in her ears, thrumming with an anxious rhythm. *Could William be outside the door?* She swallowed, forcing herself to calm down.

"I have to go," she said to Joyce, her voice lowered to a hurried whisper. Urgency clung to each word, a tightness that conveyed more than an ending to their conversation.

"Lexie? Is everything all right?" Joyce asked, her voice distressed.

Lexie squinted at the door, her mind racing through memories of William's recent behavior, his strange silences, the way he came from nowhere at the most unexpected times. Did he stand on the other side of the door listening, or worse, waiting for her to reveal something she shouldn't?

"I'll call you later, Joyce," she added, her voice strained. She didn't dare stay on the line any longer. She hung up the phone and listened as slow and deliberate footsteps edged near the door.

Did he hear what she told Joyce? Did he have his ear to the door listening to every word? Lexie tensed.

What would she say? Her mind raced, looking for any excuse he would accept. But the footsteps faded, moving in the opposite direction, leaving silence. Her ears strained for any sign of his return to the bedroom.

Lexie pulled a baby magazine from beneath her mattress and sank onto the edge of the bed; her thoughts were random and dark. She needed to relieve some tension. The magazine brimmed with glossy photos of baby clothes, wooden cribs, and toys. An ache of something missing flowed through Lexie as she flipped through the pages, her eyes scanning the images with a persistent longing. This marked the life she wanted—a life with the baby she could have. She stared at her cell phone. She needed to call Joyce back. *No, I'll text her.*

With trembling fingers, she texted Joyce.

> *I'm getting older... I want to have a baby.*

She hadn't acknowledged that fact to herself, yet now it stared back from the screen.

> *Just do it. Have a baby.*

> *Easy for you to say. You got married on a whim on a Caribbean island. This will change*

> *our lives. He's never wanted children, can I deceive him this way?*

> *He'll come around.*

> *But will he forgive me?*

Lexie paused, biting her lip, wondering what Joyce would say. She waited for what might be an unwanted lecture. But Joyce's response gave her hope.

> *If he has cheated on you, does it matter? It's time for you to fulfill your needs. Besides, a happy wife and a beautiful baby? He'll forgive you.*

> *But talk to him, Lexie. Just have the conversation.*

> Gotta go, bye.

Lexie wanted to believe Joyce. She smiled. Joyce spoke the truth, it had to be time to take control and claim her own happiness. Life is short and if she was ever intended to have a baby, she needed to make it happen—on her terms. She could give herself permission to live the life she wanted and deserved, with or without William's consent.

But could she do it? She feared the conversation they would have. Her life as she knows it now could change forever. She took one last look at her phone, she set it down and lay back on the bed, her mind a maze of tangled thoughts. And yet, for the first time in a long time, a small ray of hope. Lexie placed her cell phone on the nightstand, closed her eyes and envisioned the baby she would have.

She turned over in bed, her mind racing with impossible choices. Her fingers glided across her stomach, the idea of a future with a baby—a future filled with light—beginning to take root. But the fear lingered, like a dark cloud hovering at the edges of her thoughts.

<hr />

The Devil leaned forward, His hand hovering over the board as He studied the intricate dance of pieces. He tapped His chin, eyes gleaming with amusement. "Ah, the sweet taste of hesitation and fear. She thinks she's in control, but her strings are tied tighter than she knows. Let's add a little more weight, shall we?" With a deliberate flick, He advanced His knight, placing it in a position of calculated menace. "Hope and dread make such delicious companions."

God observed the move, His expression a mix of patience and sorrow. He rested His hand on a pawn but didn't move it. "Hope is not yours to tarnish," He said. He concentrated on the Cosmic Chessboard and the scene playing out before Him. "Even in doubt, even in fear, hope remains a spark of me. You'll see, her courage will outgrow your games."

The Devil snickered, leaning back with a satisfied smirk. "Courage? Perhaps. But real courage often blooms too late, after all the damage is done. Let her wrestle with her doubt. Let's see if her hope is worth the risk."

With a slow and deliberate move, God slid His pawn forward. "Hope always carries risk, but it also carries the promise of grace. And grace will find her, even in the shadows."

The Devil spied on Lexie, His smile dark and predatory. "There, in the shadows of her room, she wrestles with the weight of her dreams and the chains of her fear. Soon, she'll see how fragile her hope is."

God's *White-Gloved Hand* hovered for a second over His rook. He moved it with absolute precision. "Her hope is not fragile; it is resilient. In time, it will shine through the storm you've cast around her."

AN AFFAIR TO REMEMBER

The days blurred into nights, slipping past Lexie without the results she sought and prayed for. She touched her stomach, a hard knot formed instead of the baby she wanted, and the reality of failure loomed in the distance, crushing her spirit. Endless scenarios, one image after another floated through her mind. Images she now believes may not be possible.

The image kept returning to her like a photograph. A nursery painted in cornflower blue and white, her wedding colors. The musical carousel's faint lullabies rang clear as she held her precious baby, weightless, in her arms. The scent of baby powder filled her nostrils. Her precious child—an extension of herself, a living part of her heart, in her arms, proof that all the disappointments and negative tests were worth it. Her baby. The one she had dreamed of and fought for.

But the dream shattered like fragile glass, leaving nothing but cold reality. Her arms empty. Her womb empty. And the weight of failure pressed against her chest, heavy enough to steal her breath.

Lexie contemplated another choice. A choice that had lingered in her mind for days now, one that could change everything. The idea kept returning to her, though unlikely to happen. An affair?

Could she have the family she wanted if she stepped outside her marriage? Could she deceive the man she loves to have a baby?

A shameful ideal, one that William would never understand nor accept, but a whispering temptation laced with bitterness and a dark fury filled her ears. Tonight, that dark fury froze her heart, and for the first time, it became more vivid, real, and doable.

Could she give in to this idea and seek a path that would give her the family she wanted, regardless of the morality and the high standards she'd held all her life? *Is this how I want it to be?* A betrayal? William always had a hardened expression that she couldn't decipher whenever they discussed how he never wanted the responsibility of children and his lack of desire to be a father. Lexie frowned. *But why should I suffer? What about my needs? Aren't my dreams important? How could he dismiss them as insignificant?*

An undeniable truth pressed against her. William would never change. He would never give her the child she wanted. That choice—his choice—stood between them every night like an invisible wall. Also, a betrayal. A silent, selfish betrayal that had stolen her future without a single word of warning?

Yet, being with another man would be unforgivable if William ever found out. But it is so, so tempting. She could have everything she wanted in a single moment of weakness, a single calculated decision. She could carry life inside her and create the family she had always longed for.

Could she really do it?

The thought had been lingering in the back of her mind for weeks now, growing stronger with each negative test, each empty night spent in their bed, each unanswered plea for something William would never give her. She had convinced herself that they needed more time, that neither one of them were to blame. But deep down, the nagging truth—nothing worked. And the tests proved it. The bedroom became more silent, holding the weight of unmet expectations that had built between them like an unspoken barrier.

Lexie's body screamed at her about the elusive time clock, sending her signals of urgency she couldn't ignore. The ache to be a mother had become an obsession she needed to be complete. She needed a baby, and she couldn't bear the thought of William being the one who couldn't give her that.

The plan of turning to someone else, of seeking the seed she so desperately craved, would be logical, and the man could be a stranger—someone she wouldn't ever see again. The arrangement could be simple, with no strings attached. She'd get pregnant, fulfill her dream of motherhood, and return to her life with William, who would never need to know.

Words she didn't hear, but they somehow surfaced within her heart.

"Wait. You do not have to take what is already yours. Your blessing is coming. You do not have to steal it. Betrayal will not bring you peace, nor will it bring you happiness."

A calm settled over Lexie, but she didn't know why.

It's sinful. The deception, the violation of the trust between her and William. *Could she become that woman?* And yet, a small, dark, and evil part of her kept justifying it. *William cheated, why shouldn't I? I could leave. But I love him. Am I being selfish to want both a baby by another man and my husband?* Lexie convinced herself she was doing it for them. For the family they wanted. For the future they had both dreamed of.

Her fingers moved to her stomach, the gentle curve she wanted filled with a baby. She had imagined this moment so many times—her body cradling a child, William's eyes lighting up with the joy of fatherhood. But what if it never happened? What if, despite everything, their bodies weren't compatible that way? She couldn't accept that. She couldn't accept a life without children, without that piece of her heart that could only come from their love, passed down to the next generation.

The men she'd seen at work, at the gym, strangers, the man at the coffee shop whose eyes devoured her body for a second too long. Edward. *What about Edward?* The thought of him sent a strange shiver through her. A man she's only seen in brief encounters. Tall, broad-shouldered, confident. A stranger, yes—but a stranger who could fulfill her desire.

Yet, a knot of guilt twisted in her stomach. She squeezed her eyes shut, but the temptation remained. Could she really go through with it? Could she betray William like that? Even if she never told him, even if it were for a greater cause, it would still be an act of betrayal. Even if she convinced herself it served a greater purpose, it would still break something between them that could never be repaired.

Hoping and wishing to become pregnant consumed Lexie. The longing to hold her child overshadowed everything else. Even her marriage. Even her love for William. What if this were the one thing she couldn't have with him? What if no matter how hard they try, no matter how much love they shared, they would never have a child together?

Her heart raced thinking about what could go wrong, what could go right. Lexie began to spiral. What is the right choice for her? What would one moment of weakness hurt if it meant fulfilling the dream she had held for so long?

She closed her eyes, the darkness around her a mirror of the storm raging inside. She avoided facing the elusive answer that could solve the problem. *If she dared.*

There were times in Lexie's life when she'd catch a warm smile from a stranger while shopping, or the lingering eye of a co-worker. Every time, she'd look away, almost embarrassed, yet her ego swelled from the attention. Now, these incidents have taken on a new meaning. These were doors she could now open and give herself the right to explore. Would it create a new life for her and William or destroy the one they already have?

She touched her stomach again, willing the growth of a baby through the sheer force of her yearning. Little arms reaching up to her, needing her comfort and love. The mornings spent bathing, dressing, and feeding him or her. How can she navigate the dark turbulent waters of her marriage with this suffocating weight of everything she'd given up and everything she'd lost?

A long time ago, the lines between right and wrong had faded, blurred by the reality of William's stubborn and selfish refusal to share her dreams and fulfill her desires. *Isn't that what husbands do?* She vowed to create the life she wanted with or without him.

But her conscience took over and reminded her of the vows she had taken, her values, and who she always believed herself to be. Lexie stood up and moved toward the window. She wrapped her arms around herself and glanced outside at the darkening sky. A little torn between not changing her life and leaving it as it is or choosing to change her life and having the baby she craved, regardless of the cost, it amounted to an endless hole of blackness and every day she sank further and further down. Did she want to trade the life she has with William for a fleeting chance at something more, something that she thinks will bring her the happiness she wants? Lexie didn't know how much longer she could waffle and continue to be indecisive. She had a choice to make. And time no longer waited.

***

God moved His knight into a guarded position, His touch deliberate and filled with a firm tenacity. "She stands on the precipice of her desires," He stated. "But her heart holds more strength than she knows. I will guide her, though the choice is hers to make." His move created a barrier of protection, subtle yet unyielding, symbolizing faith and hope.

The Devil leaned forward with a sardonic smile. He slid His queen across the board, her dark presence casting a shadow over God's defenses. "Ah, but what is faith when desire speaks louder?" His voice flowed smooth, seductive, like a whisper curling into Lexie's ears. "The yearning is stronger than the chains of morality. She's beginning to see that love and betrayal often walk hand in hand."

The pieces on the board glimmered, reflecting the weight of Lexie's silent battle. Her love, her pain, and her doubts became the forces shaping the game, every move an echo of her indecision. But God remained steady, His hand poised, His resolve unshaken.

"The game is not over," He said, His eyes filled with compassion. "And neither is her story".

TESTED

L exie stands in the dim light of the bathroom, the soft silk of her nightgown brushing against her skin. The reflection in the mirror dared her to make a choice. She stood there naked and vulnerable.

The small, familiar container of birth control pills rested on the sink. Pills she had taken month after month, year after year. But now, she will live the life she wanted and have the baby she wanted, regardless of the cost of that decision. And there would be a cost. There always is.

Each footstep stretched like an eternity as she inched her way to the toilet. Trembling, she lifted each pill from the container. She emptied them, one by one into the bowl. Little white dots floated in the water. *Can I do this?*

William would never understand, but if she didn't take control of her life now, she never would.

Lexie closed her eyes and reached over for the lever. She hovered over it steadying herself, waiting for the fear to evaporate. She held her breath, her heart pounding in her chest. With determination she pushed the lever down, flushing the toilet.

The pills disappeared, twisting in the aqua-blue water. Her new life began to take shape in ways she had only imagined. Her eyes drifted to the mirror. A woman stared back, a new woman, a strong woman. A woman in complete control of her life. She would get what she wanted.

Lexie gasped, knowing a choice had been made that could not be undone.

⸺◆⸺

Life with William changed in the days that followed. Every night with the pink hue of the lamp warming the room, their bodies moved together expressing desires and promises that neither spoke of, but each had their very own personal agenda.

Lexie bit her lip as she squinted at the display window of the test tube, waiting, wondering, and praying if this would be the day she would begin her journey of motherhood.

Not Pregnant

A shooting twinge pierced through her, but she brushed it off.

She threw the test into the bathroom trash and forced herself to regain her composure. No way could William see her wet, dull eyes. *Be patient; it's just a matter of time.*

The cycle of intimacy and waiting continued, hope rose and fell like the tides. Lexie grew restless with each test that not only tested her hormones but also tested her will. *Why can't I get pregnant? What's wrong with me?*

Another night, another still moment, her heart pounding in her chest as she read the simple words on the tiny screen:

Not Pregnant.

Lexie became resentful and on edge each time she read those words, as though something essential remained withheld, lingering just out of reach. She bit her lip and tossed the test in the trash. She would have to keep brushing off William's concerned glances with a forced smile and the constant reassurance that she had everything under control.

And again...

Their bodies met in the quiet of their bedroom, Lexie holding onto William as if he were her savior and provider of her dreams. In the darkness, they whispered to each other, murmuring sweet endearments and sharing their thoughts on futures they couldn't yet name.

She clung to the hope that this time would be different. But she found herself staring at yet another test strip with the same disheartening result:

Not Pregnant.

Nothing changed over the next few weeks, but Lexie kept trying as she became obsessed with wishing the results to be different. Each night presented a possibility that she could become pregnant. So, with a mixture of hope and dread, she tested and tested again, bracing herself for the possibility that lay beyond her control. But each time, the words remained the same, taunting her with their stark clarity.

One morning, Lexie stood alone in the bathroom. Heavy disappointment weighed on her as she read yet another negative result. She began to hate the woman in the mirror; her own reflection made her flinch. Bleary eyes and tiny lines filled her face, but nothing would deter her. She touched her stomach, her baby's future home, and promised that no matter the odds, or the numerous failures, she refused to stop trying.

Lexie leaned against the counter, her palms pressed flat against the cool surface, grounding herself as a wave of emotion threatened to pull her under. The disappointments and the fierce loneliness she didn't dare voice aloud consumed her every thought.

She glanced back at the mirror, her eyes searched her face as if looking for answers.

"What's wrong with me?" she whispered.

The bathroom walls absorbed the question, offering no reply, no reassurance. She swallowed hard, blinking back the tears that pricked at the corners of her eyes.

Lexie straightened, forcing her shoulders back. She couldn't let herself crumble, not here, not now. The clock ticked louder and louder every day, ticking away in the background of their lives, a relentless reminder of what she feared—a fear of running out of time.

She pulled open the cabinet beneath the sink. In the far corner, safe from William's eyesight, she pulled out a lockbox. She unlocked the box, revealing a collection of prenatal vitamins, ovulation kits, and pregnancy tests. Each item, a symbol of hope and a reminder of how many times that hope had been dashed. Her fingers brushed over the box of prenatal vitamins that she may never need. She shut the box and put it back, closing the cabinet door with more force than intended.

The sound echoed in the small room, startling her. Lexie pressed a hand to her chest, willing her heart to slow. She took a deep breath, counting to four as she inhaled and exhaled. *You're stronger than this.* Her hand rested on her stomach. *One day it will happen. And when it does, all of this will be worth it.*

Lexie glanced down at the test strip and tossed it into the nearby trash can. *William can't see this. He can't know, not yet.* She reached down and pushed the test strip deeper into the trash, covering it with toilet tissue, making sure it bore no visible evidence of her ultimate betrayal. *He may never forgive me.*

Lexie stepped back, her hands trembling. The weight of her actions pressed against her chest. She wrapped her arms around herself, the empty room suffocating in its silence.

William's voice reached Lexie from the living room. "Lexie? You've been quiet, everything okay?" Her heart jumped, panic bubbled, rising in her throat. "Fine," she replied, her voice strained but steady enough. "Just... I just needed a moment."

———◆———

The Devil laughed, reclining in His chair. "Ah, but what fun is the truth without a little chaos first? Her impatience, her guilt, all simmering exactly as I planned. Push too hard, and even the strongest bond cracks."

God's eyes flickered with something unspoken, His hand resting on a bishop. "Bonds tested by fire can emerge stronger if only they choose to hold on."

The Devil tilted His head, watching Lexie's reaction with a gleam of satisfaction. "See? Even now, she weaves her own web. Let her stew in the lies and secrets. The cracks are forming, and soon they'll shatter."

God moved His bishop into a critical position, His tone resolute. "The lies may weave a web, but love has its way of cutting through even the thickest tangles. Observe, for even in despair, light can find a way."

BETRAYAL

L exie trudged down the hallway to Edward's studio apartment. Her walk of shame. She had walked down this corridor
many times, yet tonight, for some reason, her steps were heavier,
the weight of guilt and anxiety pressed down on her, both inter-
twining like vines around her ribs. This necessary evil would enable
her to have the baby she wanted, the baby she dreamed about. She
had to make this happen. No matter the cost.

She reached his door and hesitated for a moment before knock-
ing. Behind her back, she held a long-stemmed rose. An offering, a
distraction—even an apology she couldn't bring herself to voice.
The door opened, and Lexie's eyes roamed over Edward's bare
chest. His smooth, sculpted torso glistened, and tingles spiraled
throughout her body.

"Hey," she said, extending the rose. "This is for you."

Edward raised an eyebrow, taking the flower with an amused
smile. "For me? I've never received a rose from a woman before."

"Good, I like being your first."

Lexie stepped into the tiny apartment—their love nest—well,
their nest.

She eased off her coat, revealing nothing underneath. Edward's
eyes darkened. He must have been pleased—so pleased, in fact, that

the rose slipped from his fingers, forgotten, as he pulled her into his arms. Their lips met in a hungry collision, and he moved her backward until they tumbled onto the bed. Edward smothered her with kisses, and their bodies tangled, moving in a perfect, familiar rhythm, hands searching and claiming. They dissolved into the throes of lovemaking, their bodies moving in a perfect rhythmic sync. His fingers laced through hers as they reached the crest together, their pleasure spilling into breathless whispers and gasps.

Afterward, Edward rolled onto his back, an arm slung over his forehead. Lexie turned to face him, a satisfied smile lingering on her lips. He exuded sexuality. Everything about him—the chiseled features, the thick dark and wavy hair, the way he carried himself—radiated confidence and charm. An Adonis. She didn't stand a chance.

Edward let out a deep sigh. "We need to talk."

Lexie lies there with this huge glowing smile. "Right now? At this moment?" She traced lazy circles on his chest, pressing soft kisses along his jawline.

He didn't react, his expression turned serious. "Sheila moved out."

Lexie's hand froze. "Oh."

"We can spend more time together now."

Her stomach knotted. She sat up, pulling the sheet around her. "I'm here all the time."

Edward pushed himself up on his elbows. "No Lexie, you're not. You slip in and out like a ghost, and I can't be out on this limb alone."

Lexie glanced at Edward, trying to find the right words and tone. How could she avoid hurting him? With the goal of having a baby so close, she couldn't end this now. Not yet.

"You're not. It's just... it's difficult. He's difficult."

Edward's jaw tightened. "Will he hurt you?"

"Not physically. But my situation is different. Your wife doesn't care anymore. She's already checked out of your life."

"But Lexie, he controls you."

"He doesn't control me." Lexie bit her lips. The words tasted like a lie.

Edward flared. "Then what is it, Lexie? Why are you still there?"

She swallowed hard, her heart pounding. "Because I have to be."

"You mean you choose to be."

"You don't understand."

"Then help me to understand." His voice rose. "Sheila's gone. I cut ties, just like you asked me to. But you—" He shook his head. "You keep making excuses. I know it's hard, but—"

"You don't know." Lexie stood, grabbing her clothes from the floor. She dresses. "You couldn't possibly know what goes on in my home."

"Edward's voice softened. "Then tell me."

Lexie turned her back on him, slipping into her skirt and blouse. "I can't."

"Because you don't trust me?"

"It's not about trust. I can't explain my marriage to you."

"Then what is it?" He sat up, gripping the edge of the bed. "Lexie, is this all you want, is this just about sex for you?"

Hell yes... But she couldn't say that.

"Have you ever tried to let go of a puppy who adores you?"

Edward scoffed. "He's a grown man, not a puppy. He'll survive."

Lexie exhaled, rubbing her temples. "I need more time. This is moving way too fast."

Edward stood. "Too fast? We've been sneaking around for months. I thought we were on the same page."

"We are—I... I need time to work this out with William."

"How much longer do you need?"

Lexie grabbed her purse and headed for the door but paused, glancing over her shoulder. "We'll get there. Be patient."

Edward brushed a knuckle along her cheek. His lips found hers in a lingering kiss, but she sensed an undercurrent of tension—of frustration and a definite ultimatum.

Lexie pulled away, offering a small, forced smile.

Edward stepped back, studying her as if trying to decipher a puzzle. With a resigned nod, he opened the door. "Patience is overrated. Go... do what you need to do, woman."

Lexie hesitated for a fraction of a second before stepping into the hallway. The door clicked shut behind her, and she exhaled, her chest tight.

Edward wouldn't wait forever. And she couldn't tell if that fitted into her plan... or marked her biggest mistake yet.

The Devil leaned back in His chair, a satisfied smirk playing on His lips as He advanced a pawn, symbolizing Lexie's recent departure from Edward's room. "See how easily they succumb," He mused, fingers lingering on the piece. "Lexie has stepped further into the shadows, her resolve crumbling."

God observed the Cosmic Chessboard, His expression serene yet contemplative. With deliberate calm, He moved a knight, positioning it to shield a vulnerable piece. "Her journey is fraught with missteps," He acknowledged. "But the light of redemption still lights her path."

The Devil chuckled, eyes gleaming with mischief. "Redemption?" He echoed. "When she deceives and betrays? Even now, she plots further falsehoods to conceal her actions."

God's *White-Gloved Hand* rested on the edge of the board. "Within every soul lies the capacity for forgiveness and change," He replied. "Lexie's heart is burdened, yet it is not beyond the reach of grace."

The Devil's smile widened, a glint of challenge in His eyes. He purred. "Then let us see whether grace can mend what has been so thoroughly fractured." He advanced another piece, eyes locked onto God's. "The game is far from over."

God nodded, a gentle yet resolute light in His eyes. "Indeed," He agreed, moving a bishop to support the knight. "And hope remains ever steadfast."

The pieces stood poised. The outcome uncertain, as the celestial game continued, mirroring the trials and choices unfolding in the lives of Lexie and William.

THE GHOST OF THE BREADWINNER

T he evening cast long, heavy shadows through the window
over the kitchen table where William sat alone. The silence
of the room reminded him of the hollow ache in his chest he
couldn't seem to escape. His hands were, at one time, tools, in-
struments he used to provide for Lexie and to give her the life
she deserved, but now they had failed him, they weren't his, they
belonged to someone else.

William winced at the huge stack of bills and red-stamped over-
due notices on the kitchen counter. A constant reminder of his
inability to provide. He picked up an envelope. *William Grant.*
How could he have let their finances sink to this level? When had
he last sent money to cover those bills—money he'd earned himself. This is not the man he wanted to be or expected to be. How
will he get out of this mess? His marriage was already crumbling
under the weight of every unpaid bill.

William remembered the years when he could provide for Lexie.
He brought home a paycheck, and it thrilled him to do so. And
it had never been about the money—it came down to that look
from her, that look of respect that made him the man, her man, her
king. She admired him. She expected him to be the provider, the
leader, and the protector. But now, everything unraveled, thread

by thread, dissolving into nothing and he didn't know how to put the pieces back together.

Aside from the continuing financial strain, although stifling, Lexie, working overtime and never complaining about it, made him feel guilty. Or when she mentioned another bill coming due but maintained that slight polite smile. Pure disappointment, and the weight of that disappointment suffocated him.

William pressed his palms into his eyes. Lexie had listened to him the last time he attempted to share his feelings, or maybe she just tolerated them, as though his fears were an inconvenience she had to endure. And that awareness hurt him to his core. Lexie paid the household bills, carrying them both while he lounged at home, useless. The man he used to be, wouldn't recognize the self-loathing man he had become.

One night, years earlier, they had spent celebrating one of his promotions. Lexie, her eyes shining with such pride, leaned over, and whispered, "You're my king." Those words touched him. He could conquer the world. But now he had become an imposter in his own life.

William swallowed hard; his throat tightened. If he didn't provide financially, the situation would only get worse and their home, once filled with laughter and love, would be replaced with insurmountable resentment that even Lexie might not be aware of. Nothing and no one could keep that from happening but himself. He had to find a way to reinvent himself and become the man he used to be. The man she once called her king.

If only she would yell or curse at him, anything to release some of the pressure that had been building between them for a long time. Their life seems to have changed in the last few weeks. Their happiness had become elusive, and Lexie had become guarded and distant. He caused it—the hopes and disappointments. Interviews, but no jobs. It demanded more than either of them could give. When he lost his job, he lost a part of himself that he wasn't sure he'd ever find again. A shadow of the man he used to be, that's all he saw now, and deep down, he knew it and without a doubt, Lexie knew it too. So how long will she stay with him, not being happy, not getting what she wants or desires? Having to skimp one bill and pay the other to keep the lights on. How much is too much?

He should call someone, anyone. But what good would that do? William would have to share things only Lexie should know. Their finances were no one's business but their own. There was no one to talk to. And this burden—his alone to carry. His failure to own. He should've been the strong one, the provider, and he couldn't stand the thought of anyone discovering how far he'd fallen made him ill.

William paced the length of the living room, his footsteps muffled by the plush carpet that Lexie had insisted on getting years ago, back when their home and future stretched wide and their future security limitless. Now, that same carpet reminded him of everything slipping through his grasp—every choice he'd made to keep Lexie happy, to maintain the facade that nothing had cracked.

On the small table by the door lay a huge stack of unopened envelopes. The red lettering on a few of them glared at him like an accusation: FINAL NOTICE. He clenched his jaw, shoving his hands into his pockets to stop himself from sweeping the entire pile to the floor in frustration.

What would Lexie think if she knew the truth? The delinquent payments, the mounting debt, the lies he told himself to justify every decision that had brought them here. She deserved better—better than a man who couldn't hold it all together. The thought made his chest tighten, a weight settling over him like an anchor dragging him deeper into his own despair.

He rubbed the back of his neck, his eyes darting to the framed photo of the two of them on their wedding day. Lexie's radiant smile leapt out of the frame, her eyes full of trust and love. William remembered the vows he had made to her that day, his voice steady and sure as he promised to be her king, to protect her, to give her the life she deserved.

But now, standing in their living room surrounded by shadows of the life they had built together, William felt like an imposter. The man in that photo no longer resembled him. He wasn't strong. He wasn't capable. He was drowning.

A sharp pang of guilt hit him as he thought of Lexie upstairs, sleeping. She trusted him and believed in him even when he couldn't believe in himself. He hated the idea of shattering that trust, of letting her see how far he had fallen.

But wasn't that what marriage meant? A partnership? Sharing the load, even the unbearable ones? The thought tugged at him, tempting him to wake her, to confess everything, to ask for her help. But fear crept in, that gnawing voice in the back of his mind telling him she might not see him the same way again.

He sighed, running a hand through his hair. "Get it together," he muttered under his breath.

Silence pressed in, thick and airless. He walked to the window and peeked out at the darkened street, the world outside oblivious to the storm raging within him.

Could he admit he couldn't make this work, surrender the weight of the disappointments, the bills, the stress. What would that feel like? He shook his head. This mess belonged to him. His failure to fix. He wouldn't drag Lexie into it.

Early dawn marks the beginning of a new chapter, one that he made possible through his own efforts. If all goes well, the change would be profound and none of this would even matter. Not at all.

But tonight, nothing cloaked him—just William, bare and alone—a man who had lost his way, sitting alone in the dark kitchen, waiting for a chance to be worth something again. *But how? Will the early dawn gift be enough to change everything?*

The silence continued to envelop him like a suffocating blanket. The hum of the refrigerator, the soft tick of the clock on the wall—everything so still. He shifted in his seat, fingers idly tracing the chipped edge of the mug in front of him, his mind racing in circles. He couldn't shake the image of Lexie's face from earlier, the way she peered at him with that sadness in her eyes, as if she were waiting for him to say something, do something, anything to break the wall that had formed between them.

But distance crept into their lives. More than bills or the stress of work— It lived in the silence between their words, the emptiness in their touch, the stark awareness that he couldn't quite reach her anymore. She withdrew, not in obvious ways, but in the small, subtle shifts—those moments when her presence faded, when she spoke in lower tones, when her eyes no longer lit up the way they used to.

He couldn't blame her. He hated being inadequate. It gnawed at him like a constant reminder that he no longer matched the man she married, the man who had promised her the world. But promises? Easy to speak, but keeping them, that had always been the hard part. And lately, none of his promises have rung true.

William leaned back in the chair, closing his eyes, trying to remember the man he had been—before all the stress, before the bills piled up, before the tension seeped into every corner of their home. He remembered how he used to make Lexie laugh, how they talked for hours about everything and nothing. A lifetime ago. What happened? How could they have drifted so far apart?

Will dawn bring a new beginning? Will it be enough? To make up for all that's wrong? He couldn't say. He couldn't keep sitting here in the dark, hoping for a miracle. He had to act. He had to fight for them, for her.

But what if she didn't want to fight anymore? What if the love they once had— had faded beyond the point of return? He couldn't bear the thought. The fear of losing her, of being the one who let them slip away, made him sick to his stomach. The weight of that fear, the responsibility for their fractured relationship, settled on his shoulders, a burden he struggled to carry.

He stood up, pushing the chair back with a groan, his hands resting on the counter as if trying to steady himself against the wave of emotions threatening to overwhelm him. The light from the streetlamp outside flickered through the window, casting faint shadows across the kitchen.

Too late for us?

William's heart tightened. He loved her. He had always loved her. But sometimes love alone couldn't hold a life together. Sometimes, it demanded more than saying the words—it required action, sacrifice, and the kind of vulnerability that stripped you bare. He had been so consumed with trying to fix everything that he had forgotten the one thing that mattered most: he had to show up. He had to be the man she deserved, the man he promised to be all those years ago.

Dawn would come, and it would be his chance to change everything; to make things right again. To become her king once more.

The Devil smirked as He studied the board. "William clings to hope," He mused, moving a rook forward with practiced ease. "Desperation disguised as devotion. He thinks if he fights hard enough, he can undo the damage I've caused, but he can't." A low chuckle rumbled from His throat. "But doubt festers. Fear will paralyze him soon enough."

God's expression remained unreadable as He moved a knight with deliberate precision. "Fear is not the end, he still stands, and he still loves."

The Devil leaned forward, resting His elbows on the table. "Love?" He scoffed, shaking His head. "Love isn't enough. Not when failure weighs heavier. He's drowning in it, and soon, he'll see there's no way out."

God studied the board a moment longer before placing His bishop in defense. "Fallen Angel, the game isn't over."

The Devil's grin widened. His fingers tapped lazily against the table. "No, but the fall is always more interesting than the climb." His eyes gleamed with anticipation, watching the board as if he could already see the moment William would break.

Unwavering, God replied. "And yet, he climbs."

DINNER WITH LEXIE

William strolled through the living room to the dining room, setting the last piece of Jean Dubost silverware beside the plate, its polished edge catching the glow of the lights above. He stepped back, examining the symmetry, the way the utensils framed each plate with a beautiful elegance. Satisfied, he fanned out a linen napkin and folded it into an intricate design, the last touch of grace on an otherwise simple setting. Everything had to be perfect tonight.

The soft amber light from a pair of candles flickered in the corner of the room. William arranged the candles on both sides of a vase filled with deep red roses, their petals velvety, the blooms perfect. *I must thank my florist.* With his hands on his hips, he stepped back and admired the arrangement. The entire evening would unfold in front of that bold and vibrant centerpiece of roses. They had to be perfect. Everything had to be perfect.

William moved into the kitchen and opened the pantry; he pulled out the champagne bucket, its sleek silver surface gleaming. He slithered to the wine rack; he ran his fingers along the bottles, reading the labels until he found what he was looking for. His hand stopped at a bottle of Veuve Clicquot Vintage Rose 2015. He held it high, examining the label with a smile, the weight of the bottle heavy in his hands. No ordinary night, so no ordinary champagne. This champagne marks an extraordinary celebration, a toast to something... significant.

Did you take care of it? he recalled asking her.

The champagne bottle sat in the bucket as he carried it over to the refrigerator, his mind distracted by another voice, one that lingered like a shadow at the edges of his thoughts.

Everything's been taken care of, she responded, calm and confident. *I've done what you asked.*

With his hands on the champagne bottle, William's grip tightened. He shrugged it away. No nerves tonight. He scooped a handful of ice from the freezer, pouring it into the bucket until the bottle was secure, the ice filling up the sides. He carried it back to the table and sat it down with a sense of completion, standing back to view the table. Perfect. A perfect night and a special dawn.

He checked every detail as he walked by the table. The room was silent. What's missing? He crossed to the small cabinet in the corner, where he kept the Bluetooth speaker for evenings like this. As he positioned it on the side table, he allowed himself a small smile, fingers pressing through his phone to find the right song, something soft, romantic, something with enough melody to fill the room without overwhelming it. Music Lexie would love to hear.

A smooth, romantic tune filtered through the speaker and wrapped around the room like a warm embrace, each beat coaxing a sense of calm into him as he walked to the front window. He peered out toward the driveway. Empty. He sighed and glanced down at his watch. He traced its face with one finger. Soon, she would walk through that door, elated.

Does she suspect anything? the woman's voice echoed in his mind, cool and cautious, a question layered with an edge of concern.

William's jaw clenched as he peeked out at the darkened driveway, his eyes scanning the emptiness as if searching for some sign, some confirmation. He flicked his watch face back down, his hand falling to his side.

No, she doesn't have a clue, he had responded, the words were sharper than he intended. *But then again,* a hint of bitterness threaded through his mind, *neither did I.* The line lingered, weaving through his thoughts like smoke. He shook his head, clearing it, and returned his focus to this special anniversary night.

His fingers drummed against his thigh as he eyed the driveway, the seconds heavier with each beat. He took a breath, forcing himself to step away from the window. The table called to him again, its pristine setting a testament to his efforts, his desire for tonight to go as planned. He walked back to it, eyes trailing over each detail, searching for anything out of place, any minor imperfection. There were none. He'd planned this night. The night he'd imagined.

William pictured what Lexie's expression might be when she walked in, imagined her surprise, the way her face would soften, her eyes lighting up as she took in each detail. This dinner created a promise, a declaration. He wanted her to know how much he cared and his commitment to build an unbreakable, lasting bond.

Outside, headlights cut through the dark, illuminating the driveway. William's heart gave a small jump, and his pulse quickened. A familiar silhouette slid into view. *Lexie.* He took a deep breath and straightened the invisible wrinkles from his shirt. He attempted to center himself. This is it. This is the moment he'd been waiting for, the moment that may change everything.

The soft hum of the engine cut off as Lexie's Mercedes-Benz glided to a stop in the driveway, settling into silence under the soft glow of the porch light.

She sat there for a moment and exhaled. Her fingers tightened around the wheel as she glanced up at the house. The windows reflected a warm glow, casting welcoming squares of light onto the front lawn, and it filled her with a strange mixture of comfort, apprehension, and dread.

Tonight, she will focus on talking to William about her relentless desire to have a baby. No... her need to have a baby now, not years from now. But how does she get through to him?

On the passenger's seat, Lexie's cell phone beeps. Lexie picks it up.

> *Can you call me later?*

> *I can't, it's our anniversary tonight.*

> *Think you might need some tender loving care tomorrow?*

> *Edward, I have to go. Bye.*

Lexie ended the call and dropped her cellphone in her purse. She pushed open the car door, stepping out onto the driveway.

Her nose inhaled the rich scent of fresh-cut grass and distant honeysuckle as the cool evening air settled against her skin. She adjusted her coat, clutching it a little tighter around her shoulders as she walked toward the front door, each step measured, her heels tapping against the concrete in a steady, rhythmic beat.

At the doorstep, she reached into her purse, her fingers brushing against the sleek metal of her house key. She took a breath, slotting it into the lock and turning it, listening to the familiar click as the door released. A strange hush spread over her world as she stepped into the house, leaving the night behind.

———◦○◦———

Dense, almost electric air wrapped around the Grant home in a hushed intensity. Unseen eyes peeked from the shadows, every detail of the evening poised on the edge of something larger, something woven by hands far beyond mortal understanding.

God and the Devil hovered in silent concentration, each leaning into the gameboard that sat between them. God's face was calm and serene. With a steady and silent wisdom, God considered each piece. He's poised over the board with the patience of eternity. Across from Him, a flicker of something dark, vibrant. The Devil, a glint of eagerness in His eyes, sat poised over His own pieces, calculating, waiting, His hand flexing with anticipation.

The Devil grinned, unable to contain His excitement. "Your move."

God moved a pawn forward, fingers gentle but deliberate, setting it in place with purpose. The Devil's smile widened as He reached for a pawn of His own, sliding it forward in a move that seemed casual but was meticulously planned. Each move shifted the air around the Grant home, threading through the tension between Lexie and William like a noose.

The scent of garlic and rosemary wafted through the entryway, warm and inviting, a hint of domesticity. Lexie, although amused, didn't know what to expect. Being met by the aroma of food happens perhaps once in a blue moon. She inched her way inside the door.

Unseen, the Devil leaned in closer, an eager glint in His eyes as He anticipated Lexie crossing the threshold. He reached forward, moving a bishop across the board, its path cutting close to the queen. The piece clicked into place with a tiny, resonant echo that rippled through the Grant's home.

William's face lit up when Lexie walked in. He crossed to her, wrapping her in an embrace that lingered a moment too long. Lexie stiffened, her body reacting before her mind could catch up, her muscles tensing as his arms closed around her. She could almost hear a faint hum, like something else was at work here, something she couldn't quite shake.

God observed the tension in her stance, His eyes serene as He studied Lexie's subtle resistance. He reached across the board, moving a knight forward, positioning it defensively beside the queen, a shield against the encroaching pieces.

William released her with a sigh. Lexie sensed his disappointment as he turned back toward the kitchen. His movements were purposeful as he grabbed the oven mitts and reached into the hot oven, lifting out a lasagna casserole.

"In five minutes, you will taste the most scrumptious meal of all time."

"You're cooking?"

He smiled. "Sweetheart, it's our anniversary."

With the weight of everything left unsaid between them hanging heavy in the air, she managed to suppress a scoff. But she wanted to be grateful, to appreciate the gesture, but her tone failed her.

"I'm not hungry," she muttered, the words slipping out before she could stop them.

Sitting at the Cosmic Chessboard, the Devil chuckled, watching her rejection with a hint of satisfaction. He reached forward, sliding His queen across the board with a triumphant flick of His wrist, positioning her in direct alignment with God's bishop, edging Him closer to the unforeseen and inevitable confrontation.

Lexie moved past William, setting her purse down on the counter with a dull thud. The kitchen was immaculate. *Someone's been cleaning.* Her eyes fell on his wallet, lying on the coffee table. Something inside her stirred, a mix of suspicion and resentment she couldn't quite explain. She strode over, her movements brisk. She picked up the wallet, withdrew the credit cards, and proceeded to slam them down on the kitchen counter with a force that startled even herself.

"Did Zisner's close?" she snapped, each word tinged with something bitter. "Or Dale's Steakhouse? Or even Denny's?"

Lexie glimpsed the hurt in William's eyes, though he hid it well. He took a few steps toward her, his voice low, controlled.

"Our home is more private and intimate," he said, his eyes steady. "Here we have the champagne, the music, and... lest we forget, the bed."

William leaned in for a kiss, but Lexie turned her head. His sigh brushed her cheeks. He turned back to the stove, his shoulders slumped as he lifted the pot, straining the pasta with an almost robotic focus.

———◆O◆———

God observed with patience, sliding a pawn forward, creating a new line of defense. He dared the Devil, who sat grinning as the scene unfolded. His hand was already inching toward his next move.

———◆O◆———

Lexie slipped off her shoes and plopped down on the sofa, rubbing her temples in slow, deliberate circles. Her headache grew into a dull throb that pulsed in time with her resentment. She glanced at the stack of mail on the coffee table, flipping through it with a sense of irritation, as if hoping to distract herself from the silence.

"You're needy," she responded, scrutinizing the envelopes in her hand. "You want too much."

William turned to her, spatula in hand. "I want you home, buck naked and ready," he replied.

"One of us has to work," she said.

"One of us does," William quipped, his words laced with sarcasm, each syllable punctuated with bitterness.

The words hit Lexie hard, her frustration boiling over as she sprang up from the sofa. She stalked over to the refrigerator, yanking open the door and pulling out a can of soda, the motion almost violent. She took a long, defiant sip, the tension between them stretching to the breaking point.

The Devil moved another piece forward, sliding a rook across the board with a swift, forceful motion. He eyeballs God, a smirk tugging at His lips. "A crack is forming. Can you feel it?"

God's *White-Gloved Hand* hesitated, hovering over the knight. He moved the piece forward, a small, almost insignificant adjustment, a single line of defense against the oncoming chaos.

The Devil leaned back, folding His hands together with a satisfied smile, watching Lexie's movements with hunger. God observed with a steady patience, His eyes resting on William, a silent encouragement as He moved a bishop to protect the knight, a small gesture of resilience against the inevitable.

Lexie walked to the patio door; The lake spread out before her like a soothing blanket, its calm surface glinting in the moonlight, an almost eerie reflection of the storm brewing within her.

"Lexie." William's voice snapped through the silence.

She turned, her face blank. "What?" she replied, her voice tinged with exhaustion.

William crossed the room with a glass of wine held loosely in his hand.

"Maybe—just maybe, you could divert your obviously divided attention to... I don't know... me?" William said with sarcasm.

She tilted her head. "Are you a bitch now?"

William chuckled. "Ouch. You will be spanked for that remark."

She scoffed, rolling her eyes. "Yeah? Are you calling someone over?"

He pulled her into an embrace, but Lexie's body remained tense, her arms limp at her sides. William struggled to hold her, but she stepped back, her eyes fixed on the floor.

"Is it my breath? Body odor?"

"That's all you think about," Lexie snapped.

"Don't you want to feel good?"

"You mean... at home?" This back-and-forth sarcastic quip was going nowhere, but their communication with each other had evolved into this twisted unending sarcasm.

"I'll ignore that comment. C'mon, let's have sex in the kitchen," William pleaded.

"I think we're past that."

"Speak for yourself," William uttered as he leaned in close for the kiss... again. The glass of wine he held slipped from his hand and fell to the floor, shattering into pieces. Lexie pushes him away.

"Finish cooking," Lexie insisted.

* * *

The Devil chuckled, leaning back in satisfaction. God's attention remained on the board, patient, awaiting the next move as He prepared another line of defense.

"As you wish," William responded.

"Are you ever going to write that novel?" Lexie asked. "You never talk about it anymore."

"I'm an out-of-work architect, job-searching all day. When would I have the time to write?"

"You're a writer, you'll find the time—"

"—This from a woman who's already complaining about how I'm not doing my fair share."

"Obviously, I can take care of the bills myself."

"Ouch." William said.

The Devil laughed, savoring the bitterness in Lexie's voice as He slid His queen forward, edging closer to God's defenses, reveling in the slow, creeping discord between the two.

Unseen, God moved His king, a deliberate, slow shift that fortified the center of the board, as if bracing for a blow.

The Devil grinned, reaching forward to move a piece that cast a shadow over God's queen, each movement tightening the grip on William and Lexie's lives.

William sighed, bending down to sweep up the shards of glass. Lexie peeks at him, her mind somewhere else, her thoughts drifting as she clutched her purse, glancing toward the hallway.

"Where are you going?" he asked, his voice tired, resigned.

Lexie forced a small smile. "I... the bathroom."

William throws up his hands.

Lexie dashed upstairs.

As Lexie slipped down the hallway, the Devil moved another pawn, edging the pieces closer, the shadow over their marriage growing as God contemplated, His hand hovering, waiting. The next move would be His alone.

PATIENCE

Lexie shut the bathroom door with a click, the small room cloaking her in a hush, isolating her from the simmering tension settling in the house. She leaned against the counter, her fingers brushing her forehead, her pulse racing beneath her skin. She drew her hand back, staring at her slick, sweaty, damp fingers in surprise.

The adrenaline, the unease, whatever had settled inside her, stirred beneath her skin. She teetered on the edge of something dangerous leading her along the wrong path.

Lexie reached into her purse, her hands shaking as she pulled out her keys, tossing them onto the counter. Her fingers fumbled around the bag's depths until they wrapped around a small box—*Early Pregnancy Test* printed in bold, clinical letters.

She stood still for a moment, staring down at it, a surge of conflicting emotions washing over her. The weight of possibility, the delicate balance of hope and fear flooded her as she flipped the box over and read the instructions. The right path was unknown, but she dared herself to take the next step. Again.

Satisfied with the instructions, Lexie took a small cup from the counter and crossed to the toilet. Her movements were deliberate and tense, as though each step cemented the choice she made. She caught the stream, her hands trembling as she placed the cup on the tile floor, her mind racing as she straightened, pulling up her panties and turning back to the counter.

———◄O►———

God, with a calm, almost serene focus, reached forward, moving a piece in careful response. The queen glided across the board to shield the king. A graceful move against the Devil's encroaching threat. God's *White-Gloved Hand* lingered for a moment as if drawing strength from the move itself before He settled back, His gaze fixated on Lexie, on the shift within her heart.

The Devil leaned in closer, His eyes narrowing as she pulled a slim test stick from the box, the tool that would determine her fate. He flicked a pawn forward, a smug smile on His face as He readied Himself for her reaction of triumph or despair.

———◄O►———

Lexie dipped the stick into the cup. Her hand shook as she laid the test on the counter, her eyes trained on the word or words that could soon change her life. She set the timer on her phone, the soft glow of the numbers ticking down one second at a time. Every moment stretched thin with tension, each second a whisper of what could be.

Her fingers drummed against the counter, a crisp echo in the silence. She couldn't sit still. She paced from the door to the sink and back again, her eyes flashed toward the bathroom door. She crossed over, turning the lock with a decisive click. Whatever the result, she needed this moment alone.

From the vanity drawer, she pulled out a small woven basket, her hands searching through it until she found what she needed: a magazine on childbirth. She flipped through it, her fingers brushing over the glossy images of mothers cradling newborns, small bundles swathed in soft blankets, moments of love and promise captured in still frames. A strange longing tugged at her, an ache for something she couldn't fully explain.

The game continued. God exuded a gentle calm as Lexie's hope rose from a fragile flame held steady against the Devil's maneuvers. His fingers moved another piece, a bishop that cast a protective line along Lexie's path, a subtle shield against the encroaching forces of doubt.

The Devil's eyes glinted as He surveyed the board, His fingers hovering over a pawn. With a single flick, He advanced it, the piece falling into line with another move that tightened the game. He leaned back, His smile widening as He imagined Lexie's turmoil, the potential discord He'd planted, waiting to unfurl.

Lexie's timer buzzed, the sound startling her out of her reverie. She set the magazine back in the basket, her hand lingering over the cover for a moment before she turned back to the test, her breath catching in her throat. The silence stretched out, deepening around her, her fingers trembling as she picked up the test.

Nothing and no one existed at that moment as her heart pounded in her ears.

Lexie's lips quivered, and she squinted, her eyes half-closed as she peeked at the test strip. She read one single definitive word.

Pregnant.

The impact of it hit her like a wave, the weight of the word resonating through her. She gasped, her hand flying to her mouth, her eyes blinking as she read the words again.

Pregnant.

Her mind swirled with images, glimpses of a life yet unlived, of a child who was, at this moment, a real possibility.

A delighted laugh bubbled out of her, her whole body filled with the thrill of it, the beautiful, yet terrifying truth. She leapt, her feet lifting off the tile in a joyful, almost childlike jump, her heart soaring as the thought of giving birth wrapped around her like a warm embrace. She clutched the test in her hand, her smile stretching wide, her face softening in a way it hadn't in years.

Lexie pressed her free hand to her abdomen, the realization sinking in deeper with each passing second. Beneath her palm, she imagined the faintest flutter, a life she hadn't planned for but now couldn't bear the thought of losing. Tears sprang to her eyes, blurring her vision as she laughed again, the sound echoing in the bathroom.

"This is real," she whispered, her voice low with a mixture of awe and disbelief. "This is real."

She sat on the edge of the tub, her legs weak as the weight of the moment settled over her. A thousand thoughts raced through her mind, each one colliding with the next. What would this mean for her and William? Could this baby mend the fractures between them, or would it drive them further apart?

The thought of William caused her smile to falter, a pang of doubt creeping in at the edges of her joy. He made it clear that he didn't want children—hadn't wanted them for years. But this... this changes everything.

Lexie shook her head, pushing the doubts aside. For once, she wanted to savor this moment, to hold on to its pure, untainted joy before reality came crashing down.

She paused in front of the mirror, her reflection catching her off guard. Her cheeks were flushed, her eyes bright and alive. A younger Lexie—the lines of stress and worry softened by the glow of happiness radiating from within.

"I'm going to be a mom," she said aloud, testing the words on her tongue. She laughed again, a nervous, giddy sound that filled the room.

Her mind wandered to the life growing inside her, the possibilities unfurling like the petals of a flower. She imagined tiny hands clutching at her fingers, the soft cry of a baby cradled against her chest, the sweet, powdery scent of newborn skin.

Lexie picked up a tissue and wiped her tears, a focused determination settling over her. No matter what challenges lay ahead, no matter how William reacted or how complicated things became, she would love this baby with every fiber of her being.

The significance of the test in her hand grew heavier with each beat of her heart. It was a new life, a new beginning.

Her thoughts turned to God, and a prayer formed in her mind. "Thank you," she whispered, her voice filled with gratitude. Thank you for this gift, for this chance to feel alive again." *I'm no different than all the other people who thank God when only something good happened in their lives and at other times, his presence is ignored.* Lexie bit her lips. It was a miracle, surely, but miracles didn't come without purpose or consequence.

Unbeknownst to her, the Cosmic Chessboard glowed in the dark, the pieces shifting as unseen hands moved them into place.

"She feels joy," God said, His voice filled with both hope and concern. "She sees this child as a blessing."

The Devil smirked, leaning back in His chair. "Joy is fleeting, and she doesn't believe in you. Let's see how she handles the weight of what's to come."

"She is stronger than you think," God replied, His tone steady. "And love has a way of enduring through any storm."

The Devil laughed, His eyes gleaming with mischief. "Perhaps. But even the strongest resolve can crack under pressure."

Lexie ran her hand over her stomach once more, a protective, natural gesture. She thought of William again, her heart tightening with uncertainty. Would he see this child as a miracle, or would it only deepen the divide between them?

She closed her eyes and whispered to herself, "No matter what, I'll protect you. I promise."

The house also held its breath as the next chapter of their lives unfolded. And for the first time in a long time for Lexie, there was hope. Now she will have to force herself to be less bitchy toward William, he must accept and believe that this baby is his.

Lexie placed the test back on the counter, staring at it, a profound sense of hope blossoming within her. The voices of doubt, the bitterness, the weariness dissolved in that one clear moment, her world narrowing to a single, perfect point of light. She smiled and touched her stomach, the hint of life there filling her with a strength she hadn't known she possessed, her soul ignited by the fragile, powerful promise of a new life.

The Devil's smile faltered, a flicker of frustration crossing His face as He leaned in, scrutinizing Lexie's expression. The reaction wasn't what He had expected, the spark of happiness lighting her face throwing off the tension He'd cultivated. His fingers tapped against the edge of the board, a scowl forming as He surveyed the pieces. He reached for His queen, His hand steady as He set it forward, dark energy coiling around it as He angled it toward God's defense.

But God remained unflinching. Lexie's joy satisfied God. His hand moved forward, placing a knight between the Devil's advancing queen and the king, a protective move almost imperceptible in its subtlety, yet unyielding in its strength.

The game continued, each piece carrying the weight of its unseen influence. God and the Devil remained locked in a silent, dangerous conflict, each turn of the game rippling through the lives of the unsuspecting couple.

DOMESTICITY

Lexie wandered into the dining room, clutching a small stack of bills as if they were proof of everything left unsaid between them. She paused, taking note of the room, he'd so carefully arranged: tiny candles flickered around an elegant vase brimming with red roses, casting warm shadows across the table. The romantic gesture should have brought comfort, but instead, it brought indifference. She observed William sitting there hunched over, his shoulders slumped. His look was one of exhaustion and weariness.

The Devil leaned forward over the Cosmic Chessboard, He gleamed with satisfaction. He advanced His queen, positioning it with a deft touch that cast a shadow over God's knight. "The illusion of love," He noted to Himself, watching Lexie's discomfort as she glanced around the room. "It frays so easily, doesn't it?"

God observed without words, His expression calm. He moved a rook in subtle counterpoint, creating a line of defense around Lexie, His eyes never leaving her as she crossed the room to join William.

William stood; he pulled out her chair with a practiced, almost forced smile, gesturing for her to sit. She eased into the seat, she set the bills on the table.

"Things are about to change," she said, her voice soft but laden with meaning. "I... I'm going to need your help."

William sat reaching for his wine glass. "I'll get a job. This is temporary—"

"Temporary?" Lexie interrupted, a note of frustration creeping into her tone. "I don't want to be the breadwinner. You should provide. Not me." Her voice faltered. Lexie held the bills in front of her, their presence like a stale accusation between them. A tangible reminder of everything they were pushing aside.

William kept eating, no doubt, miles away, and it stirred a mix of frustration and sadness in her chest.

"William, I need you to look at this," she said, sliding the stack of bills toward him. "These are due, and we're behind on two already."

He glanced at the papers, shrugging. "I'll get around to it. Why don't you pay them online, like you usually do?"

"It's not about that," she replied, her voice firmer. "It's the fact that we keep falling behind, and I feel like I'm managing everything on my own. I could use your help here."

He glanced at Lexie, his eyes searched her eyes for a moment, but the familiar distance lingered. "Lexie, I don't know what you want from me. I'm doing my best," he paused. "Soon, you won't have to worry about bills or anything else."

She pressed her lips together, gathering her thoughts before speaking again. "It's not the bills, William. It's... it's you. I want you to be here with me. I want you to see what's happening between us. How much distance there is."

He shifted in his seat, the usual shield of indifference creeping over his face. "So, you're saying I'm not doing enough? That I'm the reason we're falling behind?"

Her voice softened, almost pleading, as she shook her head. "No, it's not that. I wish you'd notice me, William. I feel invisible sometimes and only here to keep things together while you... I don't know, focus on everything but us."

William's expression faltered, and Lexie cringed as guilt flickered across his face. But he masked it, leaning back with a sigh. "I'm trying to keep my head above water here too, Lexie. I know what you want, and I know what you need from me. You're not the only one dealing with pressure."

She nodded, the familiar ache of disappointment settled in her chest. "I get that. But occasionally, you could say something that shows me you care about me, about us. It's like I'm just here to manage things."

William paused for a moment, his fingers tapping against the table. "You're not just here to manage things. You're my wife. I do care."

She crossed her arms, taking a shaky breath. "Then show it. I don't need grand gestures; I need you to be present with me, see me, even when there's no problem to solve."

A silence fell between them, heavy and full of unspoken words. Lexie wanted him to reach out, bridge the gap between them. But he just nodded, offering a small, distant smile.

"I'll try," he said.

Lexie swallowed back her frustration. The conversation had veered off course once again, slipping back into the same empty promises. She picked up the bills, tucked them back into the envelope, and turned away, her chest tight with the ache of what she couldn't seem to say.

The Devil's smile widened as He observed the tension between husband and wife. He leaned over the board, His fingers brushing the pawn closest to God's king as if savoring the moment. God's face remained impassive; His eyes filled with patience as He noted William's will.

William took a slow, deliberate sip of his wine before slicing his food, his movements controlled. He took a bite, ignoring the frustration simmering in Lexie.

"You need to pay these."

"And how do you suggest I do that?"

"You're smart, figure it out" she shot back, her voice cracking.

William's eyes hardened, the mask of patience slipping. "Are you sure you want to change the power dynamics of this relationship?"

"Yes," Lexie replied. "I want... I need you to step up."

William's lips quirked. "Then how would you lead?"

"I'll find a way," she answered.

———◆◦◆———

God moved a bishop forward, positioning it near His king, a firm response to the Devil's encroaching queen. His expression softened, a silent encouragement flowing across the board, shielding Lexie as she fought to reclaim her voice in the silence that stretched between them.

———◆◦◆———

William sighed, gesturing to the food. "Let's eat. Our dinner is getting cold, you can rage about my shortcomings tomorrow."

Lexie picked up her fork, her fingers curling around it out of habit rather than hunger. She skimmed over her food, pushing it around on her plate as she peeked at William. Each movement of his fork tortured her. The slow and deliberate bites were a reminder of the growing distance between them, a chasm that widened with every passing day. As he ate, her sense of isolation deepened, leaving her a stranger at her own table rather than a partner in the life they had once promised to build together.

With a soft clang, she let her fork drop onto her plate. She leaned back, crossing her arms, glancing past him to the wall behind his head. There, in a frame hung their wedding photo, capturing a version of themselves she didn't recognize. In it, they portrayed no burdens, no disappointments, and a sense of easy laughter. Her eyes lingered on the details—their clasped hands, the way they had fit together as if they were made for each other. Every laugh, every touch, a promise that the future would be calm and blissful.

Lexie remembered the sensation of his arm around her that day, his solidity, how he had whispered something that had made her laugh, and the photographer captured that snapshot of joy. Pure excitement bubbled up inside her; she was so sure of the life they would share, so blind to the struggles that would one day cast shadows over that brightness. The photo, a painful relic now, a snapshot of a couple who had believed in forever without question, two people who had yet to learn how life could chip away at even the deepest bonds, one subtle fracture at a time.

Lexie's chest tightened as she peeked at him, sitting across from her now, his expression closed off, focused solely on his meal. How did this happen? Two people sharing a table, yet worlds apart. The weight of her own disappointments pressed down, as heavy as the silence between them. This wasn't the life she'd envisioned when she stood beside him in that white dress, vowing to stand by his side through everything, for better or worse.

For better or for worse. The words echoed in her mind now, a stark reminder of the promises they had—

"Isn't this better than an overcrowded restaurant?"

"No," Lexie whispered.

He reached across the table, covering her hand with his.

"Next weekend, we'll go to a crowded, impersonal restaurant," he said with a half-smile. "You can flirt with the waiter."

"Works for me," she replied, forcing a small smile.

"See?" William said, pouring more champagne into his glass.

"I can compromise."

He picked up her glass, refilling it as well, but she pushed it away, her fingers brushing the rim.

"Sparkling water for me."

William's brow furrowed, taken aback. "No champagne? Are you okay?"

"Uh... new diet. No alcohol," Lexie replied, the words stumbling out, a quick shield to mask the truth. "Joyce and I have this contest. Whoever goes the longest without an alcoholic drink, gets a pair of Jimmy Choo shoes."

"Joyce will never know."

"I'll know. What about sparkling water?"

"Sparkling water it is."

William shrugged, taking her glass and drinking it himself before heading into the kitchen for sparkling water. When he returned, he poured her a fresh glass, raising his own in a toast. "Happy Anniversary, darling."

Lexie, a bit uncomfortable, forced herself to smile. She lifted her glass to meet his. "Happy Anniversary."

They drank, and William's eyes fell back to his plate as he resumed eating.

"It's amazing what can be done when you actually use seasoning and follow the recipe," he muttered.

"You didn't marry me for my cooking," she said, a faint smile tugging at her lips.

"So, so true." William reached down, his hand grazing his crotch. "What do you think, Big William?" he joked, smirking at her. "He agrees."

Lexie let out a laugh, the tension breaking for a moment as she shook her head. "Silly."

He leaned in, his tone softening. "I have an anniversary surprise gift for you... at dawn."

She raised an eyebrow, intrigued despite herself. "Give me a hint."

William smiled; he leaned back with a mischievous glint in his eyes. "Patience, grasshopper."

"You know I have many virtues. Patience isn't one of them."

"Many virtues? Many? he teased, an eyebrow raised.

"Many," she replied, narrowing her eyes, the faintest hint of a smile at the corner of her mouth.

"I have a plan. Don't try to mess it up. You'll see... tomorrow."

"Did Compton hire you? Did you get that Project Manager position you applied for?"

"Baby, relax, a guessing game was not my intent," William replied between bites.

"You do want to be my baby, right?"

"Lucky me." Lexie quipped.

William laughed, pouring himself another drink, the silence between them settling into something lighter. But as he filled his glass, God reached across the board, advancing a pawn, a small but vital move in the game's intricate web.

Lexie took a deep breath. "Speaking of bab—"

"Expect to be surprised at dawn."

"Why dawn?"

"Here we go."

"Why does everything have to be a big production with you?"

"Why? Why? Why? Why?" William said, annoyed.

"Am I nagging you?"

"Yeah, you're ruining the mood."

"Why tell me about it at all?"

"There's that 'why' again."

"I hate it when you're vague."

"As long as you don't hate me," William said smiling.

Lexie bit her lower lip. She smiled. "I have some news too. I'm

—

--Buzz

William's phone cut her off, vibrating on the table. He picked it up, reading the message with a faint scowl Lexie couldn't decipher.

"Give me a minute, honey, this won't take long," he muttered, fingers already texting a response.

"Do what you gotta do," she replied, irritated.

William continued to text, his eyes met hers, she didn't flinch, daring him to explain. "Something important?" she asked, voice laced with suspicion.

"It's... something I have to respond to," he said.

"Why?"

William peers up at Lexie. Lexie makes a face.

"Anyone I know?" Lexie questioned.

"Uh... No."

Lexie chewed on her bottom lip, annoyed, as William continued to text. He stood up and moved toward her, kissing her forehead, but Lexie ignored the gesture.

As he left the room, the hollow ache inside of Lexie deepened. She picked up the plates, clearing the table with practiced ease, the words of an old song slipping from her lips as she worked. "Yes sir, she's my baby, no sir, I don't mean maybe..."

The Devil's smirk faltered, His eyes narrowing as He studied her response. He moved His knight, positioning it aggressively, His face a mask of concentration.

God, with a smooth intensity, lifted a rook to shield Lexie's path, protecting her from the Devil's assault.

William returned, leaning against the doorway, observing her. "You're in a good mood," he said, his tone light.

Lexie turned, offering him a guarded smile. "What's this surprise gift you have for me? Is it something I want or something really meant for you?"

William moved closer to Lexie wrapping his arms around her. "No, it's not lingerie."

"Why not give it to me now?" she asked.

William grinned. "Right here, right now? On the floor, the table, or in bed?"

She rolled her eyes, the moment of levity darkening as the weight of her hidden news settled between them. "I... I have a headache," she said, pulling away.

William's face fell, the smile fading as he stepped back. "And?"

Lexie made a faint smile, but it didn't reach her eyes. Her fingers brushed over the surface of the table as if searching for something to hold onto. So many unsaid things pressed down on her, an entire storm of thoughts she'd kept hidden beneath her calm exterior. A world of secrets lay veiled in that simple look where the shadows danced. He's clueless.

"I need to finish the kitchen." Her voice low, almost swallowed by the silence of the room. Her eyes didn't lift as she spoke, instead focused on an invisible speck on the table. Her mind churned as she added, "Give me a few minutes."

She could sense William's presence without looking at him—he nodded, a motion she caught in her peripheral vision. A routine gesture that meant he accepted her words but didn't necessarily hear them.

"I have to go into my cave first," he said, his tone brisk, already laced with the disconnection that had grown between them. He reached for his phone, his fingers tightening around it as he glanced down at the screen. "So, take your time."

With that, he disappeared, both physically and mentally, his attention drawn back to his phone. He was already moving on, unaware of the emotions she'd kept under the surface like tightly wound wires. The familiarity of the moment stung; it was a reminder of how often she found herself in this limbo, where her own thoughts and emotions were kept in check, unseen and unheard.

Lexie walked into the kitchen, her steps measured and purposeful. She let out a breath, there was a faint sense of relief in the solitude of that space. Here, she could be alone with her thoughts, the ones she'd kept hidden from him, from herself, even at times. She reached for a dishrag, her hands moving on autopilot as she wiped down the counter, her mind drifting.

The kitchen had always been her sanctuary, a place where she could escape and lose herself in the simple rhythm of cooking or cleaning. Where things made sense in a way they didn't in other areas of her life. Each swipe of the rag against the countertop grounded her, as she let the familiar task take over, creating order in this one small part of her world.

But tonight, the cleaning ritual could not soothe the ache in her chest. The restlessness made her movements hollow, her purpose lost. She stared down at the rag in her hand, her grip tightening with the weight of all the unspoken words; the truths she had swallowed back time and time again. It was easier this way, she told herself—easier to keep going, to do what needed to be done, to maintain the appearance of order. But in this space, the cracks in that well-maintained facade continued to surface.

She glanced toward the doorway, his parting words still hanging in the air.

"I must go into the cave, so take your time."

The words were so casual, so detached, yet they carried the weight of everything that had changed between them. She could still remember a time when he would have stayed, when he would have wrapped his arms around her and offered to help, when he would have made her laugh while doing the dishes, all the time maintaining that familiar warmth in his eyes, a warmth she hadn't seen in far too long.

And that hurts the most—the knowledge that they had once been different and shared something deeper, something stronger. Now, she holds fragments, pieces of a life they had built together, scattered like dust on the counter she now wiped clean. The disconnect between them grows wider with each passing day, a distance that no amount of conversation can bridge.

Her lips twitched into a faint smile. Love had been easy. It hadn't mattered that they did not have money or own secondhand furniture. He had made her the center of his world, and she'd loved him for it. A fire existed between them, an unspoken connection that needed no words. His touch had been her solace, his laughter her favorite song.

But now, the warmth of those memories faded, leaving her with a hollow ache in her chest. How had they gotten here—to this place where silence stretched between them like a chasm, and he skimmed over her without seeing her? She couldn't pinpoint the exact moment things had begun to shift, but now the weight of the problems pressed down on her.

She thought of the way William used to reach for her without hesitation, his hand sliding across the bed in the middle of the night to find hers. Now, there were nights when they lay side by side, worlds apart, the space between them cold and unyielding. It wasn't that she didn't love him—she did, in a way that almost scared her—but was she holding onto a version of him that no longer existed?

A part of her wanted to believe that they could find their way back, that the man who had once danced with her in the rain and kissed her breathless still existed somewhere beneath the layers of stress and distance. But another part of her—the more fearful part—questioned whether they had drifted too far for too long, to ever close the gap.

Lexie whispered, "Where did we go wrong? Why do we treat each other like this?"

The silence offered no answer, but the memories lingered, bittersweet and persistent, pulling her back to a time when everything had seemed possible. And for a moment, she let herself hold onto them, every single memory woven into her, some good and some not so good.

Lexie placed the dishrag on the counter as a deep ache settled in her chest. She pulled her sweater tighter around her. The kitchen had taken on the weight of her thoughts, echoing them back at her in the silence. *"I don't want to be a father, Lexie, I don't want kids."* That simple statement threw a dark cloud over their marriage, looming over every meal, every conversation, everything big and small. She turned off the light, casting the room into a dim shadow, and stood momentarily as the loneliness touched her soul, spreading a cold breath of air over her light.

Lexie glanced down, her hand resting on her stomach and beneath her hand, the first flicker of something precious, fragile, yet unbreakable.

She always believed that love could fix things. Naive, maybe even foolish, but it was a lie she had clung to for as long as she could remember.

A deep and persistent desire and longing for a baby consumed her, a hunger that had never been fed. It had settled inside her long ago, taking root in the hollows of her childhood, in the spaces where warmth and affection should have been.

If you asked other people, she had grown up in a perfect home—a house surrounded by luscious rose bushes and a well-manicured lawn—polished, magazine-spread kind of life filled with glittering dinner parties and forced smiles. But beneath the chandeliers and pristine furniture, a suffocating emptiness. Her mother, beautiful, cold and sharp-edged, a woman who spoke elegantly. Her father, nothing but a shadow, always present yet distant, existing in a fog of silent indifference.

Lexie had never been enough for either of them.

"You ruined my figure," her mother had told her once, sipping from a crystal glass as if she were discussing something as trivial as the weather. "Do you know how hard it was to get into my jeans again? And the sexy dresses? Well, no longer sexy. What the hell was I thinking, I should have left you with the nurse."

Lexie had been five years old.

Words like that didn't fade; they burrowed deep, carving themselves in the soft parts of her mind until they became truths she could never shake. She had spent her life trying to prove herself worthy of love, care, and anything real.

And then she met William.

In the beginning, William had become the center of her world, a force so steady and sure that everything else seemed to fall into place around him. His presence carried an unshakable certainty, the kind that made life seem simple as if the weight of decision-making had been lifted from her shoulders.

He had a way of walking into a room that commanded attention, not with arrogance, but with the confident assurance of a man who always knew what to do. When he reached for her, his touch carried intent—firm, protective, promising. His hand on the small of her back in a crowded space, the steady grip of his fingers as they danced, the way he drew her close at night, tucking her safely against him as if daring the world to try and take her away.

There had been laughter once, the easy kind that spilled out in stolen moments over breakfast, in the car with the windows down, in the middle of the night when neither of them could sleep. He had a dry wit, sharp and quick, and when he leaned in and whispered something conspiratorial in her ear at a formal event, she had to bite her lip to keep from laughing too loud. Those nights always ended the same way—his hands tracing her skin, his mouth following, pulling her into a world where nothing else existed.

William knew how to take charge, how to steady the chaos. During those times of uncertainty, his words wove a path forward, clearing away the doubts she hadn't even spoken aloud. He could dissect a problem in seconds and find an answer before she even asked a question. There had been a time when she trusted him completely, when the surety in his voice had been enough to calm her own storms.

He was never cruel. Not then.

In the early years, he spoke her name like it was something sacred, as if saying it meant claiming her in the best possible way. And there had been gifts—small, thoughtful things that showed he had been paying attention. A book she had casually mentioned in passing, a vintage ring he said reminded him of her, a handwritten note tucked into her purse before she left for a trip.

There had been passion, yes, but more than that, there were small everyday gestures. Every morning, he placed a K-pod in the coffee maker and a cup underneath with a spoon alongside it. Every morning. When he left for work or when he returned home, the hug came first, even if he only went to the store. A loving hug. A loving man, a kind man and Lexie counted her blessings daily. She recalled the way his thumb brushed absent-minded circles on her wrist when they sat together, his mind elsewhere but his body still tethered to hers. The way he had once, without hesitation, stepped between her and a stranger whose attention may have lingered a little too long, as if the idea of someone else laying claim—unthinkable.

For a long time, she had believed she was his greatest treasure. And maybe, in those early years, she had been.

A family of three, their baby would change everything for them. And for her.

Selfish? Manipulative? Like one of those foolish women who thought a child could repair a broken marriage. *Perhaps.* But not naïve. She wasn't looking for a fairy tale ending—she had stopped believing in those long ago. This wasn't about fixing something. This was about *restoring what they had before, a long time ago. This baby could be the answer.*

William a man who thrived on control, a man who valued legacy above all else. A child would tether him to her in ways he wouldn't be able to unravel. He might soften again, might stop looking at her as if she were a burden he regretted carrying. And if he didn't?

At least she would have something of her own.

Because the real truth, the one she didn't say aloud.

She wanted something of her own... her own baby.

Something no one—not William, not fate, not even the ghosts of her past—could ever take away.

And if she had to lie, if she had to manipulate, if she had to play this game where the stakes were higher than she could afford to lose, then so be it. She had been playing a game in other people's worlds since birth.

Lexie continued to sing, "*Yes sir, she's my baby, no sir, I don't mean maybe.*"

God and the Devil exchanged glances over the board, their unspoken battle continuing, each move drawing Lexie and William deeper into the intricate, unseen game.

Lexie froze. William's voice drifted through the house, soft but firm, its low cadence weaved through the stillness. The words held an edge, carrying intimacy and urgency that sent a chill prickling down her spine. She glanced toward the sound, her curiosity drawing her closer. With measured steps, she tiptoed down the hallway, every instinct on high alert, her pulse hammered in her ears.

The Devil's lips curled into a wicked smile as He leaned over the Cosmic Chessboard, fingers brushing over His queen. He slid it forward with a deliberate, predatory grace. His eyes gleamed as Lexie inched down the hall, her expression flickering with suspicion and fear. God, across the board, admires her with a protective intensity, His fingers resting on His knight, poised to intercept whatever blow might come next.

As Lexie moved closer, William's voice grew clearer. She pressed herself against the closed door, her heart raced, as her ears strained to catch every word.

"Tomorrow at dawn..." William's voice, calm but firm, filtered through the door. "It fits... That's the best time."

Lexie's breath caught as her fingers pressed against her lips to stifle any sound. The unease brewing within her sharpened, a sinking realization beginning to take shape.

The Devil nudged a rook forward, eyes glittering as He cast a glance toward God, savoring the discord between husband and wife. "Suspicion," He whispered, to Himself. "It sows seeds so easily." He chuckled, His fingers tapping on the board as He moved His bishop, reinforcing the line between Lexie and William with an invisible, impenetrable wall of distrust.

God's expression remained calm. However, there was a glint of sadness as He reached forward, positioning His queen near His king, a small, unwavering line of hope stretched across the board. His movements were slow and deliberate, the touch of His hand gentle yet purposeful as He fortified Lexie's side of the game.

Lexie pressed closer, a strange sense of dread twisting in her stomach as she continued listening.

"I do... No, she doesn't." William's voice lowered, carrying an almost confessional tone, like he was speaking to someone with a connection that Lexie herself could never understand. "I know, I know... But remember, it happens at early dawn... it will be a new beginning for us."

Her heart skipped a beat. *A new beginning for us.*

The words echoed in her mind, lingering with a bitterness that she couldn't shake. A surge of anger and betrayal was building within her, and her hands balled into fists at her sides as she steadied herself.

The Devil viewed her reaction with rapt attention, His grin widening. He slid His queen forward, cutting off any potential escape route for Lexie, trapping her in a maze of suspicion and doubt.

God moved a bishop in defense, the pressure building, the Devil's moves crowding in on the board, the tension closing in around her.

Lexie's mind whirled, pieces of conversation and fragments of moments from the past few days coming together, painting a picture she wanted to ignore. She had been right—her instincts, her suspicions, the late nights, the secrecy. It was all there, tangible now, and she spiraled to a conclusion she wasn't prepared to confront.

"Don't forget... Yes, of course... It's our anniversary." William's voice softened; a hint of sentiment woven through the words.

Her eyes widened, a sharp breath catching in her throat. She covered her mouth, the weight of everything she'd overheard pressed down on her, filling her with a mixture of anger and disbelief. The romantic dinner, the promises, the dawn surprise—empty lies, like a cruel pretense built to conceal a truth she hadn't wanted to see.

How could he?

The Devil leaned back, basking in her torment, savoring each flicker of pain as if it were fuel for His own fire. He moved His rook, sealing the trap, His eyes meeting God's with a look of triumph. "Pain," He replied, "is the surest way to fracture loyalty. The easiest way to turn hope to ash."

God observed Lexie's despair. His fingers moved, sliding His knight forward in a protective shield, blocking the Devil's advances. His actions were gentle and unobtrusive yet filled with a strength that remained unyielding against the Devil's encroaching forces.

Lexie backed away from the door, her heart hammering, her mind reeling. She turned on her heel, moving back toward the living room. The warmth of the dining room, with its candlelit table and bouquet of roses, complete mockery, a setup meant to deceive. She stumbled, her feet carrying her away from the scene, away from the whispered promises and words she could never unhear.

Reaching the living room, Lexie clutched the sofa's edge, trying to steady herself. The soft fabric under her fingers grounded her enough to keep her from falling. The devastation was unnerving. The world narrowed, closing in on her, her chest tightening as her breaths grew shallow.

The Devil smirked as His fingers traced the edge of His queen. "Well, isn't she fragile?" He mused, as he regarded Lexie's pain with evil delight. His eyes gleamed with satisfaction as the fracture between husband and wife deepened.

But God, always a step or two ahead of the Devil, held firm. His hand rested on His queen, His fingers hovered over it as if offering a silent reassurance. "It isn't over yet."

The Devil raised an eyebrow, intrigued by God's intention. He chuckled as he moved His bishop into position, reinforcing His queen's influence over Lexie. "Hope's a stubborn thing, isn't it?" He tilted His head, watching Lexie's tears glisten in her eyes, her confusion turning to anger. "But despair... Despair lingers."

***

Lexie bit her lip, the sting of her teeth grounding her as she fought against the tears that threatened to spill. She replayed his words in her mind, trying to untangle their meaning and rationalize something irrational. The weight of betrayal suffocated her, and the revelation—a slap upside the head. But underneath, there was still a spark—a refusal to let go—to get to the truth. She couldn't run from this. She straightened and lifted her chin; the embers of her newfound courage sparked life. She would confront him.

***

God observed Lexie, His fingers moving to a pawn, sliding it forward, His eyes filled with compassion. His movements were small and measured, but each piece He moved fortified Lexie's side of the board, providing the shield she would need.

The Devil's smile faded as He checked God's maneuver, an almost imperceptible irritation crossing His face. He leaned over the board, examining the positions with renewed focus, His fingers curled around His rook. "She's fighting it," He muttered, His voice laced with frustration. But He advanced His rook anyway, casting a shadow over her path, forcing her closer to the edge.

FRACTURES BENEATH THE SURFACE

L exie entered the room where William lay stretched across the bed. She moved with calm deliberateness, every step measured, as if she were holding herself together with sheer will. The silence stretched taut between them, thick with words left unsaid.

William turned, his eyes meeting hers, the years of distance and resentment falling away and for a moment her heart clenched, not with fear or suspicion, but with a longing she had forgotten.

"I miss us," he said, his voice cracking. "I miss the way we used to be."

His words struck a chord deep within her. She remembered the man he had been—the man who would dance with her in the kitchen, who kissed her like it was the first time every time. A glimmer of that man stood there, vulnerable and waiting.

Lexie swallowed hard, her fingers clutching the edge of the blanket.

"I miss us too," she admitted.

William moved to sit beside her, his presence grounding her. He reached out, his fingers brushing against her fingers, sending ripples of electricity racing through her body. It was the same spark—back when they were young and fearless, and love seemed simple.

"I know I've hurt you," he said, his voice filled with regret. "I know I've let you down. But I want to try, Lexie. I want to be better—for you, for us."

Her chest tightened, memories flooding her mind: the way he had kissed her on their wedding day, the warmth of his arms around her on cold nights, the promises they had made and the dreams they had shared. She wanted to believe in those promises again. But she was skeptical.

Lexie's eyes flickered with a blend of disbelief and frustration. "A lot could have been avoided," she replied, her voice cool, distant.

William's brow creased. "What could have been avoided?" he asked, searching her face.

She hesitated, the words poised on her tongue, heavy with everything she wanted to say but couldn't bring herself to. She shook her head, her voice soft. "It doesn't matter now, nothing matters now."

Irritation crossed his face, and he straightened. "Not playing that game." He softened his tone, reaching out a hand toward her. "Come, let's forget this for now. Let's make love."

Lexie's lips quirked, a bitter smile flickering at the corner of her mouth. She glanced at him with a challenge. "You don't want me to just lie there, do you?"

William's smile was faint. "I don't mind. I can work with that."

A reluctant smile slipped onto her face despite herself, it was a glimmer of the old ease between them, but it faded.

"I can't," she sighed, shaking her head.

"Of course not."

A look of resignation settled over him, and he shrugged. Rising from the bed, he stepped to the dresser, retrieved a set of pajamas, and headed to the bathroom.

Lexie stood motionless as he disappeared behind the door, the faint clicks echoing in the room as he closed it behind him. She sank onto the bed, the weight of her emotions settling heavy in her chest, pressing down with a force she couldn't contain.

The Devil peered at her from the Cosmic Chessboard, His fingers curling around a bishop as He moved it forward, His expression gleeful, savoring the division growing between them. He leaned in closer, whispering, "Secrets and silence—perfect ingredients for destruction."

God observed, His hand moving to rest on His knight, steady, protective. God lingered on Lexie, a silent encouragement radiating toward her, an unspoken plea to hold firm.

From the bathroom, the shower broke the silence. Lexie glanced toward the door. The hum of the water was almost hypnotic in its steadiness. She reached into her nightstand, pulling out a brush, running it through her hair in slow, methodical strokes, each brush a small release from the tension building within her.

Lexie brushed her hair, but the awareness of William's sexual need hung in the air. She set the brush back into the drawer and strolled to the bathroom door, her hand lingering over the door-knob for a moment as if questioning herself.

The Devil moved His queen, casting a shadow over God's king, His eyes alight with satisfaction as Lexie rose to her feet, her decision made. God scrutinized the Devil. His hand hovered over His rook, ready to intercept and protect.

Lexie stood in front of the bathroom door, the steam curling out from the edges, creating a thin, misty veil between her and what lay beyond. She took a slow breath; the robe slid over her skin and fell to the floor, leaving her vulnerable and exposed. With a gentle push, she opened the door.

Inside, the steam clung to the air, the mirrors fogged, obscuring the details. Through the glass shower door, she could make out the faint silhouette of William. His body moved with a rhythm she recognized, yet it took her a moment to understand, to comprehend what he was doing.

The realization hit her with a strange mixture of shock and betrayal, there he was, caught in his own moment, his hand moving in what could only be described as a private ritual. It was a final, painful rupture between them. She took an involuntary step back, the heat of the steam mixing with the cold that swept through her, leaving her frozen in place.

***

The Devil's eyes glittered with triumph as He moved another piece, His fingers gliding over the board with a gloating satisfaction. "Distance," He said, watching her retreat. "The more they keep hidden, the deeper the wound."

God moved His bishop, blocking the Devil's advancing knight. "Not all wounds break," He whispered, a quiet conviction underlying His movements.

***

Lexie slipped out of the bathroom, her breath shallow, her face a mixture of confusion and hurt. A hollow ache curled in her chest as she braced herself against the sink for a moment, her fingers gripping the cold porcelain like an anchor. She tried to steady herself, to will away the shaking in her limbs, but the image burned behind her eyes—an unwelcome truth seared into her mind.

She swallowed against the lump in her throat. *Wasn't she enough?* The question looped in her head, clawing at her, refusing to be silenced. *Does he need something beyond what I can give?* The thought sent a sharp, twisting, humiliating pang through her. She had given everything—hadn't she?

Her thoughts spun wildly, desperate for a foothold, for an explanation that wouldn't sting. But every answer she landed on cut just as deep. She had been fooling herself all along. This—*they*—had been unraveling longer than she wanted to admit.

Her hands trembled as she gathered her robe, her movements stiff, jerky. She wrapped it around herself, knotting it tight, as if the fabric alone could shield her from the raw vulnerability pressing in on all sides. A hollow laugh nearly escaped her. As if it could erase the sense of exposure, of being *less than*.

Her mind screamed with questions, yet they tangled together, an incomprehensible mess of anger, hurt, and confusion. What was she supposed to do? Confront him? Walk away? Pretend she hadn't seen?

A sharp breath cut through her chest. She didn't *do* weak. She didn't stand idle, hoping for scraps of attention or empty reassurances. That wasn't her. But right now—God, right now—she didn't recognize herself.

Lexie turned on her heel, each step more urgent than the last. She needed space. Distance. Something to separate herself from the stifling weight of betrayal—or insecurity? Both hurt more than she cared to admit.

Her bare feet didn't make a sound against the floor as she stepped into the hallway, but inside, she was crashing, shattering with every movement.

The silence of the house wrapped around her, thick and suffocating. She couldn't tell if she wanted to scream or cry, but Lexie would not do either. Strong-willed, she simply walked, forcing herself forward, her pace quickening as if she could outwalk the heaviness pressing against her ribs, threatening to crush her.

But no matter how much distance she put between herself and that room—between herself and *William*—the ache followed, clinging to her like a shadow.

———— ◄O► ————

God stared. He observed Lexie's pain and disappointment. His hand moved His rook to form a protective barrier of strength.

But the Devil leaned back, a slow, satisfied grin spreading across His face. He moved His queen forward, His fingers caressing the piece as if savoring each twist in their lives that nudged them closer to the edge.

THE INTERROGATION ROOM

Lexie's fingers trembled as she picked up an old picture from the mantel, a snapshot of her and William from a long-ago vacation to the Bahamas. Their arms were slung around each other, their faces bright with laughter, their expressions open and full of love, they were happy. The pang of nostalgia hit Lexie, the memory of that moment too vivid. For a fleeting second, a smile softened her face.

"That was fun," came William's voice from behind her, his tone warm, almost wistful.

She turned, startled, the memory fading as she faced the man standing before her. The ease, the joy of those days no longer existed.

William's expression softened. "But... remember the interrogation room we set up in our tiny closet?" he continued, a faint grin on his lips, as if trying to resurrect an old inside joke.

Lexie's lips quirked in response, but her eyes held a weariness, a sadness that hadn't been there before. "That was a long time ago," she muttered, her tone guarded, almost distant. She took a small breath, her mind going back to the conversation from earlier, the words that had cut through her like a knife. The question slipped out before she could stop herself.

"Who were you talking to on the phone earlier?"

The briefest flash of something crossed his face, but it was too quick for her to decipher.

"No one you know," he replied, his voice even.

Lexie's eyes searched for any hint of truth or deception. She decided not to push the issue. At least, not yet.

He forced a small, encouraging smile, extending his hand. "C'mon. Let's do it. It'll be fun."

Her eyes narrowed, studying him, before she tilted her head to the side. "If you wish," she said. "But outside, near the lake. There's a full moon tonight."

"That's my baby," he said, a note of affection softening his tone. He glanced toward the bottles. "Let me guess—sparkling water?"

"Yeah, sparkling water," she replied, watching him as he moved to the wine rack. She caught a hint of the old William in his movements, the ease with which he selected vintage champagne and then pulled a bottle of sparkling water from the fridge, his hand moving like he was assembling a scene he'd long rehearsed.

⚬

The Devil slid his bishop forward, casting a shadow over the board. His eyes gleamed, watching the unease that settled over Lexie and William. The questions that were still unanswered between them. He leaned back, satisfied, savoring the tension.

God remained calm, His hand moving a rook forward, a strength emanating from His every movement, shielding her piece by piece, guiding her with determination.

Lexie grabbed two champagne glasses, eyeing William as he mo-
tioned for her to take his hand. She hesitated, her mind flickering back to the secrets she sensed, the evasions she'd glimpsed.
But something in his expression softened her defenses, and she
reached out, letting her fingers slip into his. He led her to the patio,
their steps in quiet synchrony, as if echoing the silent years, they'd
walked together.

Outside, William released her hand, placing the wine bucket on
the table with an ease that belied the tension between them. Lexie
arranged the glasses, setting them down with precision, as if each
movement could mask the turmoil beneath the surface. The night
was charged and heavy, like the world was holding its breath. She
glanced at the lake, the moon casting silvery reflections across the
water's surface, a serene scene, mocking in its calmness compared
to the storm brewing within her.

"I'll get a candle," she said, retreating into the house.

When she returned with the candle and the remote, William
had rearranged the small table and chairs between two palm trees,
facing the lake. She held back, watching him for a moment, the familiar silhouette of him bathed in moonlight, the strange intimacy
of the scene stirring a longing for something she couldn't quite
name. She tapped the remote, casting a soft glow over their setup.

William glanced over, chuckling. "Remember how in college,
we used real candles."

"It's too windy," she replied, her tone cautious.

He shrugged, still smiling. "Still romantic. Still perfect."

She studied him, the words lingering in her mind, as if trying to convince herself they were true. He poured champagne into his glass and sparkling water into hers; looking up, he witnessed the faraway expression on her face.

"Earth to Lexie," he said. "If you really don't want to do this, we don't have to."

She glanced at him, his concern was touching and Lexie managed to smile. "No. I want to. We do have reason to celebrate."

They raised their glasses, clinking them. "To the interrogation room," William toasted, his voice soft with nostalgia.

She raised her glass letting the weight of their shared memories settle around them like a fragile peace.

"To the interrogation room."

"No holds barred. No lies, in this space, we speak the truth and only the truth. We say what we mean and mean what we say."

Lexie nodded, but did either of them have the courage to honor those words?

The Devil moved His knight closer, hovering near God's queen, casting an ominous shadow over the board. He smirked, glancing at God, who remained unflinching, moving a pawn forward, a small yet powerful shield.

"Okay, first question," Lexie began, the faintest smile tugging at her lips. "It's been ten years. Do you still find me hot and sexy... and will you at seventy?"

William chuckled, sipping his champagne. "That's two questions. But yes, your beauty takes my breath away." He paused, his smile faltering for a moment. "But as for seventy? I'll plead the fifth... for now."

Lexie laughed, lifting her glass to her lips.

"But grasshopper, you're also extremely cold and just like a box of chocolates, I never know what I'm going to get."

Her smile faded, a shadow passing over her face.

He leaned forward.

"When you're with your girlfriends, do you talk about our sex life?"

She hesitated with a mixture of defiance and vulnerability. "Yes... but not often," she replied, her voice quiet. "Why depress them?"

He laughed, breaking the tension, and she found herself smiling.

"That's my Lexie," he teased. "Always honest."

She turned, her expression sobering, the question slipping out before she could stop herself. "Is there someone else?"

William's face softened. "You know very well that I would never cheat on you again."

"Do I?" she whispered.

"There's only you, there's no one else."

She cocked her head, studying his expression, the layers of truth and hidden secrets etched there.

"There better not be."

He leaned closer, a faint, hopeful smile tugging at his lips. "Can we go back... try to..."

"Did hell freeze over?" she replied, her voice tinged with sarcasm.

The Devil laughed at Lexie's statement, he slid a black pawn forward, slamming it into place with satisfaction, the board rattling under the force, a vibration rippling through their lives.

William exhaled. "You don't mean that. This is the interrogation room. Say what you mean, mean what you say."

"Anyhow, other than lack of sex, what else about me makes you crazy?"

"Sarcasm," he said without missing a beat. "Unrelenting sarcasm."

She smiled, defiant. "It's part of my charm."

He shook his head, a half-smile playing on his lips. "No, no, it's not."

The question that had haunted her for so long slipped from her lips, raw, exposed. "Did there ever come a time when you felt regret about... about us? About marrying me?"

"Yeah, the worst day of my life," he said with a playful grin, breaking the tension. "Crazy, maybe... but I'd do it again, grasshopper. Gladly."

William peered into her eyes; his voice faltered as he braced himself. "Would you really be okay with... not ever having sex with me again?"

"That's the problem. I would be okay with it." Her honesty caught her off guard.

The Devil grinned, advancing His queen, leaning closer to God, savoring the bitterness in her words.

William clutched his chest in mock pain. "Ah... so brutal."

She studied him with a strange mix of sadness and hope. "Are you hiding something from me?"

"Yes, I am," he said, his voice a whisper, "till early dawn."

Her eyes widened. "Early dawn? What is it?"

"Patience, grasshopper," he replied, reaching for her hand, his voice filled with a quiet plea. "It's a surprise. Don't ruin my joy."

Lexie exhaled, a bitter smile on her lips. "I'm frigid, resentful, sarcastic, and a terrible cook. Tell me, exactly, what joy is there?"

"If I told you," he replied with a grin, "I'd have to kill you. Then you'd be a killjoy."

She laughed a real laugh this time, softening the tension between them. "Ha, ha. I do get it."

"That's what I like," he said. "You, laughing at my corny jokes."

William's smile faded. "Give me a little more time, don't pull away from the dock just yet."

But her response was hollow, her face now hard.

"That ship has sailed and is headed straight into an iceberg."

Desperation flickered in his eyes as he reached for her hand, squeezing it, silent plea in his touch.

"I'm listening. What do you want, what can I do?"

The wheels turn inside Lexie's head. *Now... Say it now.*

God moved a white pawn forward, positioning it beside His queen, offering a glimmer of hope.

"How do you feel about... having a baby?"

The question landed between them, heavy and unexpected. He dropped her hand, his face unreadable. "You know how I feel. We talked about this... years ago."

Lexie's voice shook, her vulnerability slipping through. "I was hoping you'd change your mind."

"I won't change my mind," he replied, his voice a whisper, a quiet finality.

"You're being selfish."

William sipped champagne. He looked at her the way you look at a two-year old having a tantrum. "I understand your need to have a baby, but—"

"Then change your mind."

"I won't change my mind because I can't change my mind. I—"

"What?"

"I...I..."

Lexie becomes hysterical. "What is it?"

William exhaled. "I can't give you a baby... I had a vasectomy. Years ago."

Lexie jumped up, glasses fell, and the table tipped over.

"What?! Why didn't you tell me? I've been taking birth control pills for years."

"I said I didn't want kids, and I wasn't about to rely on you taking those pills. I made sure it wouldn't happen. Not then, not now, not ever."

Lexie became aware of an unimaginable problem and the weight of the secrets and lies pressed down on her, shattering her world.

"I don't want to do this anymore," she whispered, her voice trembling.

The muscles in William's face tightened. "And what Lexie doesn't want... doesn't happen."

Lexie stormed away, leaving William behind.

God and the Devil observed the invisible Cosmic Chessboard with focused intensity, each move on the board rippling through the emotions of William and Lexie. The Devil's fingers brushed over His knight, sliding it forward with an amused glint in His eye. "Secrets," He whispered, leaning toward God with a grin. "They're like shadows, always lurking, ready to break even the strongest of bonds."

God remained impassive, His fingers steady as they moved a pawn in defense, placing it near His king. "But light reveals," He replied as He studied Lexie. "The truth has a way of bringing healing, even if it first causes pain."

The Devil raised an eyebrow, His grin widening. "Let's see how much pain they can withstand." The Devil slid His Black knight forward, sealing the space between them, His laughter echoing in the stillness.

God protected His rook, but the Devil's laughter rang out as He advanced His knight, reveling in the fracture between William and Lexie.

MEMORIES

The tension in the Grant home thickened like a storm cloud ready to break. Lexie paced the living room, her thoughts whirling, words bubbling up inside her that she didn't dare speak. She stopped, glancing down at the coffee table, where a stack of mail lay. Reaching for the remote, she knocked the pile over, bills scattering. With a sigh, she gathered them. Her eyes fell on the credit card statement. Something about it attracted her attention, pulling her from the fog of her thoughts.

As she scanned the list of transactions, her pulse quickened, her mind racing with questions. She remembered the receipt in William's pocket.

Zisner's Restaurant.

There it was, right there on the credit card statement, along with Snyder's Restaurant and Delta Airlines. A small gasp escaped her lips as she processed the list. This wasn't the life they had built together. This life is filled with secrets and distances widening with every unspoken truth.

The Devil's eyes gleamed as He leaned over the Cosmic Chess-board, savoring the look of shock flickering across Lexie's face. With a precise movement, He advanced His knight, pushing it closer to God's defenses. "Truth hurts," He whispered, delighting in Lexie's reaction as she held the statement in trembling hands.

God's expression remained calm, His fingers moved the rook forward to block the Devil's knight. His eyes softened as He wit-nessed Lexie's struggle, the battle within her as she held the credit card statement like a piece of undeniable evidence.

William sauntered into the kitchen, his face neutral as he strolled to the refrigerator, grabbing a beer. He closed the door with ca-sual ease that grated against Lexie's tension. Without a word, he flopped down onto the sofa near her, popping the cap with a low hiss. She turned to him, eyes narrowed.

"What have you been up to?" she asked, her voice laced with a forced calmness.

William glanced at her, his expression shifting to mild irritation. "What is it now, Lexie?"

She held up the credit card bill, waving it in front of him like an accusation. "Care to explain?"

He took the bill from her, studying it with a detached expression that she couldn't decipher. Her pulse quickened, waiting for an explanation that didn't come.

"Dinner receipts," she demanded, her voice rising. "What the hell, William?"

He peeked up at her, a faint smile touching his lips. "My dear, why so hostile?"

Her face flushed with frustration, her grip on the statement tightening. "What is going on?"

"It's not what you think," he said, though his eyes flickered with something darker.

Lexie's voice lowered to a dangerous edge. "We haven't been to dinner in ages, yet you have numerous restaurant charges on this statement."

"How careless of me," he replied. "Next time, I'll be sure to use cash."

A pang of hurt shot through her body. "You find this amusing?"

"Amusing? he replied, taking a slow sip of his beer. "Frankly, I find it... confusing."

Lexie's fingers gripped the edge of the coffee table. "My only interest is to control the bills, not your shenanigans."

"Shenanigans?" He laughed, the sound grating. "I swear, I've never heard you use that word before. It doesn't suit you."

"Is my vocabulary bothering you?"

William shook his head, his eyes meeting hers with a dark edge. "I expected more from you."

She swallowed hard, a familiar ache deepening in her chest. "So, we're both disappointed."

The Devil ogled their exchange with relish, His fingers moving His queen forward, positioning it with precision, enjoying every flicker of pain that crossed Lexie's face. "Disappointment, it breaks down the walls they think will hold."

God reached for a pawn, moving it with quiet determination, shielding Lexie from the Devil's encroaching pieces. He remained steady, unyielding.

William drained his beer. "What do you want to know?"

With a fierce intensity, she turned to him. "The truth."

"I've never lied to you," he replied, though his voice faltered.

She narrowed her eyes. "Have you been meeting a woman for lunch? At Zisner's?"

"Yes, I have," he answered, his tone almost challenging.

She gasped, the words cutting through her like a knife. "And you're not having an affair?"

"No, I'm not," he replied, his voice flat, his expression unreadable.

Her mind raced, grasping for the truth William hid from her.

"Why are you meeting with her?"

Silence.

"Omission is a lie," she pressed.

His eyes returned to hers, cold and resolute. "There's no omission. The truth is, I simply choose not to discuss it, at this time."

The distance widened, like a huge abyss opening between them.

"Fine. Do you also choose not to pay this bill? Or do I finance your shenanigans?"

He glared at her, his jaw tightening. "Lexie, I'll pay the bill."

"With no job?" She scoffed, her tone sharp, unforgiving.

"I'll get the money," he replied, his voice low.

She laughed. "Yeah, probably from her."

The Devil grinned, watching her accusation hit its mark. He moved His bishop, closing the space around Lexie, he gloated as she pieced together the story that shifted with every answer.

"If I didn't know any better, I'd think you were jealous," William said, his voice a mix of amusement and accusation.

Lexie's face flushed, and her voice rose. "I'm definitely not jealous!"

"Of course not," he replied, his tone mocking.

"What is there to be jealous of?" she shot back. "Our sex life is a joke."

"Hey... hey... Can we leave our sex life out of this conversation?" he snapped, irritation flashing in his eyes.

"Why would you have a vasectomy?" Her voice trembled with each word loaded with anger. "It's so... so final." She rose, pacing, the walls of the room closing in around her. "Your... uh, lady... doesn't see what I see. If she had any sense, she'd wise up to who you are."

William's expression darkened, his voice hardening. "Again, I'm not having an affair."

"Just go! Be with her tonight," she snapped, her voice raw.

He took another sip, leaning back with a smirk. "I like how you've decided I should be the one to leave."

Her voice broke, a note of desperation slipping in. "It doesn't matter! I'll leave!"

She turned toward the door, but he caught her arm, his grip firm. "You need to be here for your early dawn gift."

She wrenched her arm free, her voice suspicious. "Why dawn?"

He smiled, his eyes gleaming. "Humor me."

Lexie exhaled, her anger simmering but unresolved. She walked back to the sofa and sat down, her mind raced as she fumbled to piece together the fragments of their life, the secrets lurking behind his eyes.

William rose, heading to the kitchen. "More sparkling water?" he offered. "We'll drink to happier times."

Her heart ached, a mixture of longing and bitterness churning inside her. "So, only a few drinks?" she replied, forcing a smile.

He nodded, giving her a soft grin. "That's my Lexie."

Despite herself, she returned his smile, a flicker of the old warmth resurfacing.

"I'll admit, sometimes I do miss the old William," Lexie admitted.

"I haven't changed," he said.

As he poured their drinks, the silence stretched between them, heavy and thick. He brought her a glass, raising his own in a quiet toast.

"To surprises," he said.

She raised her glass. "I hope it's something I want."

"This is our anniversary celebration," he acknowledged. "Let's get lively."

He reached for her hand, pulling her to her feet. She allowed herself to be drawn into his arms, her mind whirling, his touch both familiar and strange. He held her close, his voice a whisper.

"I was afraid you'd leave if there was no chance I could give you a baby... I didn't want to fight about it."

Lexie said nothing, her heart a mix of anger and longing, the dance between them both an embrace and a struggle.

———◆◇◆———

God slid His knight forward, protecting Lexie's position, He remained calm and steady as she wrestled with her emotions.

"Come dance with me."

"You mean, come 'sway' with you?" Lexie teased.

"Dance, sway, it's all the same. Come sway with me."

She found herself intoxicated by the sweet, sexy rhythm, his hands on her hips as they swayed, her mind racing. In that moment, the weight of the years, the secrets, and the unspoken questions hung between them, a silent third presence in their embrace.

The night air settled over the Grants' home, a tangible force pressing down as they moved through the fractured dance of their marriage. As they swayed in each other's arms, Lexie forced herself to smile, a hollow gesture masking the uncertainty gnawing at her. William's hands moved through her hair, gentle and familiar, as if he could stroke away all that lay between them. He twirled her, and for a moment, a glimmer of something close to happiness flowed around them—a faint echo of who they used to be.

William's hands cupped her face as though they were still those same young lovers from long ago. "Remember how we met and how awkward it was?"

Lexie let out a soft laugh, unable to hold back the memory. "You were awkward."

He chuckled, his smile widening. "Yeah, you're right. I was quite awkward."

"But adorable. You were so nervous; you could barely speak."

His voice softened, a hint of vulnerability seeping through his words. "Woman, you stunned me. It was truly a slam-dunk."

She rolled her eyes. "You had this god-awful Christmas sweater—"

"Hey," he interrupted, a playful protest in his tone. "That sweater was the bomb."

"It was loud," she countered, allowing herself to languish in the nostalgia, even as a part of her held back.

They moved in sync, her hand in his, the years slipping away, if only for a moment.

"Those early years were special. No drama, no expectations." William said.

Lexie's smile fades as she looks into his eyes. "No bills. No job. No money. We didn't know what we didn't know."

The song wound down, with it, the brief spell of their laughter and ease. The silence pressed in as William stopped dancing. He held her hands in a tight grasp. "Am I still your king?"

The question hit her harder than she'd expected. "Were you ever?" she replied, a hint of doubt flashing across her face.

The silence stretched, his eyes searching hers, waiting. "I'm here aren't I?" she added.

"That's not an answer."

She shifted, her discomfort evident, the weight of what had been left unsaid growing. "If you have to ask…"

He continued to stare, his expression unreadable as he waited, but her response never came. Instead, the words that slipped out carried a raw edge. "I don't know how I feel, especially when I see my husband… jacking off in the shower, and I'm right in the next room."

A shadow fell over his face, his jaw tightening. "See? That—that right there. That's who you've become. All sarcasm and insults."

He released her hands and walked toward the sofa, sinking into it. She hesitated before following, sitting beside him with a sense of defiance.

"Everything isn't all about you, Lexie," he muttered, a dark edge to his voice. "If you performed your wifely duties, maybe I wouldn't need to jack off… well, at least not as much."

Her eyes narrowed, a chill in her tone. "Oh, I see. So, it's my fault?"

"You're never in the mood," he shot back. "And for what it's worth, my vasectomy only made me hornier."

She scoffed, crossing her arms. "Hornier maybe… better, not so much."

A flicker of anger crossed his face. "Ice is hard to melt."

She shrugged, her tone calm. "No… it just requires heat."

William jumped to his feet, towering over her, his fists clenched.

Lexie froze, holding her breath, her body tense, bracing herself.

William stepped back, releasing heavy breaths as he calmed himself. He walked over to the champagne bucket, grabbing a bottle. From the cabinet, he retrieved a single glass. With one swift motion, he popped the cork, and it flew across the room, hitting Lexie square on the forehead.

She gasped, clutching her head. William rushed over to her side, fussing over her. "Are you okay?"

"Yes, I'm fine." She brushed him off.

"Lie down," he insisted, guiding her to the sofa. He ran to the sink, wetting a towel before placing it on her forehead. She swatted his hand away. "Stop fussing."

He pulled back, settled onto the sofa beside her. They sat in silence.

William, a hint of vulnerability in his eyes. "We can do this, Lexie."

"Too much has happened. It's too late."

"Tomorrow will be different," he whispered.

Lexie, her expression skeptical. "What are you hiding from me? Why are you being so secretive?"

"At early dawn, all will be clear."

"Why early dawn?" she demanded, the frustration spilling out of her. "It won't change the fact that I want—no, I need to have a baby."

William's expression was dark, his voice filled with resignation. "I can't give you a baby, nor do I want to adopt one."

She narrowed her eyes, the accusation sharp in her voice. "You can't be that selfish, denying me motherhood, yet you're spending money on some... some woman. Who are you spending our money on?"

He shot her with a steely look. "Our money, Lexie. Whom am I spending *our* money on."

Lexie stared at William. Her voice was low, dangerous. "Then it's true... you're—"

"Hate to disappoint you," he interrupted, his voice thick with irritation. "But I'm not having an affair."

Her voice rose, cutting through the room. "We don't fuck."

He moved closer, his face inches from hers, his words harsh. "I know! Why do you think I jack off all the time? Woman not needed."

Lexie leaped from the sofa, her voice sharp, unyielding. "Then go fuck yourself!"

In a flash of anger, he slapped her. She slapped him back, harder, her hand stinging as it connected with his face.

"I know what you think, but you're wrong—there isn't another woman."

Lexie's eyes narrowed, a bitter edge to her tone.

"So, it's not another woman. Okay, a man?"

William's expression grew distant, his eyes glazing over as he shook his head. "It's clear, you don't know me at all. Just what do you want from me?"

She let out a short, mirthless laugh. "Why? Are you going to hear me now?"

"If it's something I'm capable of," he said, his voice soft, almost pleading. "I'll do it."

The sadness in her eyes deepened. "Nothing. I want nothing."

William leaned closer. "Seattle, I'm listening."

Against her better judgment, a small laugh escaped her. "You always make me laugh... even when I don't want to."

He fluffed his collar with a faint smile. "It's what I do."

He grabbed her shoulders. "You can talk to me. What do you want, Lexie?"

"Nothing now... but I did... a couple of years ago."

He shook his head. "I couldn't read your mind. What did you want years ago?"

She glanced toward the door, before turning and walking out to the patio, the cool night air hitting her as she stepped outside with William on her heels.

The Devil leaned forward, his eyes gleaming as the bitterness flickered between them, savoring every wound they reopened. He moved His queen forward, trapping one of God's pieces with a calculated satisfaction.

God observed them in silence, His hand poised over His knight, ready to defend even in the bleakest moment. The Devil, however, grinned as Lexie and William walked into the night, moving His rook with a smooth, deliberate motion that closed another door on their chances for reconciliation.

And as the night deepened around them, the final moves of their marriage lay waiting, shadows lingering between each beat of silence.

WILLIAM'S DILEMMA

O n the patio, the stars cast a cold, distant light that echoed the hollow ache within William. He took a deep breath, the scent of damp earth mingling with a faint hint of salt. He followed Lexie outside, his steps slow and hesitant, stopping behind her.

William admired the lake. It had been years since they purchased their home, but he still appreciated the beauty surrounding him. He loved the way the moonlight hit the lake, leaving ripples of light. He loved the birds' building of nests and the turtles strolling; even the occasional alligator didn't deter his enjoyment. This—he would never tire of. But he couldn't enjoy any of it when Lexie was sad.

Lexie spoke in a quiet voice as if speaking to the darkness itself rather than to him. William hugged her from behind as he listened.

"I wanted you to call me at work, ask me how my day's going. Buy me flowers for no reason. Make love to me in the morning, like you do at night. Open the car door for me."

"Wow," he said. "You could have told me this long before now."

"It's not the same if I have to ask you to do it," she replied, her tone tinged with sadness.

Behind them, the Devil leaned over the Cosmic Chessboard, His fingers moving with quiet confidence as He slid a bishop forward, positioning it to cut off God's knight. His eyes glinted with satisfaction as He observed the silent tension between the couple, relishing the widening rift. "Unmet needs," He whispered, His voice like silk. "They rot the soul and sour the heart."

God studied Lexie. He had seen every possible version of her and loved each one. He focused on the board. His hand hovered over His knight as He moved it, blocking the Devil's bishop. "Understanding can heal," He willed her to acknowledge the deeper truth beneath her pain.

William sighed, stepping closer to her, wrapping his arms around her from behind, holding her as though he could shield her from the emptiness they'd allowed to grow between them. "You mean all I had to do was buy you a rose, one that would die, open the car door, and call you at work?"

A faint smile tugged at her lips despite herself. "Well... don't forget the morning love."

With tenderness, William turned her around to face him, his hands resting on her shoulders as he gazed into her eyes.

"I've been an idiot, Lexie," he admitted, his voice hushed. "I've let you down. Neither of us has been getting what we need."

Lexie, unwilling or unable to meet his eyes, shrugged out of his grasp, stepping back as she shook her head. "Doesn't matter now. I just want a baby."

The words were simple, but the weight behind them was like a stone dropped into the quiet of their evening, rippling out, reshaping everything in its path. William stood there, frozen, the shadow of realization creeping over him.

"I can't give you a baby," he replied, his voice thick with a mixture of helplessness and regret.

Her head snapped up, and she leered at him with a fierceness that startled him. "Then what good are you?"

The words landed between them like a slap, cold and unyielding, a brutal statement of the distance that had crept between them. William's face fell, the impact of her words visible, his expression raw, stripped bare by the intensity of her rejection.

The Devil's smile widened as He moved His queen with a slow, calculated grace, setting it down with a quiet *click* that reverberated like a warning. He glanced at God, a glint of triumph in His eyes. "Rejection breeds resentment," He said. His voice filled with satisfaction. "Resentment that ripens into hate."

God's eyes filled with a profound sadness as He surveyed the growing fracture. He moved His bishop, His hand steady as He countered the Devil's queen, His voice soft but unyielding. "But love," He replied, "is stronger than rejection. It can bridge the deepest divides."

William took a shaky breath, trying to gather the strength to respond, but the weight of her words held him silent. He had never experienced such inadequacy, such utter powerlessness. All the quiet moments they'd shared, the laughter, the dreams of what could be—shadows now, remnants of something that once was, slipping from his grasp like sand.

"Is that really all I am to you?" His voice choked. "Just... a way to get what you want?"

"No, William, but I need this. I need something real, something... lasting."

"And I'm not real?" he asked, his tone sharp, his eyes flashing with pain.

Lexie's face softened, her voice breaking as she replied, "I don't know anymore, William. I don't know who you are, who we are." She whispered. "My heart and soul want a baby, but you don't—how do we move forward?"

Delight danced in the Devil's eyes as He leaned closer to the board, His fingers tracing the edge of His knight. He moved it forward, aligning it with God's bishop, a move designed to further isolate Lexie. "Distance, once they feel it, they will always look for a way out."

God's expression remained calm, but His hand trembled as He moved a rook to intercept the Devil's knight. His voice was a whisper, a prayer. "Hope remains. Even the smallest spark can rekindle what is lost."

———◄O►———

"Why couldn't you have just told me?" she whispered, her voice fragile. "Why did you keep it from me, let me go on hoping for a baby that would never come?"

William shook his head, his voice low. "Because I didn't want to lose you. I thought... I thought maybe if I didn't say it, you wouldn't leave."

"But you already lost me, piece by piece, when you allowed me to assume that one day we could have a family."

His face crumpled, the weight of her words breaking through the last of his defenses. "And if I could change it? If I could give you what you want, would it be enough?"

"Maybe... but it's too late now. Too many things are broken, and I don't know if we can fix them."

The tension between William and Lexie simmered, the silence pressing down on them, heavy and suffocating. William gawked at her retreat, his fingers twitching with the impulse to reach out, to pull her back from the precipice she stood on. William twisted his wedding band, the metal cool and familiar against his skin, yet foreign, like a relic from another life. A life he didn't need and wouldn't accept.

"Lexie—" his voice tentative, almost pleading.

She cut him off, her tone sharp. "I have nothing more to say."

"But I do." His voice was firmer now, holding a finality that defied her indifference.

She sighed, shaking her head. "What's the point?"

A flash of desperation passed over his face. "I think I can change your mind."

"Not anymore."

Lexie turned and strolled back into the house. She slumped down on the sofa. William followed her, his steps slow but determined, refusing to let her slip away without a fight.

He eased onto the sofa beside her. "Lexie, we were in the middle of a conversation," he said, his voice thick with frustration.

"No, *you* were in the middle of a conversation." Her voice was flat, distant.

He let out a breath, his hand reaching for her shoulder, but he stopped short, his hand hovering above her. "What can I do?" The question came out as if he were asking it himself.

She let out a bitter laugh, looking at him with eyes that had grown cold. "Nothing. As usual."

In a surge of desperation, he cupped her face, pulling her into a kiss, pouring all his unspoken words, his apologies, his need into it. But Lexie's lips remained still, unyielding. She endured the kiss, her body rigid, her lack of response a stark rejection of his efforts.

He continued to press his lips to hers with a quiet urgency, but the silence between them remained unbroken, her indifference driving a cold spike of frustration through him. Stepping back, he let her go, his mind racing as he searched for something, anything that might bridge the gap between them.

"Maybe we should go away," he suggested, his voice strained. "A trip. A few days to ourselves. Nantucket is nice this time of year."

"You're not hearing me, William."

His frustration mounted, his voice rising. "At early dawn, none of this will matter."

She bit her lip, her eyes narrowing. "What happens at early dawn, William? What aren't you telling me?"

He smiled a faint, cryptic smile. "Aha. That's the mystery."

"You're only prolonging the inevitable. This marriage... it's over. Our needs, our desires—they're worlds apart. I'm done. I don't want you anymore!"

Something shifted in him, a darker intensity flashed in his eyes as he closed the distance between them, his voice lowering to a threatening tone.

"You think you can leave me? Just dump me like garbage?"

"You can't imprison me here."

He took a step closer, his voice growling. "I'll chain you to the bed if I have to."

Her eyes widened, and she took a step back, her face a mixture of shock and anger. "You're insane."

A smirk touched his lips, though his eyes held an unsteady gleam. "I absolutely am insane. I thought you knew that."

"Now, who's being sarcastic?"

There was a beat of silence before she continued, her voice softer but filled with a deep-seated yearning that almost broke his heart.

"I want a baby, William. You don't."

He studied her, a flicker of vulnerability crossing his face. "Do you? There was a time when I was unhappy too, Lexie. Unhappy with our marriage, with the day-to-day... so I got involved."

Her eyes narrowed. "So, you did have an affair?"

He laughed, a hollow sound. "An affair is temporary, a band-aid on a broken bone. I needed something more than that." He dropped to his knees beside her, his voice softening. "I needed to have a relationship with myself. I needed to find... me."

She let out a dry laugh, bitterness lacing her words. "You're more of a woman than I am."

A smile tugged at his lips. "That's been established, hasn't it?"

They stared at each other, the weight of their resentment, their lost dreams, hanging heavy in the air between them. He reached for her hands, holding them reverently.

"Lexie, find your joy outside of me, outside of a baby. You're a strong woman; you don't need a baby or a man to define you."

He rose, guiding her toward the hallway. She resisted.

"Where are you taking me?"

He gave her a faint smile. "Quiet, grasshopper."

She shook her head but allowed herself to be led, their footsteps echoing down the hall.

The Devil's eyes emitted a predatory gleam. His hands hovered over the Cosmic Chessboard as He moved His queen, sliding it dangerously close to God's king. "Joy outside of love is no joy at all."

God was filled with compassion as He moved His bishop in a quiet but steadfast defense. "But love," He whispered, His voice filled with a gentle strength, can be reborn in the simplest of things."

———◆O◆———

In the spare bedroom, William stopped, gesturing to a painting on the wall. Lexie stared at it, her face softening as her fingers touched the canvas. The painting was a beautiful, abstract swirl of colors, filled with energy and warmth unlike the life she now led.

"This was you," William said, his voice filled with an old pride. "All you."

She let her fingers trace over the image, her eyes distant. "Life gets in the way, William. There's no time. Unlike you, I work."

His eyes flashed with frustration and sadness. "It's up to you to find the time. Isn't that what you always told me?"

"It's not that simple."

He shook his head, his voice firm. "It's just that simple."

She turned to him. "I know what will fulfill me. I know what will bring me joy. Something you can't give me William... a baby."

His face fell, and he took a deep breath. "No, I can't give you a baby."

She stepped closer, her eyes blazing. "Exactly. That's why I must leave you."

He grabbed her shoulders, his grip gentle but firm. He needed the truth. "You're not being honest, Lexie. I don't remember a baby being part of our vows. There's something else, isn't there?" *Or someone else.*

Her face twisted, her eyes darkening. "We all have our dark secrets, William... even you."

"My secret doesn't lead to ending our marriage."

She shrugged out of his grip, her expression unreadable. "Talk to me, Lexie," he whispered. "Tell me the truth."

She peered at William, quiet finality in her voice. "I just want out."

"Lexie?" he pressed, his voice filled with desperate hope. "The truth."

Lexie's voice rose, cold as steel. "The truth? I want a baby more than I want you. That's the truth."

He flinched, as though she'd struck him. "So, if I can't give you a baby, you leave? You just... walk?"

She turned away, her voice breaking. "Let's not do this."

Lexie sat on the edge of the bed, hands folded in her lap.

William's heart ached as the evening light softened around them. How could he make her understand that a baby could never fill that void? And neither could he.

"Can I sit with you?" he asked, his voice low, warm.

She nodded, watching as he crossed the room and took a seat beside her. The bed dipped under his weight, and for a moment, they sat, unsure of where to begin. Lexie held a small object in her hands, her fingers brushing over its smooth surface. William sat at the edge of the bed, his head bowed, tension still clinging to his shoulders. Without a word, she reached for his hand, turning it over and pressing something into his palm. His fingers instinctively curled around it, but his eyes stayed locked on hers.

"His brow creased. "What is it?"

Her lips curved in a soft, knowing smile. "You know what it is."

He glanced down at the small chess piece resting in his palm. "The king," he whispered.

Lexie nodded, and her fingertips touched his hand. "You've always been my king, William." Her voice quiet but filled with emotion. "No matter what happens. No matter what we've been through." She swallowed— "You still are."

William's jaw quivered, his grip firming around the chess piece as if holding onto precious gold. William sighed as a wide smile crossed his face. "And what does that make you?"

A small smile played on her lips. "Your queen."

William exhaled, his breath slow and careful, as if gathering the words he'd held back for too long. "Lexie..." he began, his hand reaching out, hovering near her own. She gave a faint nod, and he took her hand, his thumb tracing circles over her knuckles, grounding them both.

"I know things haven't been easy between us," he said, his voice thick with emotion, "and that part of it is on me and the choices I have made." He swallowed, and his eyes searched hers. How could he explain that he never meant to hurt her, that he regretted not communicating his decision to have a vasectomy? "The vasectomy—years ago—I thought it was the right thing. The right decision for both of us. I was sure of it. But I realize now... it wasn't about me. It was about you, too."

"It hurt, William. Knowing that you'd made such a big decision... without me."

He squeezed her hand, his brow creasing with remorse. "I know. I was so caught up in trying to control things, to keep everything manageable, that I didn't think about what it would mean for you. For us."

Lexie glanced down at her lap, but William's hand tilted her chin up, urging her to meet his eyes. "You deserve to know... that I regret it," he continued. "Every day. Every time you looked at a child or held a friend's baby... I knew I had taken that possibility away from us. And you deserved better."

"It's not too late, William," she whispered, the words trembling on her lips. "But... I don't want to be the only one who wants this."

He reached up, brushing a tear from her cheek with the gentlest touch, as if afraid she might disappear. "I don't want that either. But I do want this, Lexie. I want to try, for us... and because I see how much it means to you."

"Are you saying... you'd consider it?"

Her voice cracked with emotion, her eyes pleading.

He nodded, a soft, bittersweet smile forming as he took her face between his hands. "I would. I'd give anything to go back and undo what I did, Lexie... but I can't. All I can do now is tell you... that I want a chance to make it right."

"William... it means so much to hear you say this. I've felt so alone—like I was asking too much."

"You weren't," he whispered, his forehead pressing against hers, his voice low, like a promise meant only for her. "I was the one who took something away from us, something you deserved. I was afraid of losing control, but in the end, I lost something more important. I lost that chance with you."

For a moment, they stayed like that, their breaths mingling, their hands clasped as if letting go might shatter this fragile moment of shared understanding.

William pulled her close. *This is my woman. My Lexie.* He must protect her and be the man she needs him to be.

"Thank you," she whispered, her voice cracking. "For being willing to try."

He held her tighter, his hand moving in soothing circles along her back, grounding her, anchoring her in his warmth.

"I love you, Lexie," he declared. "I know I don't say it enough... but I do. And if this is what it takes to be the man you deserve, then I'll do it."

As they held each other in the quiet of the evening, William allowed himself to believe that they could find their way back to the life they'd dreamed of together—one where love and forgiveness could heal the wounds left by regret, and where a new beginning was still possible.

But William couldn't shake a darkness that he couldn't understand or adjust to. A terror gripped his emotions.

As she retreated, God's eyes filled with a deep sadness. His hand moved His knight forward in a protective stance, His fingers steady as He prepared for the Devil's next move.

But the Devil only smiled, His fingers hovering over His queen as He eyeballed Lexie as she retreated. "Sometimes, leaving is the only truth they know," He stated with dark amusement. "And in that lies all the beauty of an ending."

PROMISES &
SECRETS

L exie rummaged through her nightstand drawer, searching for a hairbrush. Her fingers brushed against something thin and folded, tucked beneath an assortment of small items. She paused, pulling it out—a single, fragile sheet of paper with the words *Wedding Vows* scrawled at the top.

She hesitated. Did she need to read what she wrote years ago? Are the vows she took on that day still valid on this day? Lexie unfolded the paper. The words drifted through her mind, haunting in their simplicity.

"I promise to always trust you, I promise to always love you, I promise my fidelity, I promise to always be by your side."

Lexie closed her eyes for a moment; the weight of each promise, the weight of each syllable, echoed back to her like a distant memory from a time when such vows had seemed effortless to keep. With a weary sigh, she refolded the note and tossed it back into the drawer, shutting it with finality. Her hand drifted to her wedding band, twisting it, the metal cold against her skin as she paced the room, her mind whirling in a thousand different directions.

The Devil spied on her from the shadows, His fingers curling around His queen as He moved her into position, ready to strike. "Promises are brittle things," His eyes gleamed. "So easily shattered, so easily discarded."

God's focus remained calm, His hand rested on His rook, a quiet strength radiating from His every move. "But the heart remembers," He whispered, watching Lexie with a mixture of hope and sorrow. "Even when promises falter, the heart remembers."

Lexie stopped pacing, glancing toward the bed. Taking a breath, she lifted the mattress, pulling out the *Early Pregnancy Box* and a well-thumbed baby magazine. She pulled out the test tube and reveled in the words still visible under the plastic.

Pregnant

A small smile crept across her face, tentative and hesitant, but real. She placed the test on the bed and flipped through the magazine, her eyes grazing over pictures of baby clothes and nursery setups. A page with a colorful food dish caught her attention, and a sudden wave of nausea crashed over her. She dropped the magazine and bolted to the bathroom, reaching the toilet as her stomach heaved.

Meanwhile, William walked into the bedroom.

Scattered remnants of Lexie's hidden dreams, the magazine, the book of baby names, and the pregnancy test lie exposed and vulnerable on the bed. He froze, his face draining of color as he picked up the test, his hand shaking as he read the result:

Pregnant

The Devil leaned closer, a smirk curling His lips as He moved His bishop, pressing forward. "And now, he will believe she has betrayed him." He whispered, savoring the turmoil he brewed in William.

God's *White-Gloved Hand* moved over the board, sliding His knight forward. "Even in doubt, there can be understanding," He watched William's reaction with quiet compassion.

For a moment, he couldn't move, the word searing itself into his mind. *Pregnant.* His hand trembled as he turned the small plastic device over, half-hoping he'd misunderstood. No mistake. The letters spoke the truth in large black print. *Pregnant.*

A strangled sound escaped William's throat, like a wounded animal. His pulse roared in his ears as the weight of the realization crashed down on him. A child. Lexie was pregnant. His wife carries a child. But a darker thought slithered in, cold, and insidious: *It couldn't be mine. I had a vasectomy.*

The question struck him with such force that he fell onto the bed. His eyes darted between the test and the glossy magazine beside it, its cheerful cover featuring a radiant woman cradling an infant. The image, meant to inspire hope and joy, displayed a cruel parody of their fractured marriage.

Why hadn't she told him? Why had she kept this a secret?

The answer formed on its own, unbidden, and devastating. His mind flashed back to every whispered conversation she'd had when she thought he wasn't paying attention to the nights she'd stayed out later than usual, and the way she avoided his touch. A suffocating wave of doubt clawed at his chest. Could there be someone else? Had she turned to another man to fulfill the dream he couldn't give her?

William's fist tightened around the test as anger flared within him, sharp and hot. His face flushed, his throat constricted. William forced himself to breathe. They had struggled, yes, but had it really driven her to this? To step outside their marriage, to find someone who could succeed where he had failed? The thought twisted like a knife in his gut; the idea of Lexie sharing the intimacy they once cherished with another man—too much to bear.

A countercurrent of guilt surged through him. Was he jumping to conclusions? Lexie had been distant, yes, but wasn't he as much to blame as she was? He'd buried himself in his own frustration, in the silent shame of his failures as a husband. If he were being honest, could he claim to know her heart anymore?

He set the test down carefully, as though it might shatter under the weight of his spiraling emotions and raked a hand through his hair. His thoughts were a chaotic tangle of suspicion, sadness, and longing.

He glanced toward the bathroom door, half-expecting Lexie to walk in and offer some kind of explanation, something that could anchor him in this storm of uncertainty.

William's eyes fell back to the magazine, its pristine pages now smudged with faint fingerprints. He picked it up, flipping through its contents, scanning the articles filled with advice for expectant mothers. The words blurred as his mind drifted. *How could she have hidden this? How could she have gone through the discovery, the emotions, the decisions—without him? And if the child was the result of a botched vasectomy? What then?*

His heart clenched at the thought of Lexie carrying another man's baby, the ultimate symbol of betrayal. Yet, even as the idea consumed him, another part of him clung to the possibility that he could be wrong. He wanted to be wrong.

Closing the magazine, he set it down next to the test and leaned forward, his elbows resting on his knees as he buried his face in his hands. His shoulders shook with a mix of anger and sorrow, emotions he wasn't sure he could untangle.

What do I do?

The question hung heavily in his mind, unanswered and echoing in the silence. *Did he confront her? Demand to know the truth? Or did he wait, or let her come to him when she was ready?*

But another, darker thought whispered in the back of his mind: *What if she never told him? What if she'd planned to keep this secret forever, to let him believe the lie if that's what it was?* The possibility chilled him to his core.

He stood and paced the length of the room. His movements were driven by a restless energy he couldn't contain. He wanted answers. He wanted the truth.

But most of all, he wanted to rewind time, to go back to a point where their love hadn't been weighed down by so many unspoken words and unmet needs. He wanted to find the version of Lexie that believed in him completely and he wanted to be the man who deserved that belief.

His pacing slowed. The faint murmur of her voice seeped through the walls.

Was she talking to someone? Or to herself.

He didn't know if he had the courage to face her yet. Not with so many unanswered questions swirling in his mind. However, he couldn't stay in this limbo.

The truth would come out. She couldn't hide it much longer. He glanced toward the open bathroom door, Lexie's retching hit him like a physical blow. For a moment, he stood there, paralyzed by a rush of emotions—fear, anger, disbelief. His hand went slack, the test slipping from his fingers onto the bed, he stood and left the room, retreating down the hallway, his expression torn with a mixture of anguish and confusion.

Part of him wanted to confront her, to demand answers. But his promises held him back.

He pressed a hand to his face, his fingers digging into his temples. His mind raced back to the vows he'd once spoken, the promises that were as solid as stone. How had they come to this?

He leaned heavily against the wall, the cool surface grounding him as his thoughts spiraled. He remembered their wedding day, the way Lexie had adored and admired him with absolute certainty, as if nothing in the world could ever shake the foundation they'd built. Now, that certainty was gone, replaced by something unspoken but unmistakably present in her eyes. A distance.

The quiet of the house pressed down on him like a weight. The hum of the refrigerator in the kitchen and the faint creak of the wooden floor beneath his feet were the only sounds. He took a hesitant step towards the bedroom. His feet remained planted, as if stuck in quicksand, caught between the need to act and the paralyzing fear of what confrontation might bring. Instead, he stayed in the kitchen.

Filling a glass with water, his hand trembled as he raised it to his lips. The cold liquid did little to ease the heat of frustration simmering inside him. He set the glass down with a little too much force, the sound reverberating through the empty space, a hollow echo of his own turmoil.

<hr>

Lexie returned to the bedroom, pale and shaky, wiping her mouth with a tissue, unaware that the pregnancy test had been moved, or that William had been there at all. She padded to bed, her movements slow and deliberate as she lifted the mattress and returned the *Early Pregnancy Box* and magazine to their hiding place, securing her secret once again beneath the weight of their shared bed. She lay down, curling up on her side as her hand rested on her stomach, the faintest hint of a smile tugging at her lips as she imagined life growing within her. A small flicker of hope stirred in her heart; it was a tiny spark, fragile yet resilient.

Lexie stared at the wall, the shadows cast by the streetlight outside forming shapes that shifted and danced. She needed that flicker of hope, she needed to focus on the image of tiny fingers curling around hers, a sweet laugh filling the air, and a future that she could make happen.

Doubt crept in, weaving through her thoughts like a shadow. What kind of life would this child have, born into a marriage teetering on the edge, held together by threads of unspoken resentment and unmet dreams? Would the baby be enough to mend the rift between them, or would it only add to the cracks they were desperately trying to ignore?

The questions came in waves, each one pulling her deeper into an ocean of uncertainty. She thought of William's silence—how it had grown heavier, more suffocating over the months. There were times when she could almost hear him screaming in his mind, words he refused to say aloud. And yet, despite it all, in his own way, he held on as much as she did.

Her fingers traced slow circles over her stomach, her mind flickering back to the early days of their relationship. They had laughed so much and shared everything without hesitation. When did that change? When had the laughter been replaced by strained smiles and the easy conversations by careful silences?

Tears pricked at her eyes, but she blinked them away. No, she couldn't fall apart. Not now. Not when a chance existed, however slim, that they could find their way back to each other.

———— ◆ ————

In the kitchen, William stood staring at the empty glass in his hand. He'd been gripping it so tightly that a dull ache spread through his palm. He set it down and leaned against the counter, his shoulders slumping.

He thought about walking into the bedroom, sitting down beside her, and saying everything that was on his mind. He wanted to tell her about the guilt that kept him awake at night, about the fear of failing her and their future. But every time he imagined speaking the words, his throat tightened, and the weight of his pride held him back.

So instead, he wandered to the window. The faint glow of the streetlights outside illuminated the driveway where their car sat, a silent witness to countless nights like this one. The nights he was a stranger in his own home, longing for the connection they once shared, a connection now lost.

⸺◆⸺

Lexie's eyes fluttered shut in the bedroom, sleeping a distant possibility. The steady rhythm of the ceiling fan above her mocked the chaos in her mind. She imagined William in the kitchen, pacing or sitting in the dark, as lost in his thoughts as she was in hers.

She wanted to call out to him, to ask him to come to bed, to wrap his arms around her and tell her they would figure it out. But the words were trapped in her throat.

What if he didn't come? What if he didn't feel the same pull she did, the desperate need to stay close.

She sat on the edge of the bed, wrapping herself in the cool sheets, her mind spinning as she reconciled her joy with the sinking weight of all that was left unsaid.

In the kitchen, William paced, his thoughts racing in erratic circles, the realization crashing over him like waves, unrelenting. *This was why she'd been so distant?* His heart thudded in his chest, and his mind replayed the quiet desperation in her voice, the way she'd eyed him with a mixture of love and bitterness.

The Devil's eyes glinted as He moved His knight into position. A calculated smile twisted His lips. "The illusion of happiness," He said, savoring William's torment. "It crumbles so easily under the weight of truth."

God leaned forward, His hand hovering over His rook as He whispered, "Love endures beyond the illusion. Even if it takes courage, even if it takes faith."

William stopped, his expression torn. Part of him wanted to con-front her, to demand answers. But another part of him, the part that recalled the faint embers of their promises, knew that no matter what she did, he would always be there for her.

He pressed a hand to his face, his fingers dug into his temples. His mind raced back to the vows he'd once spoken, promises as solid as stone. How had they come to this?

In the bedroom, Lexie closed her eyes as doubt crept in, weaving through her thoughts like a shadow. *What kind of life would this child have, born into a marriage teetering on the edge, held together by threads of unspoken resentment and unmet dreams?*

The Devil's voice drifted over the Cosmic Chessboard, dark and triumphant. "The seeds of doubt have been sown," He declared. "And once doubt takes root, it consumes all."

But God's eyes remained kind, His hand decisive, as He slid His bishop forward, a move that offered quiet protection. "Yet love is resilient," He replied, His voice filled with quiet strength. "Even in the shadow of doubt, love endures."

As the night deepened, the Cosmic Chessboard between God and the Devil gleamed with the stark contrast of light and shadow, each piece strategically placed, each move a quiet reflection of the turmoil swirling within Lexie and William. Their lives hung in balance, the choices they made poised to either mend their fractured hearts or break them beyond repair. And as the first light of dawn approached, the game awaited its next move, the pieces standing still, each one a silent witness to the battle raging within.

DEADLY INTENTIONS

L exie moved through her closet, her hand grazing over the soft fabric of her nightgown as she retrieved it, hanging it on the hook near the bath. She turned to the large bottle of bubble bath on the counter, pouring a generous amount into the running water. The scent of lavender and chamomile wafted up with the steam, filling the room with a soothing warmth.

With a slow exhale, she slipped out of her clothes, letting them fall in a gentle heap on the floor, and stepped into the tub. The warmth of the water wrapped around her, relaxing her tight muscles as she leaned against the bath pillow. Her eyes fluttering shut, she let the day's chaos drift from her mind.

A faint sound—a squeak—broke through the soft hum of the running water. Her eyes snapped open, and William stood in the doorway. She gasped, clutching the edge of the tub.

"William."

He held up his hands, a gentle smile playing on his lips. "I didn't mean to startle you."

"Why are you in here?"

He hesitated, his eyes scanning the room, returning to hers, his voice soft. "Would you like tea or sparkling water with your bath?"

The simple offer caught her off guard. For a moment, she studied him, noting the unusual warmth in his expression, the quiet intent that lingered. *What is he up to now?*

"Tea," her voice softening. "Uh... thanks."

He gave a small nod, a faint smile still tugging at his lips, he turned and stepped out, leaving her alone once again with the warmth of the water and the faint scent of lavender.

The Devil leaned forward over the chessboard, his eyes gleaming as he moved his rook, positioning it in line with God's bishop. "Little comforts," a smile curling his lips, "They mask the bitterness, which make it all the more acrid when it returns."

God's *White-Gloved Hand* hovered for a moment before He shifted a knight into a protective position, His face calm, unfazed. "Or they offer a glimmer of healing," He replied, His tone filled with quiet conviction. "A chance to rebuild."

Lexie reached over to her cell phone and pressed a button to play a tune on the nearby Bose speaker. The soft strains of a familiar song drifted through the air, filling the room with a gentle, soothing melody. She leaned back once more, her mind torn between the lingering tension and the unexpected comfort of William's offer. The bubbles surrounded her, the music settled over her like a soothing balm, her heart caught in a quiet place between unease and a faint, lingering hope.

The quiet hum of the refrigerator filled the kitchen as William pulled a lemon from the crisper, a cutting board from the cabinet, and a large knife from the knife block. His eyes fixed on the knife, his fingers gripping its handle with a tension that seeped into his whole body. He held it aloft for a second longer than necessary and brought it down with a heavy *thud,* slicing the lemon in half with an almost violent precision. As he did, the blade nicked his finger, a bright bead of blood welling up and trailing down his skin. The sting didn't register. The lemon sat split on the cutting board, its scent sharp in the air, its juice bleeding onto the worn wooden surface. He pressed his thumb against the sting of the cut, the blood mixing with the citrus. The pain remained distant, an afterthought.

His thoughts, however, were anything but.

The pregnancy test had been left on the bed, discarded, yet obvious, its result unmistakable. *Pregnant. Lexie was pregnant!*

His grip tightened on the knife, the blade glinting under the soft glow of the overhead light. The kitchen, once an impersonal space meant for meals and get-togethers, now held a pungent odor, its walls closing in, thick with something unspoken, and that something constricted his throat and left a bitter sour taste in his mouth. He inhaled through his nose, slow and controlled, but the effort did nothing to steady the slow burn rising in his chest.

His eyes drifted to the lower cabinet as he crouched down to retrieve a bandage. But as he reached inside, his eyes wandered to the box tucked in the corner—*a box of rat poison*. His hand paused, lingering on the bandages as his eyes stayed fixed on the box, a small shadow of something dark flashing across his face.

His free hand hovered over the box of rat poison in the cabinet, fingers flexing, hesitating. A cruel irony. A tool meant for extermination, for removing pests—unwanted intrusions. His stomach twisted. The thought came unbidden, dark, and venomous.

Unwanted.

His mind recoiled from the word, but it settled in, stubborn, burrowing beneath his skin. He clenched his jaw. *How could she betray him like this?* It tore at his gut, and he grabbed the bandage with more force than necessary. *Who was the father? It certainly wasn't him.*

The muscles in his neck became taut, like a rope tightening around his throat in a painful suffocation. He hadn't prepared for the thought of a child, Lexie's child—maybe by another man—growing inside her. A devastating situation he never anticipated. He knew how to control a situation and manipulate the hand he was dealt. But this? This was chaos wrapped in delicate human fragility, something unpredictable that could change everything.

His lips pressed into a thin line as he reached for the lemon again, slicing deeper this time, the blade biting into the rind with a wet snap. The juice spattered across the board, its tang filling his senses. A fitting contrast—bitter and sharp, much like the thoughts spiraling in his mind.

Lexie. Had she left it there for him to find?

His fingers drummed against the counter. Of course, she knew. Lexie never did anything without intention, not when it came to her games. A bold move on her part, a play that left him calculating his next steps.

A deep exhale pushed past his lips.

He would need to speak with her. No, not speak—corner her. Make her answer. Because one thing he couldn't afford—uncertainty. And Lexie, for all her beauty, her clever little manipulations, her charming deceptions, had just introduced a variable he hadn't accounted for.

William discarded the knife, rubbing his bandaged finger. The pain had settled in now, dull and pulsing, a quiet reminder of carelessness. With Lexie, he wouldn't make the same mistake.

No, this would require precision.

And he had always been very, very precise.

With a faint shake of his head, William turned away from the poison, straightened, and wrapped his finger with a bandage. But as he returned the bandages, he cast another glance at the *box of rat poison*, as if drawn to it despite himself.

From above, the Devil leaned over the Cosmic Chessboard, His lips curling as He moved His knight forward, encircling God's bishop with deliberate care. "Ah, temptation... such a subtle friend. So often, it needs no words, only a look," He observed William's hesitation with delight.

God's fingers guided a pawn into a protective line. His voice was calm and filled with compassion. "Temptation exits everywhere, I have faith that William will find a path that leads to light and redemption."

The door swung open with a quiet creak, and Lexie glanced up, startled, as William entered, carrying a tray with a cup of tea resting in the center. His face was calm, his eyes distant. She accepted the tea, her fingers curling around the warm cup, but her eyes never left the large, gleaming knife beside it, its blade catching the light.

"What's with the knife?" she asked, a faint unease in her voice.

William picked up the knife, his lips curling into a faint, unreadable smile.

"Oh, this," William said, his voice light. But his hand hovered in the air for a moment, holding the knife a bit too high, and Lexie recoiled, her body shifting away. His smile grew sheepish, and he lowered the knife, his tone softening. "I meant to leave it in the kitchen."

William set the knife down and turned to leave, but his eyes caught on the hair dryer lying on the counter, inches from the edge of the tub. He reached for it, lifting it with a curious expression, turning it over in his hands before glancing back at her.

A chill ran through Lexie as he leaned over, holding the dryer above the water with a thoughtful expression. "Not smart, Lexie. If this falls into your bath... well, it might not kill you, but why chance it?"

She studied his stoic face, looking for a hint of the danger that lay behind his dark eyes. Her heart raced as he lowered the dryer to within inches of her bathwater.

"William..." Her voice was steady, though her eyes betrayed the fear pulsing through her.

He straightened, unplugged the hair dryer, and returned it to the counter. With a sheepish smile, he turned to leave. Lexie let out a long, tense breath, the blood rushing back to her face as she leaned back against the bath pillow, her body relaxing inch by inch.

William paused outside the door, his mind a swirl of restless thoughts. He nudged the door open peering through the narrow crack, watching as she lifted the tea to her lips. His heart hammered in his chest, each beat reverberating with a strange, unexplainable urgency.

<hr />

God's *White-Gloved Hand* moved with quiet assurance; His knight repositioned to block the Devil's advance. "There is still a moment, William," He said, His voice steady and filled with compassion. "Even now, redemption can be embraced."

The Devil leaned in, a sly gleam in His eyes as He slid His queen forward, casting a dark shadow over the Cosmic Chessboard. "Redemption, perhaps," He said with a chilling chuckle. "But every decision carries its weight, and not all burdens can be so easily laid down."

Back in the bathroom, Lexie raised the cup, the tea hovering below her lips when William burst through the door.

"Hey, don't drink that." his voice sharp with urgency.

She stopped, the cup poised in mid-air, her eyes narrowing as she stared at him. "What?"

"That's... that's the wrong tea bag," he stammered, reaching for the cup. "You won't like it. I'll... I'll be right back."

Lexie released her hold on the cup and passed it to William. She kept her suspicion and disbelief to herself, having no reason to question his actions.

Shaking her head, she leaned back, closing her eyes, letting the warmth of the bath soothe her, though a faint tension remained in her chest. She let the quiet darkness behind her eyelids offer a brief respite from the tension between them. The silence in the bathroom was soothing, a small break in the storm that had become her marriage.

Clack. William's footsteps returning jolted her back to the present. She opened her eyes. William stood in the doorway with a cup of tea in his hands. His face was unreadable, the steam curling around him like something ghostly, something that could dissipate at any moment.

"Chamomile tea," he said, stepping forward and kneeling beside her, offering the cup. For a brief, strange moment, Lexie wanted to reach out and touch his face, to search for the man she once loved beneath the hardened expression.

She took the tea, her hands grazing his, but she didn't recognize the touch. *Was he already slipping away?* She glanced down at the tea, her reflection wavering in the amber liquid. "Thank you," she responded, unsure if the gratitude was for the tea or for his unexpected gentleness.

"I thought you needed it," he said.

With raised brows, Lexie hesitated, unsure if it was an opening or another test.

Sipping the tea, she forced herself to search for something familiar, something safe, but his eyes only reflected the deep void between them. The warmth of the tea seeped through her, but it did little to dissolve the coldness that had settled in her chest.

"William," she said, her voice breaking the quiet, "I'm so tired of all of this."

Her words hung between them, and she waited, hoping he'd say something that could bridge the unspoken chasm that had grown between them.

He stared at her with a strange intensity, his movements stiff, his expression faltering between a smile and a frown as he stepped back, his eyes flickering over her face.

"I don't know you anymore."

———— ◆◆◆ ————

From the Cosmic Chessboard, the Devil studied William with a smirk, His fingers tapping lightly against the side of His queen. "Fear, hesitation, guilt," He teased savoring each word. "They grow like seeds in silence, feeding on doubt."

God remained steady and quiet. His White-Gloved Hand hovered over the board, his rook frozen in mid-air.

As William left, his footsteps fading, Lexie lay back against the bath pillow, her fingers tracing the rim of the cup. Lingering uncertainty resided in her mind, a quiet storm of questions and doubts swirling beneath the surface as the night drifted on.

TIL DEATH DO US PART

A quiet heaviness settled in the house. Unspoken words and contained rage filled the air. Lexie eased onto the sofa beside William, who had fallen asleep, his face softened at rest, the edges of tension smoothed out by unconsciousness. His tall frame lay outstretched on the sofa, one arm draped over his chest, the other resting at his side, fingers curled. His brow, often furrowed with tension, had smoothed in sleep, making him look younger... softer.

She hesitated, the familiar ache in her chest tightened. This man—the man she had loved for so long, now had a calm, peaceful face—like the man she married years ago. Asleep, there were no sharp words or guarded stares of disgust and disappointment. He wasn't the bitter storm that tore through their marriage.

He was just... William.

The room carried the faint scent of his cologne, warm and musky, and for a moment, she stood there, inhaling his scent and watching the steady rise and fall of his chest. She reached for the blanket draped over the back of the couch; she placed it over him, letting the soft fabric settle across his body, and pulled it up to fully cover his shoulders.

A sigh left her lips quiet and almost wistful. There were things she couldn't say right now, things neither of them could fix. But at this moment, in this small act of care, she allowed herself to love him without expectations, pure love in the quietest way possible.

A tear slipped from her eye, trailing down her cheek. Lexie wiped it away, afraid he might wake up and see it. Kneeling on the sofa, she examined the rings on her finger, their once-bright gleam now dulled by the darkness of the room. With a deep sigh, she rose, ready to walk away when William stirred.

His eyes opened, heavy with sleep, squinting as he focused on her. "Hey, baby," he mumbled, his voice thick and disoriented.

The word stunned her. "*Baby...*" she echoed, in a whisper, grasping the full weight of it. That one word sharpened her thoughts, and the reality of their fractured marriage and its demise crashed down on her with a force she couldn't ignore. Her resolve hardened.

"I don't want to do this anymore," she said, her voice low but firm. "I want out."

His eyes sharpened as he came fully awake, pushing himself upright. "There is *no* out."

"Don't make this harder than it has to be." Her voice was a fragile mix of pain and determination. "I can't be the woman you need, and you're not the man I want."

A darkness flickered in his eyes as he sat up, his voice lowering to a growl. "Till death do us part, remember?"

Lexie's face tightened, a glimmer of fear in her eyes. "If we don't part, death is certain."

He crossed the space between them in an instant, his posture menacing as he loomed over her. "Listen carefully," he hissed, his voice laced with fury. "I'll kill you before I'll divorce you."

She didn't flinch. She became defiant. "Then kill me." she spat, her voice raw with frustration and despair.

His face contorted in rage, and before she could react, his hands shot out, closing around her neck. She gasped, her fingers clawing at him, but his grip tightened, his anger boiling over in a violent surge. She struggled, her movements growing weaker and weaker as she fought for air, her eyes widening in panic.

William's hands loosened. He threw her down on the sofa, releasing his grip. Lexie gasped, clutching her throat, the remnants of his fingers' pressure still lingering on her skin. She pushed herself up, her breaths coming in shallow, panicked gasps, and she stared at him with a mixture of fear and disgust.

"You... you bitch," he spat, his hands clenched into fists as he took a step back. "What kind of woman cheats on her husband?"

"A lonely one." Lexie screamed.

The words landed like a slap. He staggered, his shoulders slumping as he sank down onto the sofa, burying his face in his hands, his elbows braced on his knees.

"I thought I could trust you," he muttered.

She glanced at him as the bitterness softened. "You can," she replied, her voice steady.

As he raised his head, she witnessed disbelief and desperation. "I can? Then..." His voice trailed off, something dark and questioning settling in his eyes. With a sudden burst of fury, he lunged at her, his hands finding her throat once again.

She shook her head, her voice breaking as she struggled to speak.

"What's wrong with you?"

"I know." He released her, stepping back with a pained expression, his boiling anger replaced by something raw, something wounded.

She staggered away from him, rubbing her neck. "You're hurting me."

"Hurting you?" He hissed, his voice laced with accusation.

Lexie searched his eyes, but it reflected the same mixture of confusion and fear that clouded her own.

He made a move toward her, stopping short, his body taut with rage. "You think I'm stupid, don't you?"

"If this is how it's going to be between us, then maybe we should get a divorce."

The word cut through the air, and William flinched.

"I can't live with you looking at me like this every day," she continued, her voice tight with hurt. "I never thought we'd end up here." She let the silence linger, bracing herself, searching his face for any sign of understanding. "We can't go on like this. If this is what we've come to... it's time we go our separate ways."

His expression darkened further, a dangerous edge in his voice. "I'll never divorce you. Never."

Lexie's eyes held his, her voice calm but unyielding. "Couples divorce all the time—besides—it's not up to you."

A cold smile twisted his lips.

"Think carefully, Lexie. It *is* up to me. And unlike you, I take my vows seriously."

She shook her head, as she turned her attention to the TV, pretending to watch it, using it as a barrier between them.

"Who is he?" William asked, his voice sharp and demanding.

She switched off the TV. "I'm leaving."

Before he could react, she bolted up from the sofa, but he grabbed her shoulders, his grip firm.

"Your threat—"

"It's not a threat," she interrupted, her voice cold. "Let go of me."

Lexie broke free from his hold, stepping back with a look of rebellion etched on her face.

"Nothing you say or do will make any difference."

William peers at her, his face filled with a mixture of sorrow and anger.

"All that I'm capable of, all that I am, I have given to you. I have nothing left."

Lexie opened her mouth to respond, but the words caught in her throat, the weight of everything between them pressing down. She sank back onto the sofa, a blank TV screen before her coupled with silence stretching between them like an unbridgeable void.

As the night deepened, they sat on opposite ends of the sofa, words unspoken, promises forgotten, both clinging to the fraying edges of a marriage slipping through their fingers.

From the Cosmic Chessboard, the Devil's *Red-Gloved Hand* hovered over His queen, a smile of dark satisfaction curving His lips as He moved her forward, cutting off God's knight with a swift, decisive strike. "And so, it crumbles," He whispered, His voice filled with delight. "The bonds they once held sacred, torn asunder."

God's *White-Gloved Hand* moved. His heart and soul filled with compassion as He repositioned His rook, His voice a soft, steady whisper. "Even in the brokenness, love still remains, it waits in the silence, ready to mend."

There was a shift, the air thickened the moment William crossed the threshold of their bedroom, like the room itself was bracing for impact.

Lexie didn't move. Her body stiff beneath the thin blanket, her hand resting just above the swell of her stomach, as though it could shield the life inside her from what she feared would come.

He knew about the baby, and he knew it wasn't his.

A subtle hint of awareness burned through her. She'd seen it in his eyes that morning. Confusion and devastation.

He knew.

And now he's here. And he's silent.

William closed the bedroom door with a click, slow and deliberate. The sound echoed louder than it should have.

Her throat tightened. "William?"

He didn't answer. He didn't need to.

He stood in the dark, face cloaked in shadow, his outline illuminated only by the faint moonlight slipping through the blinds. His hands hung at his sides, too still.

Lexie sat curling her arms around her stomach. "Whatever you're thinking—"

"Don't," he said, low and flat.

The word cracked like a branch breaking underfoot.

Her heart pounded. She didn't dare blink. He stepped closer, bare feet soundless on the floorboards, like a ghost.

"You were going to let me believe it was mine." His voice soft, but not tender. "You were going to carry that lie into our house, into our bed."

Lexie's voice faltered. "I didn't mean—"

William lunged at her, grabbing her shoulders. "You did mean it."

She wanted to run, to scream, but she couldn't move. She could barely breathe.

He stood at the edge of the bed, looking down at her. A fleeting expression appeared on his face before he composed himself.

His jaw clenched, eyes wild and wet. "I told you," he said, "you aren't going to have another man's baby."

She flinched. The words struck like a blow.

His hand twitched. Just one subtle movement. It hovered near her throat for a fraction of a second. Long enough for her to see it. Long enough for the cold brush of possible death wash over her.

Lexie's body cringed, trapped, waiting for the blow. Behind her a wall, beneath her the bed.

His fingers hovered. Inches from her skin. Inches from ending everything.

She held her breath. If he touched her, she would die.

Not because of his strength but because his eyes blazed with intent.

Tears burned at the edges of her vision.

She couldn't speak. Her tongue lies thick and heavy in her mouth.

And then—just like that—he dropped his hand.

Not in mercy. Not in forgiveness.

He stepped back from her the way you step back from a thing of disgust.

Lexie exhaled, and the breath came out jagged and loud. Her lungs burned with it. She hadn't realized she'd stopped breathing.

William stared at her. His eyes weren't angry anymore. They were hollow.

He turned and walked toward the door.

"William," she said, her voice hoarse, cracked.

He didn't stop. Didn't look back.

He left her sitting there in the dark, heart-racing, hands trembling, a scream lodged deep in her body where it couldn't come out.

She pressed her palms to her stomach and whispered to the baby, "I'm sorry. I'm so sorry."

Because now, she understood something she hadn't before: He hadn't killed her. But he could have. And the next time... He might.

God and the Devil continued the game, still unfinished, the final moves waiting to reveal themselves in the darkness.

TRUTH IS MISSING

T he tension in the room had thickened to an almost unbearable weight, pressing down on them both. William moved to the refrigerator, pulling out a beer with a jerky, frustrated motion. He popped it open, taking a long, forceful gulp before returning to the sofa, his eyes darting between Lexie and the blank TV screen.

Lexie peered at William for a moment. Her jaw tightened, and she stood and grabbed her car keys from the counter, her voice steady but tired. "I do need some air. I'm going for a short drive."

William lounged at Lexie, his hand snapping out like a vice as he yanked the keys from her grip.

"You're not going anywhere."

The force of his words hung in the air, his tone sharp and unyielding. He gripped her arm and pushed her back onto the sofa.

Lexie jerked away, her heart pounding with a mixture of fear and defiance. She pulled out her phone, her fingers fumbling in her attempt to dial, but before she could press a single button, William tore the phone from her hand and slammed it onto the counter, the sharp crack echoing through the room.

"William!" she shouted, her voice edged with shock and fury. "What the hell? Have you gone mad? Don't you want out of this mess?"

He stared at her, his face twisted with an intensity she hadn't seen before. "Not like this."

She scoffed, crossing her arms, her eyes blazing with challenge. "You have other plans?"

A strange, unsettling smile flickered across his face. "I do, and at early dawn, you'll know what they are."

A chill ran down her spine at his words. She didn't understand his expression. "What are you hoping to accomplish?"

He shrugged, moving back a step, he kept his eye fixed on her with an unnerving calmness. "You're so impatient, grasshopper... just wait. Don't force me to do something I'll regret. That we... will regret."

Their eyes locked, the weight of unspoken threats and words thick between them. She studied him, her heart pounding, trying to decipher the meaning behind his calm exterior, the restrained anger that simmered beneath the surface.

Without another word, he turned and stalked into the kitchen, opening cabinets with growing impatience. The metallic clink of utensils filled the silence as he rummaged, his movements agitated.

Lexie, bewildered and wary, took a tentative step closer. "What are you doing?"

He growled as he bent down to check a lower cabinet. "Didn't we buy new knives? Sharper knives? I can't find them."

Her eyes narrowed. "Why are you searching for knives in the middle of the night?"

"It'd be nice to get a straight answer sometimes, instead of a damned why."

She rolled her eyes, exasperation tightening her tone. "We bought new knives when we were in Ontario last year."

"Where... the hell... are they?" He slammed another cabinet shut, his expression darkening with each fruitless search.

"I don't know," she replied. Her anxiety grew. "What's the emergency?"

He took a slow breath, his voice lowering as he straightened, glaring at her. "These knives are dull, and I plan to gut a fish soon."

He didn't blink, not once, and the danger in his eyes was unmistakable and clear. Lexie's mouth went dry as she registered the threat beneath his words.

"You can't gut a fish with a dull knife," he continued, his tone calm. "Where are they?"

She swallowed, her voice coming out in a whisper.

"Use the Dragon Knife."

"No," he said. "That one's special."

She sighed, her patience fraying with increasing aggression.

"Fine. Look for them tomorrow. It's late."

But he ignored her, tearing through the drawers. His movements were sharp and erratic, each cabinet slamming louder than the last. Lexie cringed with each loud bang, the sound sending jolts of anxiety through her chest.

The Devil leaned over the Cosmic Chessboard, His fingers tracing the edge of His queen as He regarded William with a delighted glint in His eyes. "Ah, rage—the simplest fuel for action, the quickest way to fracture the already broken."

God's *White-Gloved Hand* hovered over the board, not searching, not hesitating—simply waiting for the piece to know its time. There was a deep sadness in His eyes as He moved His rook. "Yet in that rage, there is still a chance for restraint, a moment to choose peace."

William's hand stopped, his fingers gripping the edge of the counter as he stared down at the disarray of the open cabinets, his breathing heavy and uneven. Lexie took a step back, her voice tentative as she searched for something to defuse the tension. "This isn't helping. Can we just talk about it?"

He spun to face her, his expression unreadable, his eyes dark and intense. For a moment, he said nothing, searching her face as if trying to gauge her sincerity—or her fear.

William tore through the remaining cabinets, each door slamming with a force that echoed through the room. The clanging and banging of metal and wood made Lexie flinch with every slam. Her pulse raced. His frustration had spiraled into something more—a simmering fury that ignited with each cabinet he found empty, each drawer that held no trace of the knives he sought.

"Stop," she said, her voice low, but it did nothing to break his focus. He was too deep, too absorbed, his movements becoming more frantic.

He yanked open the last cabinet, gripping the edges of the counter as he leaned down, his breathing heavy, his hands clenched tight. He straightened as his eyes found hers, blazing with an intensity that made her take a step back.

"Are you even looking for knives or is this about something else?" she asked.

He took a step toward her. "I'm looking for the truth, Lexie. For answers. For something real."

She gestured at the mess. "And you think you'll find it in the cabinets?"

His eyes narrowed. "What are you hiding from me?"

Lexie crossed her arms, her jaw tightening as she fought to keep her voice steady. "I'm not hiding anything. You're losing it."

His mouth twisted into a bitter smile. "Am I? Or are you just afraid of what I might find?"

* * *

The Devil's lips curved into a satisfied smirk as He leaned over the board, His fingers moving His queen with a deliberate, calculated precision. "Desperation—how beautifully it pulls them apart," He whispered, His gaze locked on the scene unfolding. "All it takes is one unsteady step, one unchecked thought."

God patiently waited. His hand resting on His knight as He spoke, His voice calm and steady. "Even now, they can choose a different path," a plea echoed in His words. "They can reach for understanding, even in the darkness."

<hr>

William's words pricked her skin. "Fine," she snapped, crossing her arms. "You want the truth? Here it is, I am exhausted. I'm tired of the accusations, the anger, the constant edge. You're tearing us apart, and I can't keep pretending everything's fine."

"Tearing us apart?" he echoed, his voice tinged with disbelief. "You think I'm the one tearing us apart?"

"Look at you." She gestured at the open cabinets, the mess he'd made. "You're obsessed with finding something that isn't there. You're spiraling, and I... I don't even know who you are anymore."

He took a step back, the words hitting him like a slap.

He had this vacant stare, his eyes drifted over the disarray in the kitchen, the fragments of their life scattered like broken glass.

William glared at her. He was furious. "Maybe you don't know who I am because you've never really tried to," he muttered. "Maybe you never cared to know."

A hint of pain crossed her face, and she shook her head, looking away. "I can't do this anymore, I just... can't."

A heavy silence settled between them, both standing amidst the remnants of a shattered moment, both unwilling to be the first to turn away, to surrender to the weight of what they had become.

William stared at her, his chest rising and falling with sharp, measured breaths. "You can't do this anymore?" he repeated, his voice low and dangerous. "What exactly is it you can't do, Lexie? Tell me."

She shook her head, refusing to be baited. "This," she said, gesturing between them. "The constant fights, the suspicion, the walking on eggshells every second. I can't live like this, and I won't."

"You won't?" His laugh, sharp and bitter, cut through the air like glass. "That's rich. Do you think you can just walk out of here and everything will be fine? That you can leave all of this behind—leave me behind—and magically be okay?"

"I don't know." she snapped, her voice breaking under the weight of her emotions. "But I know I can't stay here and keep drowning. I've tried. I've tried so hard to make this work, but all we do is hurt each other."

"So, that's it? You're giving up because things got hard?"

Her anger flared, hot and blind. "Don't you dare call this running away," she said, her voice trembling with fury. "You have no idea how much strength it takes to admit that something is broken beyond repair."

"And you think this is beyond repair?" He stepped closer, his presence looming, his voice dropping to a cold whisper. "You think you can decide that all on your own?"

Lexie held her ground, her heart pounding in her chest. "I think we've both made it pretty clear where we stand," she said, her tone firm despite the tremor in her hands. "I don't trust you, and you don't trust me. You don't see me as your partner anymore. I'm just... someone to control, someone to accuse. How is that a marriage?"

William said nothing, his jaw tightened as he processed her words. He took another step closer, his voice low and steady, but laced with an edge of menace. "You think I don't trust you?" he asked. "What about you, Lexie? What have you done to earn that trust? You think I haven't noticed the late nights, the secret phone calls, the way you pull away every time I try to get close?"

A mix of shock and anger flashed across her face. "You're paranoid," she said, her voice trembling. "There's nothing going on, I've told you that a hundred times."

"And I'm supposed to believe you?" An empty laugh escaped his lips, and his eyes narrowed as he took another step forward. "You expect me to take your word for it while you hide behind closed doors and pretend everything's fine?"

"I'm not hiding." she shot back, her voice rising. "I'm trying to survive. Survive you, survive this... whatever this is. You've turned our home into a battleground, and I'm trying to make it through without losing my mind."

"Survive me?" His voice whispered, but the venom in it was unmistakable. "That's how you see me now? As some kind of monster?"

She hesitated, her throat tightening as she peered into his eyes, searching for the man she'd fallen in love with. "I don't know what I see anymore," she admitted, her voice breaking. "All I know is that this—" She gestured around them, the chaos of the kitchen, the weight of their words. "This isn't love. Not anymore."

The words hit him like a physical blow, and for a moment, his expression softened, a flicker of pain crossing his face. A moment later, the mask returned, his jaw tightening as he squared his shoulders.

"You're wrong." His voice was cold and firm. "This is love, Lexie. It's messy and it's hard, but it's real. And you don't get to just walk away."

Her eyes glistened with unshed tears, her voice trembling as she replied. "Love doesn't look like this. Love doesn't feel like this."

"Maybe you've forgotten what love is," he said, his tone biting. "Maybe you've been too busy dreaming about some perfect, fairy-tale version of it to see what's right in front of you."

Her hands balled into fists at her sides, her anger bubbling to the surface. "And maybe you've been too busy drowning in your own insecurities to see what you're destroying," she snapped. "We could have had something real. But you let your fear, and your anger tear it apart."

The room was silent, the air between them crackled with tension.

———◆———

From above, the Devil leaned back in his chair, a satisfied smirk playing on his lips as the scene unfolded. "They're so close now," He said, His voice dripping with delight. "One more push, and the game is mine."

God moved a piece with *White-Gloved Hands* shaped by eternity, gentle yet immovable, like mountains forming under water. "The game isn't over," He said. "Not yet."

———◆———

Back in the kitchen, Lexie turned away, her shoulders trembling as she fought to hold herself together. "I can't do this anymore," she whispered. "I can't keep fighting with you."

William's hands clenched and unclenched at his sides. "Stop fighting," he said, "And start listening."

She turned to face him, her eyes filled with a mix of anger and despair. "I've been listening. I've been listening for a long time. And all I've heard is silence."

"What are you talking about?" William demanded, his tone sharp with disbelief.

Lexie's last words hung in the air, heavy and final. William stared at her for a long moment, but she didn't waver, and she didn't flinch, despite the tremor in her chest.

He sighed, running a hand through his hair as he turned away. "Silence," he muttered. "You think that's all I've given you?"

"It's not just the silence," she said, her voice weary. "It's the accusations, the distrust, the anger... the way you've shut me out of everything that matters."

"And what about you?" he shot back, spinning to face her again. "You think I don't notice the way you pull away? The way you keep things from me. Don't stand there and pretend this is all on me."

She hesitated, her throat tightening as guilt flickered in her chest. "I never wanted it to be like this," she admitted. "I never wanted us to get to this point."

"Then why are we here?" he demanded, his voice rising. "Why, Lexie? What changed?"

There was so much she wanted to say, and her lips parted, but no words came out. Her mind raced to pinpoint the moment it all began to unravel. Was it his relentless suspicion? Her own growing resentment? Her betrayal or something deeper, something she couldn't quite put into words.

"I don't know," she said. "I don't know how we got here."

His laugh sprung hollow, filled with a bitterness that made her flinch. "Of course you don't," he muttered. "You never know, do you? Always leaving me to figure it out on my own."

"That's not fair," she said, her voice trembling with emotion. "I've been trying, I've been trying to hold on, to keep us together. But I'm... I'm so tired."

"Tired of me?" he asked, his tone cutting. "Or tired of pretending you still care?"

Her breath caught, his words slicing through her like a knife. "That's not true," she said, her voice breaking. "I do care. But caring isn't enough anymore."

He stepped closer, his eyes narrowing as he studied her face.

"Then tell me something, Lexie. If you care so much, why didn't you tell me about the pregnancy?"

The room tilted, his question slamming into her like a physical blow, her heart pounded as she stared at him in stunned silence.

"You went through my phone?" Lexie stammered.

"Don't turn this on me," William shot back, his jaw clenched.

"I never meant for this to happen," she cried, her voice breaking. "I was lonely, and you were always so distant."

"So, it's my fault now?" he barked, a bitter laugh escaping his lips. "You think that justifies cheating and lying to my face?"

"I couldn't—I couldn't bear the way you would look at me. The way you're looking at me now. I wanted a baby, and I thought this was the only way."

"You would cheat and lie—betray me to have a baby?"

"You cheated on me," Lexie responded.

"Lexie, you know that was years ago, and we weren't married. We went to counseling and got past that, at least I thought we had," William said. He glared at Lexie for a long time.

"Did you cheat on me simply because you thought I'm having an affair now?"

"Aren't you?" Lexie regretted the question.

Her heart almost broke seeing the pain in William's eyes.

"No Lexie, I'm not," William said, his voice low.

She shook her head, her body trembling. "I made a mistake, a terrible mistake. But it didn't mean anything, I swear."

"Didn't mean anything?" William echoed, his voice dripping with sarcasm.

"That's an insult. You sleep with another man, get pregnant by him, and destroy our marriage, yet it didn't mean anything?"

"Please, William," Lexie pleaded, reaching out to him. "I love you. Can't we find a way to move past this?"

He recoils from her touch, pain etched across his face. "Love me?" William shakes his head. "I don't even know who you are anymore," he muttered, turning away. "Maybe I never did."

How could she explain something she didn't understand herself? Her heart raced as she struggled to form a coherent thought, her hands trembling at her sides as tears flowed down her face.

"I wanted a baby. I know it's no excuse for what I've done to our marriage, to us, to you. I don't know what possessed me to go this far, to cross the line."

"Well, you crossed it, there's no going back. And I don't know how to deal with this. I guess we both have a decision to make." William turned and walked out, leaving Lexie in the silent kitchen.

------◄○►------

Somewhere, an unseen hand moved a chess piece.

"Ah, the sweet taste of doubt," The Devil mused, His fingers drumming on the edge of the board. "It's almost too easy, isn't it?"

God's *White-Gloved Hand* hovered over the board, His face somber as He studied the game. "Free will remains, even as trials press heavy upon them," He said. "They can still choose to trust, to find their way back to each other."

The Devil chuckled, shaking His head. "Trust? Oh, how fragile it is. One crack, and it shatters like glass. Watch and see."

But God's *White-Gloved Hand* moved as well, His rook sliding forward with determination. "Despair may come, but so too can hope," He said. "The game is far from over."

The Devil moved three pieces, shaping a trap as if drawing blood with geometry. "And now, the seeds of despair." He smirked. "Let's see how long it takes for them to break."

God's eyes followed only one piece. "Even pain teaches. The ones who break the leash still know who held it." He slid a rook along the edge of the board, opening a path no one else had seen.

STRANGE
BEDFELLOWS

William's hand shook as he stared down at the gun he held, the weight of it both grounding and unsettling. He'd taken it out with the same automatic motion as one would reach for a light switch in the dark, yet now, looking at it, he couldn't remember the last time he'd touched it, let alone held it so deliberately. His gaze drifted from the cold steeliness of the gun to Lexie's side of the bed. She lay there, asleep, her breathing deep and even, oblivious to the storm raging in him... mere inches away.

With a quiet, almost mechanical step, he moved closer, lifting the gun until it hovered close to her head. The metallic glint caught the faint light filtering through the curtains, a harsh, cold contrast against the softness of her sleeping form. His eyes were heavy with a dark mix of emotions—betrayal, resentment, pain—but beneath it all, a sharp edge of curiosity, as though accessing the depth of what treacherous acts he could do or would do.

Lexie's eyes fluttered open. She took in the gun, her body jolted upright.

"What are you doing with that gun?" Her voice shook, raw and edged with terror.

"I guess I have your attention now."

Her breath came in shallow gasps, her eyes darting between him and the weapon. "Put the gun away. Why were you watching me sleep?"

William shook his head, a bitter smile tugging at his lips. "Why, why, why. Always with the questions, Lexie. You never stop asking, do you?" His voice was low, almost amused.

He twisted the gun in his hand, turning it over as if examining it, yet his eyes stayed locked on her. Cold, unreadable. The air between them thickened, charged with something electric, something dangerous. The dim light of the room cast shadows across his face, deepening the sharp lines of his jaw, the dark hollows beneath his eyes. "I've never been more... annoyed."

Lexie sat up against the headboard, the sheets bunched around her waist. "What do you want?" She asked.

William tilted his head. "Am I making you uncomfortable?" He teased, gripping the gun.

Lexie gasped. "Yes," she admitted. "I've cheated on you, and for that, you'll never forgive me."

He let out a hollow laugh, shaking his head. "You're wrong." He lifted the gun, watching the way her eyes widened, how she tensed, bracing herself. "I've already forgiven you. It's the *forgetting* that has my balls twisted."

Lexie's eyes darted to the gun. She shifted on the bed, meeting his eyes. "It's... it's creepy," she said, her voice thin and unsteady. "Standing over me with a gun, watching me sleep."

William took a step closer, his grip tightening. "Creepy?" He let out another laugh, this one softer, more dangerous. "That's what you think this is? Creepy?" He exhaled through his nose, shaking his head again. "I've been patient, Lexie. *So*, patient."

"Am I scaring you?" he asked, his voice a low murmur.

"Are you trying to scare me?" Lexie asked, her eyes still on the gun.

William wanted her to suffer, to feel the pain of having someone you love, turn against you, and deceive you in the most intimate way possible. How can he make her see that no one, not even her, wins if this marriage ends?

Her hands trembled as she reached for the sheet, pulling it up once again to shield herself. "What do you want, William?" she asked again, softer this time. "Have you watched me before?"

He turned his head, his faint outline cutting through the darkness. "Many times. But I guess tonight's different. You sensed me watching you."

"I'm keenly aware of your every movement."

He let out a low chuckle, the sound devoid of humor. "As well you should be, but I want us back."

"There is no us."

His jaw ticked. "That's not true."

"Yes, it is," she said. "You know it is."

William licked his lips, considering her words. Without warning, he sat on the bed beside her. The mattress dipped under his weight, and he sensed her discomfort.

He let the gun rest on his lap, his fingers drumming against the metal. "You know, I used to think love was something unbreakable." His voice was quieter now, reflective. "Like a force of nature. Like no matter what happened, no matter how much shit two people put each other through, love would win. Love would always make a difference." He exhaled, shaking his head. "But that's not how it works, is it?"

"William—"

"You broke us, Lexie." His voice was still calm, but it carried a weight that made her chest tighten. "And I keep thinking... I can fix it. Maybe if I just try harder. But then I realize... *I didn't break it.*"

"I know," Lexie said. But I've been honest with you."

He raised an eyebrow, his expression mocking.

"Have you ever noticed how our desire to be 'honest' is related to our own convenience?"

Lexie's face was flooded with frustration and fear.

Silence stretched between them, thick and suffocating.

"This marriage won't let you bring home another man's baby, so it's dispensable. Isn't that the truth?" William probed. "You're not getting pregnant, so you go out and get pregnant? And then you think you can pass it off as mine and toss me out without a second thought?"

"I did think about it. I did what I thought would be the best way to keep our marriage together. I want a baby, and if I'm not happy, you won't be either."

In a sudden flash of anger, he grabbed her by the hair, yanking her head back, forcing her to meet his gaze. She gasp, her hands reaching for his wrist.

"Do you love him?" His voice was a low, dangerous whisper, every word dripping with accusation.

Her face contorted in pain as she struggled in his grip. "You're hurting me."

His grip tightened, his face inches from hers, his eyes burning with a fierce, unsettling intensity. "Do. You. Love. Him?"

"No..." she whispered, her voice shaking. "No, I don't."

"So, are you lying now, or were you lying before?"

"I'll tell whatever lie is needed to keep you from hurting me."

A moment passed, his hand still tangled in her hair as he searched her for any trace of deception. He released her. Lexie's breath came in shallow, panicked gasps.

William's heart pounded as he struggled to regain his composure. The whirlwind of emotions her words stirred within him was impossible to untangle—anger, sadness, disbelief, and something else he couldn't quite name. He searched her face as though trying to reconcile the woman standing before him with the one he had fallen in love with years ago.

"You're not the man I thought you were," Lexie said.

William's expression darkened, his jaw tightening as her words cut through him like a sharp knife.

"I know I'm different. I'm not at peace with myself. I feel—I feel invaded—but you, you never bothered to look deeper," he shot back frustrated. His mind raced. *How do I explain this when I don't understand it myself?*

William turned away for a moment as if looking at her might unearth too much. "You've always had this image of me in your head. The perfect husband, the man who'd solve every problem, carry every burden. Did you ever stop to see who I really am? Or was it easier to love the man you imagined?"

"I see you, William," she said, her voice trembling. "I've seen you at your best and at your worst. But I don't know when we stopped being on the same side. When did we become...this?"

The word hung between them, fragile and accusing, as if naming the distance would make it disappear.

William shook his head as Lexie lay back against the pillows, silent tears streaming down her face; the distance, an endless chasm, each breath they took drawing them further apart.

"You know, men have been known to kill their adulterous wives."

"You wouldn't kill me."

His face twisted with a bitter smile as he leaned in close, his breath hot against her face. "Wouldn't I? I'm truly tempted."

Her lips curled. "If that's your attempt at humor—"

"Not at all," he interrupted, his voice cold, unyielding. "I seriously want to strangle your ass."

Lexie sprang to her feet, her eyes fixed on him.

"What's wrong, baby?" he taunted, his tone mocking. "Not feeling the love? Was it something I said?"

Her voice was low. "I need to get away from you."

But he moved, grabbing her arm and pulling her back down onto the bed. His grip solid, like iron, his face inches from hers as he held her there, his eyes blazing with something between anger and twisted amusement. "Don't go."

He leaned in, pressing his lips close, but she turned her face away. "This isn't happening," she muttered, her voice cracking—she pushed herself up again.

In an instant, he grabbed her hands, forcing her back down with a cruel smile.

"Don't you want to show me what he did for you?" he sneered, his voice dripping with contempt. "How he excited you? Made you come?"

She broke free, scrambling off the bed, her chest heaving as she turned to face him, her eyes blazing. "What do you want from me?"

He shrugged, his smile dark and bitter. "Love, trust, honor, sex—you know, the usual. Maybe not in that exact order."

Her face twisted with frustration, her voice rising. "Things will never be the same again. I want out."

A shadow flickered across his face, and he leaned forward, his tone shifting into something low, menacing. "You don't know me at all, Lexie... or what I'm capable of doing."

She stared at him. "So why don't you tell me?"

He let out a hollow laugh, shaking his head as he ran a hand through his hair. "That would be too exhausting."

Her tone shifted. Her voice was cold.

"Poor William. I'm your worst nightmare—a vindictive wife who screws around with lots of men."

He shook his head, a bitter laugh escaping him. "Unfortunately, I don't know if you're being sarcastic or telling the truth."

"I'm sarcastically telling the truth. You have the nerve to accuse *me*?" she hissed, her voice sharp and trembling with fury.

"After everything I forgave you for doing. After all the nights I lay awake wondering if I could ever trust you again?" She took a step back, her hands clenched at her sides, her breath coming in quick, angry bursts. "I stayed, William. I stayed and tried to rebuild what you broke. And now, you throw this at me?"

She let out a bitter laugh, shaking her head. "Do you know what it's like to spend years proving your love to someone who has betrayed you?" Her voice cracked. "I chose to believe in us when no one else would have. And now, when I'm looking to you for that same faith, you'd rather paint me as a liar, a cheater?" "How dare you. After everything... how dare you."

He recoiled. "This is not the same, and you know it. We weren't married when I cheated, we were dating, I know that doesn't make it right, but there is a difference. We made vows to each other. But this—what did I ever see in you?"

Lexie stared at William. "A reflection, maybe."

"You never should have opened your damn legs."

"You're an ass." Her voice was harsh, defiant.

William lunged at Lexie, the *SLAP* echoed through the room, cutting the silence like a blade. Lexie's head whipped to the side, and she fell to the floor.

The urge to fall to his knees and comfort her was strong, but William resisted. Caught between loving her and hating her conflicted him and tore at his heart. *How could this be our lives now? Why are we throwing words that cut like knives? What happened to us?* The questions swirled around in his mind over and over. He didn't have an answer, but this relationship could not endure. It was on the brink of dying a slow and torturous death.

Now he had once again hit the only woman he had ever loved.

A strange and cold reality settled around them, the silence of a love broke beyond repair. Both were unwilling to yield; the darkness deepened, leaving them locked in a battle that neither of them was ready to end, a crucial choice still lingering, unspoken, between them.

The weight of William's anger hung heavy in the air, and he regretted hurting Lexie, a stranger to him now, someone he didn't quite recognize... or like. He couldn't accept what she thought of him at this moment.

A mixture of fury and regret contorted his face, and he understood that the distance between them was now vast, filled with years of anger and betrayal.

The Devil's smirk widened in the darkness as He moved His queen forward, casting a dark shadow over the board. "Oh, how beautifully they unravel," He savored the chaos of emotions swirling between William and Lexie. "All it takes is a small push, and everything they held dear slips through their fingers."

God's *White-Gloved Hand* inched forward. Sorrow etched across His face as He adjusted His pieces in a quiet defense. "Yet even now, there is still time to decide," He whispered, His voice filled with composure. "A choice to see past the pain, to reach for something greater."

TENSIONS

William pulled open the refrigerator door, letting the pale light spill into the kitchen. He reached in, his fingers settling on a block of cheese, and he closed the door. Lexie moved through the shadows into the living room. She eased onto the sofa, her movements cautious. She tracked his every step as he approached the knife block and pulled out a large knife. Lexie stiffened, her eyes widening as he brought the knife and cheese to the coffee table, placing them down with an almost careless gesture.

Holding the knife, he pointed it in her direction with a faint smirk. "You want some cheese?" he asked, his tone almost mocking.

Lexie's eyes darted between the knife and his face. "You know how I feel about cheese," she replied, her voice laced with disdain. "That stuff will kill you."

"Any number of things will kill you," he said, slicing into the cheese with deliberate force. "You can't avoid death forever." The metallic scrape of the blade against the plate filled the silence as he offered her a slice. She declined with a slight shake of her head, her eyes lingered on the knife before she shifted her back to him.

"Sparkling water?" he offered, the knife lying unceremoniously on the plate.

Lexie narrowed her eyes, an unease settling into her bones. "Yes."

He rose and walked to the refrigerator, retrieving a bottle of sparkling water along with the champagne left over from dinner. He returned, filling two glasses—hers with sparkling water, his with champagne. He settled back on the sofa, holding the glasses with an air of indifference as he passed one of the glasses to her. "Now," he said while swirling the champagne, "Where were we?"

Lexie took a careful sip, her eyes glued to him.

"Visiting fantasy land," she said, her tone weary. "Maybe we should just go to bed."

"But why, Lexie? Why go to bed? I can no longer find a place in you where no man has gone before."

She clenched her jaw, refusing to let his words unsettle her. "So, who's being sarcastic now?"

William let out a low laugh. "I guess you're affecting me in a number of ways," he drawled, setting his glass on the table.

"Let's stop this," she responded, gazing away from him.

But he was already moving, slipping behind her on the sofa, his hands falling onto her shoulders.

She jumped at his touch.

"You don't have to do that," she said through gritted teeth.

"Relax, Lexie. I want to." His voice was too smooth as his hands kneaded into her shoulders. She forced herself to sit still, allowing him to continue, though every nerve in her body screamed at her to move. His hands slid up to her neck, fingers pressing with a strange firmness, Lexie swallowed hard, her throat dry.

Without warning, his grip tightened, fingers digging into her skin. Lexie's breath caught as his hands clamped around her throat, inching closer to a dangerous threshold. She squirmed as she pulled his hands away with strength, she didn't know she had. "Stop!" she gasped, heart pounding.

"So, you *do* know how to say stop," he said with an icy smirk, stepping back. "I was beginning to think you were unfamiliar with the concept."

Lexie's eyes flashed, defiance replacing the initial shock. "I only need to know it when I'm with you."

His smirk widened, a twisted glint in his eye. "I could easily snap that sarcastic neck of yours. Keep talking."

"I'm not afraid of you."

"Yet. You're not afraid of me yet.

"Why are you saying that?" Lexie asked.

William didn't respond. He moved to the window. He whispered to himself. "What happened to my best friend?"

"I didn't mean to hurt you."

"Of course you did. Well done." William clapped.

"What do you suggest I do? Get rid of the baby?"

William stumbled over to the sofa. A little drunk. "Would that be so bad? You're obviously in the early stages."

"I'm ashamed of this conversation."

William stared at Lexie. "You won't have another man's child. Not ever. I won't allow it."

Lexie rose halfway, she got in William's face. "Who the hell do you think you are?"

"Your husband. The one you chose to honor and obey."

"Obey?"

"Yes, obey. And don't forget honor. You didn't honor me, Lexie, but you will obey."

Lexie is outraged. "You don't own me. This is my body. I'll do whatever I want with it, I'll do whatever I want to it, and I'll share it with whomever I choose to share it with."

William SLAPPED her hard. "Why did you marry me? That attitude is more fitting of a single woman."

Lexie fell to the floor. She touched her cheek, which still stung from the slap. "I ask myself that question every day. I've tried to tell you, but you don't hear me."

"Oh, I hear you," he replied, his voice full of venom. "You want a divorce. You don't love me anymore. You want a baby." He sank into the sofa, his stare cold and unwavering. "But you don't hear *me*. No divorce. No baby. Not now, not ever. And that's final."

"You're not speaking to a child," Lexie shouted.

William growled. "Aren't I?"

Lexie glared, fury building as she stood up, shaking with unspent anger, a breath away from walking out for good.

Lexie clenched her fists, trembling with the force of her frustration. "How dare you talk to me like that?" she hissed, her voice shaking but growing stronger with each word. "You sit there, spewing ultimatums like a dictator, as if you have the right to control my life, my choices, my body!"

William didn't waver. His jaw tightened as his hands gripped the edges of the sofa. "I'm your husband, Lexie," he snapped. "I have every right to a say in this marriage, in what we do as a family. Or does that mean nothing to you now?"

"A family?" she spat, her voice dripping with incredulity. "We're not a family. We're two people pretending everything's fine while we rip each other apart. You can't even look at me without resentment in your eyes. And you think that's a foundation for a family?"

His eyes flashed, a storm brewing behind them. "Don't you dare twist this around on me," he said, his voice low but dangerous. "You're the one talking about walking away, about giving up. Don't put this on me."

"I'm not twisting anything." she shot back, taking a step closer to him. "I'm telling the truth, something you seem to have forgotten how to do. You say no divorce, no baby, as if those are your decisions to make. But guess what, William? They're not. You don't get to decide my future for me."

He stood, towering over her, his expression dark. "And what future is that, Lexie? Huh? One where you run off, chasing some fantasy of happiness? Where you replace me, like I'm disposable?"

She flinched at the venom in his words, but she didn't back down. "This isn't about replacing you," she said, her voice soft now but firm. "This is about saving myself. Saving us if that's even possible."

William laughed. The sound cut through the tension like a blade. "Saving us? Don't kid yourself. You're not trying to save anything. You're trying to escape."

"And maybe I have every reason to." she shouted, her voice cracking. "Do you know what it's like to feel trapped, to feel like you're suffocating in your own home? To want something so desperately, only to have the person who's supposed to love you the most dismiss it like it's nothing?"

His face hardened, his shoulders rigid as he stared at her. "You think you're the only one suffering, Lexie? Don't you think I feel trapped too? Every day, I wake up and wonder how we got here, how everything we built turned to ash. And I blame myself. I carry that weight every damn day. But you... you just want to run away from it."

Tears welled in her eyes, but she refused to let them fall. "Because I don't see another way. I don't know how to fix this when you won't even meet me halfway. All I've ever wanted was to feel like we're in this together, but all I get from you is silence and anger and walls I can't break through."

He turned away from her, running a hand through his hair, his movements jerky with frustration. "And what happens if you get your way, huh? You leave, you have your baby, and then what? You think that'll magically fix everything?"

"No," she said, her voice trembling. "But at least I'll have something to hold on to. Something to remind me that life can still be beautiful, even if this..." She gestured between them, her heart breaking as she said the words. "Even if this is beyond saving."

Her words hung in the air, heavy and suffocating, and for a moment, neither of them spoke. The clear but faint ticking of the clock on the wall was unnerving as each second dragged out like an eternity.

William turned back to her, his expression unreadable. "You're wrong," he said, his voice low and raw. "This isn't beyond saving. It's broken, yes, but it's not beyond repair. We must stop fighting against each other and start fighting for us."

She stared at him, her heart aching with the weight of his words. "And what if I don't have the strength to fight anymore?"

His face softened with a flicker of vulnerability in his eyes that Lexie found unusual.

"Let me fight for both of us," he said. "Because I'm not ready to let you go, Lexie. Not now. Not ever."

She swallowed hard, her emotions threatening to overwhelm her.

"And what if I still want to leave?"

William stepped closer, his eyes locked on hers.

"I'll wait. I'll wait until you realize that this—" He reached out, taking her hand in his. "This is worth fighting for. Until you see that I'm not the enemy, Lexie. I'm just a man who loves you, who's terrified of losing you."

Her resolve wavered, her heart aching with the weight of his words and the depth of his pain. Is love enough to heal what's broken between them? Who is this man standing before her? He keeps going back and forth. *Can I trust what he's saying? Will he accept this baby or is it simply another deception?*

In the fiery glow surrounding the Cosmic Chessboard, the Devil leaned back, His fingers steepled, a glint of satisfaction in His eyes. He had maneuvered His pieces skillfully, each one an echo of the pain and distrust reverberating between Lexie and William. His knight loomed near God's queen, positioning for a calculated strike, attempting to seal the fate of the broken couple. He relished the fragile tension, the tightening coil of bitterness, the whispered doubts He'd planted like seeds, now flourishing into a tangled web of anger and betrayal.

But God, calm and steady, moved His hand over the board with infinite care, positioning His queen in an unexpected spot, a graceful retreat that created an open path. His eyes were patient, unfazed by the Devil's smirk, as if seeing far beyond the board, beyond the chaos and conflict, to a light yet unseen.

The Devil squinted with faint irritation as God's move loosened the binds around Lexie's heart, offering her a chance to resist, and see the truth through the darkness. Their game was not yet over; and while the Devil claimed His victories in shadows and bitterness, God's moves held the quiet power of redemption, one step at a time.

DARKNESS

William's mind spun out of control, each step toward the kitchen weighed down with a dark, simmering rage he could no longer suppress. His hands clenched into fists as he reached the counter, trying to calm his breathing to clear the chaotic thoughts that pounded through his skull like a drumbeat. He had searched her face for anything that resembled the love they once shared, but all he'd seen was indifference, a cold, blank stare that hollowed him out.

In the kitchen, he yanked open the drawer, searching for anything to distract him, to ground him before the fury within spiraled further. His fingers wrapped around a knife, and he held it so tightly that his knuckles turned white. A dark thought flickered in his mind, and he squeezed his eyes shut, battling against the impulse that threatened to consume him.

The Devil's *Red-Gloved Hand* lingered over the Cosmic Chessboard, His smile widening as He moved His queen into a powerful, dominating position. "Desperation, it makes all things possible, all things forgivable."

God observed William with a sadness that softened his reserve. His fingers rested on His rook, moving it to shield Lexie's path, a quiet line of defense. "Even in rage, love can yet emerge," He whispered, His tone steady. "Sometimes, it only takes a moment of quiet to find it."

<hr />

In the kitchen, William leaned against the counter, his breath shallow as he loosened his grip on the knife. He couldn't look at her; he didn't want to. Her blank look haunted him, mocking every effort he'd made to salvage what they had. His eyes fell to the floor, the image of her indifference like a thorn burrowing deep into his heart.

Footsteps sounded behind him. He didn't turn. Her presence filled the room, quiet but cold, her voice as unyielding as ever. "Nothing you say or do will make me want to stay. I need a life beyond this, beyond us, and you keep waffling. Every day, it seems, I get a different William.

He gritted his teeth, his back still to her, a mixture of hurt and frustration churning within him. "You don't even care, do you? About what we've built, about what we've shared."

She stood behind him, the silence stretching between them, both knowing that the words they spoke now were echoes of the past, fragments of a love that had been whittled down to resentments and regrets.

"What we had wasn't enough, William. You know that as well as I do. We've been holding on to a memory, not a marriage."

He turned, his eyes flashing with pain, the depth of his hurt breaking through his anger. "You want a baby," he whispered. "And that means more to you than I ever did."

Her face softened, but she remained distant. "It's not about choosing one over the other. It's about wanting something that matters to me. I've given you everything I could. But I need this."

A bitter laugh escaped him, and he shook his head, placing the knife on the counter, his shoulders slumping with a defeated resignation. "You're right, Lexie," he said in a strange low voice. "What's left of us isn't worth fighting for. Not anymore."

Lexie took a step backward, her hand resting on the doorframe. His resistance was drained, his spirit dampened by the harsh truth. With a quiet, solemn look, she turned and walked away, leaving him alone in the kitchen, a shadow of the man he once was.

———◆———

God reflected a sadness that mirrored William's.

The Devil's laughter echoed through the room, triumphant, unyielding, savoring every fractured moment, every final, unspoken goodbye.

———◆———

Lexie sat up in bed, wrapped in her blankets, though they offered little comfort. The faint light from the hallway cast long, creeping shadows on the walls, flickering each time a draft stirred the door. The silence amplified every sound—the groaning creak of the old house settling, the distant hum of the refrigerator, the faint tick of the wall clock. But her entire body listened to the slow and measured rhythm of footsteps beyond the closed door.

William.

He was out there, pacing along the hallway. Each step measured and thoughtful as if planning something unspeakable. Lexie froze, and her throat went dry as a memory surfaced: his tight smile from earlier that night, the one that didn't reach his eyes, and the way he stared at her, a persistent stare.

She told herself it was irrational, that she was letting her mind run wild. But another part of her, the part that couldn't shake the unease coiling in her stomach, whispered that this was real. The faint, prickling sense that he watched her with something darker than love, a cold, impenetrable scrutiny that had no place in a marriage. And tonight, all her fears had manifested, hanging thick in the air like a storm on the brink of breaking.

The Devil sat back in His chair, moving a black pawn forward with a smooth, satisfied flourish. His eyes glinted with dark amusement, a smirk tugging at His lips as He studied the board, each piece carefully arranged in His favor. "She knows," he taunted, his voice like silk, seeping into her thoughts. "She knows he's waiting for her."

Opposite him, God sat, His expression unreadable, His fingers hovering over a single white pawn. He observed Lexie, His eyes filled with a sorrowful empathy that intensified the sense of dread. Lexie wanted Him to move, to do something to counter the Devil's insidious advance, but He hesitated, moving with a wisdom that bordered on regret.

Another creak from the hallway. Lexie's eyes snapped to the door, her breath catching in her throat. The footsteps had stopped. She could picture him standing outside, his hand on the doorknob, his head tilted as he listened, as though savoring the moment, drawing it out.

Her phone lay on the nightstand within arm's reach, but what would she even say if she called Joyce? She could already imagine the brush off she'd get for calling in the middle of the night to say she feared her husband. Absurd. Yet every fiber in her being screamed that William had trapped her in this house and she couldn't escape.

The Devil's laugh echoed again, rich with cruel amusement, as He slid a black bishop across the board, His eyes glinting with malicious delight. "It's almost over," He said, His voice a whisper that filled the room.

Lexie's hands trembled as she clutched the edge of the blanket, drawing it up to her chin as though it could shield her from the certainty settling over her. She strained to hear his footsteps, she held her breath, the weight of his presence lingering beyond the door and the suffocating inevitability of it all. Her mind raced back to the recent incidents—the broken brake line, the faulty stair railing, the "accidental" slip of his hand while passing her a sharp knife in the kitchen. When isolated, each one could be innocent enough. But together, they painted a chilling picture she couldn't ignore.

You're imagining it, she wanted to convince herself. *This is William. He wouldn't hurt you.* But the thought was hollow, weak, swallowed up by the crushing certainty that settled into her bones. A sense of impending danger filled the air, pressing down on her until she couldn't breathe.

The Devil's fingers tapped a piece as He turned His attention to her.

He's waiting for you to fall, Lexie. And you will. They all do.

A soft whimper escaped her lips. She slapped a hand over her mouth. *He's enjoying my terror, my fear, and my vulnerability. I won't make it easy for him.*

The footsteps resumed, slow and methodical, each step a loud echo in her chest. He wasn't coming in. Not yet. But he remained outside the door, biding his time, savoring her fear, letting it fester and grow until she drowned in it.

God moved a piece forward, a gentle, careful motion, His face grave as Lexie's torment unfolded. "Not yet," He said in a faint voice, almost to Himself. But with uncertainty, a reluctance, as though bounded by some unseen rule, some restraint that kept Him from intervening.

The Devil grinned, sliding a knight across the board with relish. "She's all yours, William," He said, His voice dripping with dark amusement. "Take your time."

Lexie rushed to the window. *Could she escape?*

She tried to raise the window, it didn't even budge. Locked. Trapped in a game William had been playing for months now, a game she wanted no part of.

Another creak. Her heart thundered, her breaths coming fast and shallow as the footsteps stopped again, outside her door. She imagined him standing there, his hand resting on the doorknob, waiting for her to make a sound, to acknowledge him, measuring her resolve, her strength—or her fear.

A shiver coiled down her spine.

Click.

Her stomach churned as the knob turned.

"Don't be afraid," came the soft voice in her mind, a voice of warmth and calm that contrasted with the terror consuming her. A whisper from God, His tone gentle, steady, filling her with a faint glimmer of hope. "You are stronger than you think, Lexie. Trust in that."

But her fear overwhelmed her, drowning out any trace of reassurance. She clutched the blanket tighter, her knuckles white, her mind racing through every scenario. Paralyzed, her body refused to move, even as her instincts screamed at her to run.

The Devil's eyes gleamed with satisfaction. He leaned back, crossing His arms as He surveyed the board, every piece aligned exactly where He wanted it.

God's *White-Gloved Hand* moved a single white piece, sliding it forward with determination. God steady, unwavering, and filled with a serene defiance, cut through the darkness.

The footsteps began again, retreating down the hall, growing fainter with each step until complete silence. She opened her eyes, her body still trembling, but her heartbeat began to steady. Although safe, the sense of dread remained, lurking beneath the surface. Lexie stared at the ceiling, but this wasn't over. The game would continue, the pieces shifting, the tension growing. But tonight, she had held her ground. Tonight, she had won a small victory, one that she clung to as fiercely as she clung to her life.

BENEATH THE PAIN

The tension between them had reached a fever pitch, each movement charged with restrained hostility, a palpable, electric current filling the room. William stormed back to the refrigerator, his hands shaking as he pulled out a brown bag. He slapped it onto the counter and reached for the Dragon Knife he wanted to keep treasured, but nothing mattered now. A calmness settled that belied the tempest raging within him.

As he unwrapped the bag to reveal a massive bass, he peeked at Lexie, who sat on the sofa, her defiance and disdain evident. Her face set. her posture unyielding, as if daring him to lash out, to release the torrent of anger he tried to hold back.

With the knife in hand, he took a deep, steady breath, each inhale filled with anger, resentment, and a hurt that he could no longer keep buried. He positioned the knife over the fish's neck and, with a swift, brutal motion, sliced off the head, his eyes never leaving Lexie's.

"I didn't expect you to cheat on me," he ranted, his voice cold. "I expected respect. I expected loyalty. I expected to rule."

Her laugh was bitter. "Rule? You have no money. You cannot rule."

The words landed like a slap, and he pressed the knife deeper into the fish, slicing through the flesh with unnecessary force. He paused, glancing up with a twisted smile. "Is this a power struggle for you?"

Lexie's expression was one of resolve. "It's no longer a struggle... I would respect a struggle."

With another vicious stroke, he hacked into the fish, his breathing quickening. "I've given you everything you ever asked for, Lexie. Everything."

"And now..." Her voice was soft, almost vulnerable, but her eyes were unyielding. "I want the madness to end. Nothing less, nothing more. Just let me go."

In one smooth motion, he dropped the fish and strode over to her, his movements quick and deliberate. The knife hovered beneath her chin, its edge glinting under the kitchen lights as he held her in place. She didn't flinch; her body rigid but unafraid as she peered into his eyes.

"I could cut your throat right now, tonight on our anniversary," he whispered, his voice low, every word laced with an unspoken threat.

Lexie's hand moved to his, her fingers curling around his fingers in a move so intimate, so unexpected, it took his breath away. Her voice was a whisper, quiet but unbreakable. "Do it... or let me go."

Something shifted in him, his grip on the knife faltering as frustration and confusion warred within him. With a low growl, he slammed her back against the wall, his hand loosening its grip on the knife, but his eyes never left hers. She held her ground, her face defiant even as his anger radiated off him like heat from a flame.

"This is unhealthy," he muttered, his voice thick with frustration as he lowered the knife.

"I'm in love with this baby," she said, her voice breaking. "I need to have this baby, William."

William began to pace the floor. He held the knife out, gesturing with each accusation. "My wife's a whore," he spat, the words tearing from his throat as he stared at her with a mixture of anger and heartbreak. "How could you disrespect me?"

Her response was immediate, sharp. "I've been a good wife. How could you get a vasectomy without telling me?"

He scoffed, the irony not lost on him. "This is my body, and I, too, will do whatever I want to do to it." He paused. "Including having a vasectomy."

The silence that followed was deafening. Each of them breathed heavily, locked in a stalemate neither could win. Frustrated, William stomped over to the dishwasher. He yanked it open, dishes and pans scraping around with a force that made Lexie jump. Every loud, clanging motion echoed with his anger and resentment... but also, unmistakably, his attachment, his inability to let go despite everything. His anger spilled over with each movement.

<hr />

The Devil's eyes gleamed with satisfaction as He moved His bishop, edging it closer to God's knight. "Attachment, the sharpest double-edged sword," He stated, savoring each bitter moment between them. "It cuts both ways, binds even as it wounds."

With deep compassion, God moved his rook in a protective arc. "Love persists, even in the most shrouded corners," He whispered. "Love endures beneath the anger, beneath the hurt."

William continued his frenzied cleaning, but his eyes darted to Lexie every few seconds, unable to fully ignore her presence. He struggled to conceal the paralyzing pain as he stabbed at the counter.

Her face, a sad blank canvas—a face he had once adored. Now, her eyes are weary, almost resigned. Had she given up on him?

William placed the last dish in the dishwasher and stood there, hands gripping the edge of the counter as he stared down at his own reflection in the stainless-steel sink. The air was thick, heavy with the words left unspoken, the fractures in their relationship deepening with each silent second.

From the corner of his eye, he peeked at her flipping through the channels, his heart pounding as he attempted to reconcile the woman before him with the woman he'd married. The woman who had once been his everything, his partner, his best friend. The woman he didn't recognize now. He thought about the early dawn gift he had planned so carefully. *Did it really matter now? Was it too late?*

His footsteps were slow as he left the kitchen. He lingered on her one last time before he retreated into the shadows, his mind still tangled in anger, but a deeper, quieter pain settled in his chest.

In the silence, the finality of it hit him, the fragile strands of their marriage unraveling with each breath he took, slipping through his fingers as he clung to a past that was already gone.

William sat hunched on the toilet, his head cradled in his hands, the words playing over and over in his mind, each one cutting deeper than the last. Lexie's voice echoed through the hollow chambers of his thoughts, relentless and unyielding.

I can't give you a baby, he'd told her.

Then what good are you? she'd replied, her words laced with disdain, echoing still like a knife twisting inside him.

He shook his head, trying to chase away her voice, but the memories came back stronger, more vivid, filling the room with the weight of everything left broken and unsaid.

You can't imprison me here, she'd shouted, the rage in her voice crackling like electricity.

I just want out. Cold words without emotion, a final declaration of her desire to be anywhere but with him.

He rose like a man shackled by invisible chains and made his way to the vanity. The sharp, pungent scent of Lexie's lipstick filled his senses as he picked it up, the cool, smooth cylinder—foreign in his grip. He stared at his reflection in the mirror—a stranger looking back at him, a man consumed by bitterness, resentment, and a loss he hadn't known could run this deep.

He uncapped the lipstick, the color a bold, angry red. Perfect. It was a manifestation of everything boiling beneath his skin. With deliberate, heavy strokes, he began to scrawl across the mirror. The pressure of each letter was a release, a purging of everything he'd bottled up, words he could never say to her face but words he needed reflected at him.

He pulled back, his breath heavy as he took in the message. Each word glared back at him, raw and unforgiving, bearing the weight of every unspoken emotion, every shattered piece of a marriage that had once meant everything to him.

With a smile, the Devil leaned forward, His hand reaching cross the Cosmic Chessboard as He slid His queen closer, trapping God's bishop in an aggressive, unyielding position. "And in an instant—love turns to hate when pride and resentment take hold."

God's fingers grazed the edges of His pieces. His posture was full of sorrow. His eyes reflecting a gentle empathy as He moved His knight to shield the bishop, creating a slim but crucial path to safety. "Amid the most burdened hearts, light makes its journey, if they choose to notice," He whispered.

In the quiet of the bathroom, William studied the message he'd scrawled across the mirror. The words stared back at him, bold and unflinching, capturing a part of himself he had once buried, a part he could no longer ignore. With the lipstick smeared, and the message blazing in the reflection, a chill settled over him. He faced a truth he could no longer deny.

The words he had written, carved in red, were a final testament to the love and bitterness that had intertwined, pulling them both into a darkness they could choose to leave behind.

Lexie sat on the edge of the bed, a soft smile playing on her lips as she absentmindedly traced gentle circles over her stomach. For a moment, all the tension and all the conflict dissolved, leaving only a quiet anticipation—a secret joy she carried within her. She reached under the mattress and retrieved the baby book, its pages filled with carefully chosen images of cribs, tiny outfits, lullabies, and all the dreams she hadn't dared to voice aloud. Flipping through the pages, she could almost picture the life she'd longed for, a life that existed in her imagination.

But as she let herself imagine it; William's muffled voice broke through the stillness. It was faint but urgent, the words distorted yet laced with frustration. Her body stiffened, clutching the book tighter before closing it and slipping it back beneath the mattress, hiding it as if it were something forbidden. With one last lingering glance, she stood, stealing herself as she left the bedroom and moved down the hall, her footsteps soft against the floorboards.

Each step brought her closer to William's voice, the familiar weight of tension settled over her again. When Lexie stepped into the hallway, a light filtered in from the second bathroom. She paused outside the bathroom door, her hand hovering near the frame as she took a breath, gathering strength to confront whatever lay beyond. She could make out William's form, his head bowed, one hand braced against the sink as he muttered to himself. She took a cautious step closer, her presence unseen, as she caught a glimpse of the mirror.

Red words scrawled across the mirror, bold and glaring under the harsh light of the bathroom. The lipstick marks were jagged, the strokes uneven, as though each word had been carved out with anger, with pain, with something darker and unresolved.

"You broke my heart, and I will kill you before I ever let you go," the message read, the letters jagged and unrelenting.

Lexie's breath caught in her throat, the weight of his accusation sinking deep, hitting her like a physical blow. She wanted to turn and walk away, to bury her head under the covers and escape back to the fragile peace she'd held onto a few moments ago. But something held her there, rooted her to the spot, forcing her to confront the raw, jagged edges of what their relationship had become.

William caught her reflection in the mirror. For a moment, their eyes met, a flicker of something unspoken passing between them—hurt, regret, even a trace of the love that once bound them. But it vanished, replaced by an expression hardened with resentment.

"You broke my heart, and yes, I will kill you before I ever let you go," he repeated, his voice low but filled with a bitterness that made her flinch.

She swallowed. "I... I didn't mean to hurt you. I never wanted any of this."

"Didn't you?" he asked, his voice rising as he turned to face her. "Because from where I'm standing, it looks like this is exactly what you wanted. You didn't want me—you wanted a child, something I couldn't give you."

Lexie's face softened. "You're not being fair."

"Fair?" he scoffed. He took a step toward her. "I was supposed to be your partner, Lexie. Your best friend. And instead, I'm just an obstacle you need to get around."

Lexie's hand moved to her stomach, a gesture so small yet filled with a meaning that deepened the rift between them.

A subtle tremor passed through her. "I didn't take everything, William. You made choices too. You... you chose not to be part of this. To be alone in what you wanted."

He stared at her for a long, tense moment, his expression unreadable as the words hung in the air, each one layered with unspoken truths neither one of them dared to say aloud.

Lexie met his eyes, her own expression shadowed with regret. She stepped closer. "We can't go back," she said, the sadness unmistakable.

"No," he replied. "I don't know how or if we can move forward, not now—not with this baby."

They stood in silence, the echoes of their past lingering between them, the path to forgiveness faint but within reach. And as they stood there, the choice waited, hovering in the stillness, waiting for one of them to make the first move.

———◆———

The Devil, squinting at the board, moved His queen forward, edging closer to God's defenses with a dark, gleeful smile. "Let them cling to the anger and hurt," He purred. "Love cannot survive in the presence of pride, and they break so easily, do they not? My defeat is not possible with these two. One secret, one misunderstanding, and it all falls apart. I love it."

Above them, God's *White-Gloved Hand* moved carefully, adjusting His rook with an enduring purpose. "Sometimes, to heal, we must first let go," He stated, as He observed Lexie and William with a mixture of sadness and hope. "It is in the breaking that they learn who they are. Pressure does not only crush—it refines. They will get through this."

"Spoken like someone who also enjoys watching them suffer."

"No, but I do believe in what they can become when the pain is faced, not avoided."

A CAUTIONARY TALE

A faint beam of light filtered through a narrow crack in the door of William's office. It caught Lexie's eye, and she hesitated, knowing he wouldn't appreciate her invading his privacy.

Tiptoeing, she slipped through the door, her heart pounding as she stepped into the cluttered room.

Inside, balled up paper and paper cups littered the wooden desk, remnants of late nights or hidden schemes; she couldn't tell which. She sank into the chair, her eyes narrowing as she faced the computer screen. Her fingers hesitated over the keys before typing *grasshopper*—no luck. She typed his middle name, *John*. Still locked.

What are you up to, William? What are you trying to hide?

Frustrated, she began sifting through the disarray on his desk. Magazines lay stacked haphazardly: *Golf Digest*, *Tennis Weekly*, *Architectural Digest*—and, to her disgust, a well-worn copy of *Playboy*. She grimaced, pushing it aside, her search becoming more frantic with each moment.

As Lexie rifled through the drawers, her gaze fell on the edge of a notepad, half hidden beneath his laptop. She pulled it out, her eyes scanning the scrawled words.

Order the book "100 Ways to Kill Your Spouse." Research how to purchase a two-million-dollar life insurance policy. It must happen at early dawn, the morning after our anniversary.

She froze, her mind reeling, the air thick with realization. *Early dawn. Life insurance policy... he's going to kill me... at early dawn.*

Her hands shook, and the notepad slipped from her grip, landing on the desk with a dull *thud*. Panic tightened her chest as her mind raced, her breaths quick and shallow. She was trapped in a plan she couldn't yet escape, her fear spiraling as the walls of the office closed in around her.

A chill ran down her spine as the weight of William's note sank in. The words burned into her mind: *Must happen at early dawn.* Her skin became moist as beads of sweat covered her forehead and her lips and chin trembled. Her heartbeat thundered in her ears, drowning out every other sound as she processed what she'd read.

Lexie sprung up and stumbled backward, bumping into the office chair behind her as she scrambled to leave. William was planning to kill her... at dawn. Her own husband, the man she'd once trusted, the man she had once loved, was planning her death.

No. This can't be happening.

She bit back the rising panic, forcing herself to inhale, to focus. Each breath was shallow, each thought like an alarm blaring in her mind. She moved toward the door but turned back. She scanned the room one last time for anything that might help. She couldn't confront him now—not with this knowledge. Not with him a few rooms away, pacing and plotting, and expecting her to stay blissfully unaware.

Her fingers grazed over the scattered papers and magazines, her mind racing, searching for answers. *Why would he do this? What had changed so drastically in him?* She clenched her fists, her nails biting into her palms. *Am I that blind?* All the anger, the resentment, the bitterness—it had twisted him into someone she didn't know, someone capable of unspeakable things.

Outside, a faint sound reached her ears, pulling her out of her frantic thoughts. She froze, straining to listen as William's voice filtered down the hall, a calm, controlled tone that unsettled Lexie, given what she'd discovered. *He's on the phone talking to her.*

"It happens at dawn. Early dawn," his voice echoed, the words familiar. *Early dawn,* the same time scrawled on the notepad. A time he'd chosen with precision, with cold deliberation and on the morning after their anniversary.

How cruel.

Lexie's stomach twisted as she inched toward the door, her movements slow and careful, praying the floor wouldn't creak beneath her weight. She couldn't let him know she'd been here, couldn't risk him suspecting that she was aware of his plan. If he caught her now, cornered her, there'd be no escaping. And she had to escape. She had to survive.

Think, Lexie, think, she told herself, willing her mind to cut through the fog of fear. *You've made it this far. You know what he's planning. Now, you need a plan of your own.*

Her eyes darted around the room, searching for anything that might serve as a weapon or a way out. But the desk had the usual papers, books, and pen holder that held pens, pencils, and a ruler. A ruler wouldn't help—*Creak. Creak*

She turned at the sound. With William down the hall, she couldn't be in this room much longer, she must hurry.

At the door, whispers of warnings raced through her mind, and she paused. Her pulse pounded against her ribs, each beat a frantic signal urging her to move, to leave before it was too late. But she couldn't, at least not yet.

The notepad on the desk was harmless, another piece of clutter among the organized chaos of his office. But amongst the chaos, there was something she needed. Written proof resided in those fragmented sentences, and scribbled lines. Proof of his plan to kill her. She might need the notepad. She couldn't leave it behind.

Her fingers trembled. The words blurred for a moment, and Lexie struggled to process what she had already read. This couldn't be real. He couldn't be planning—did he have reason to kill her? She had done some unforgivable things, but murder? Would he, could he...

A chill coiled down her spine as she committed the notepad's placement to memory. If she made it through this and found a way out, this could be her only lifeline. A shield against whatever storm was brewing in William's mind.

But she couldn't risk taking the notepad with her. He would know.

She slipped it back exactly as she had found it, smoothing down the edges as if that could erase the lingering evidence of her touch. Then, inhaling, she turned back toward the office door.

Her hand shook as she gripped the doorknob.

One step forward. Just one. Then another.

The door creaked open, the sound slicing through the thick silence. She froze, her breath caught in her throat. Had he heard?

Lexie heard no sound, nothing.

She forced herself to move, stepping into the hallway; the shadows shifted with each flicker of the dim overhead light. The long corridor stretched ahead like a dark tunnel that would never end, each footstep echoing louder than it should.

Every instinct screamed at her to run. But she couldn't. Not yet. Not when the walls had ears, when every creak of the floorboards could summon him.

She kept her movements slow and deliberate, her heart hammering against her ribcage.

A sound.

She stiffened, her breath halting.

Behind her, deep in the house, there was movement, a shift, a breath, or the rustle of fabric. William?

Her skin prickled. She swallowed against the lump in her throat, refusing to turn around. If she turned, she might see something she wasn't ready for.

Instead, she pressed forward, each step heavier than the last.

Her pulse pounded louder with every inch she put between herself and that office. The air grew thicker, more suffocating, as if the house itself was working against her, trying to trap her within its walls.

The Devil leaned over the Cosmic Chessboard, His fingers tapping idly against His pieces as He surveyed the unfolding chaos. His lips curled into a slow, satisfied smile. "Oh, how sweet the taste of fear,"

He growled, His eyes gleaming with delight. "How it unravels even the strongest resolve."

God contemplated His next move. His *White-Gloved Hand* hovered over His Knight; He whispered, "Even in fear, there can be courage. Even in darkness, a way can be found."

But the Devil's *Red-Gloved Hand* shifted, moving His bishop into an aggressive stance. "Ah, but can she find it in time?" He replied, savoring every pulse of panic that reverberated through Lexie's mind, every doubt, every fear.

As Lexie sat on the edge of the bed, her hands trembling, the weight of the note she'd found in the drawer crushed the air from her lungs: "A Killing at Early Dawn." Each word echoed in her mind like the steady ticking of a clock, each tick sent a fresh wave of fear rippling through her. Every letter of the note had been crafted to terrify her, to taunt her with some sinister plan.

She swallowed hard, her throat tight as a strange, icy thought took root in her mind.

He wouldn't, would he?

They had heated arguments, but she had never imagined that William might... that he would even think of going so far. But the pieces she had stumbled upon, the cryptic words, all aligned like clues in a twisted puzzle. She remembered the distant look in his eyes lately, the tension that had seeped into their interactions, the brief flashes of something unspoken—and now she couldn't help but question every look, every word, every subtle movement.

The bedroom was stifling, the air heavy with an unexplainable tension. Her pulse hammered in her wrists and her chest. Each beat of her pulse, like a clock on the wall, inched closer to dawn. Early dawn. The note had specified *early dawn* as if time itself had become a countdown she couldn't escape.

Lexie wrapped her arms around herself, drawing her knees up to her chest, her mind racing. *Why would he want to kill me?* She searched her mind for answers, remembering every argument, every conversation they'd had in recent months. She recalled her desire for a baby, the tension over his vasectomy, the resentment that had festered between them. She had pushed too hard, She had become an obstacle, something he wanted to erase. *The baby? I did cheat on him.*

Or he wants to be free, a clean break, one that would leave him financially unburdened. And the baby cemented the plan he had already made. The plan to kill her at early dawn.

Her breath quickened, the room tilting as her fear twisted into something sharper. Her eyes darted to the clock on the nightstand, its hands moving toward dawn. She froze, torn between the urge to run and the fear of what he might do if he discovered she'd found his plans. Her mind raced, weighing every option, trying to determine the safest course of action.

Should I confront him? Should I leave? But where would I go? She feared him, a predator lurking in every shadow. Her own husband.

There it was, clear and haunting, the words on the notepad etched deep into her mind now.

A Killing at Early Dawn.

Did he purchase an insurance policy? One that promises a financially rewarding life for himself and a life without her and the baby?"

She closed her eyes, pressing her palms to her temples. *Get a grip, Lexie.* She fought to keep her mind from spiraling. But the truth was, the trust she'd once had in William had been fractured, and all that was left were threats hiding behind every promise he had ever made. Her mind, a raging battlefield, each thought colliding with the next, her own reasoning slipping through her fingers like sand.

I need to get out of here.

Lexie stood at the front door, her fingers trembling as they wrapped around the handle. Silence shrouded the house. Too still. Only the muffled sound of the floor beneath her bare feet and the whisper of fabric as she pulled her robe tighter around her body filled the air. Yet the loud beat of her heart kept yelling... get out.

But beyond that? Nothing.

Not the sound of wind against the trees. Not the distant hum of passing cars. Not the soft chatter of birds greeting the morning.

Just silence.

A gnawing unease coiled in her stomach. She didn't understand why—until she peeked through the peephole. She gasped. There was *nothing* outside.

No porch. No street. No sky. Just blackness. Endless. Absolute. All consuming.

Panic twisted through her ribs.

She unlocked the deadbolt with frantic fingers, yanking the door open so hard it almost unhinged. A rush of cold, empty air slammed into her face.

The neighborhood was gone. The street, the trees, the sky oblit-
erated. Total blackness.

All that remained was an abyss stretching in every direction, a
void so deep that she couldn't even tell where the ground ended,
and the nothingness began.

Lexie stumbled back. Her foot caught on the threshold, sending
her sprawling to the floor.

This wasn't real. It couldn't be real. She turned toward the
windows, racing toward them.

Maybe it was just the front—maybe—but no. The windows
revealed the same things. Not darkness, not nighttime—even night
had stars, had movement, had something. This, an abyss, a black
emptiness. A void so profound it made her stomach twist, her
mind rebelled against the sheer impossibility of it. She took another step forward, pressing her palm to the glass, then jumped back,
startled by the coldness.

A whisper. A voice, soft as breath, curling against the edges of
her mind.

"*Do not leave.*"

Her entire body snapped to attention, her breath coming in
shallow bursts. She wasn't alone. She *should* have been. But she
wasn't. Something or someone hid in the shadows. Her hands
balled into fists at her sides.

"Who's there?" Silence.

"*You must stay.*"

The voice was neither male nor female, neither young nor old. It
existed beyond sound, weaving itself into her mind like a memory
she didn't know she had.

Her skin prickled, the weight of its presence settled over her like an unseen force. "I don't understand." Her own voice wavered. "Where—where is everything?"

"Beyond you. Beyond now."

Her pulse hammered.

"What does that mean?" she asked. The silence stretched thick and oppressive.

"Step outside, and you will not return. Tell William, and you will not return. Tell anyone and your baby will no longer exist."

A lump formed in her throat. Her legs refused to move, her mind battling between terror and disbelief. This couldn't be happening. Am I having a nightmare, an hallucination? Is William playing a cruel trick on me?

And yet—her instincts screamed for her not to step forward. Because something was out there. Something dark and deadly... waiting. Something she couldn't come back from. Her eyes darted toward the staircase. Had William done this? Had he locked her inside somehow, sealed her off from the world? Had he drugged her, sent her spiraled into a delusion so deep she could no longer tell reality from hallucination?

The whisper returned, threading through her like a pulse.

"Not his doing. Not his hand. But he's part of this game."

The words sent a sharp chill down her spine. What did it mean? Her knees weakened. "What game is he a part of?" She asked.

"The next move is not yours to make."

The truth pressed in. She was trapped here. Not by doors. Not by locks. By fate itself. By something older, more powerful than she could comprehend. She had been moved. Positioned. She was part of a game, and until the next move was played... She could not leave.

But her body froze, the impulse to move stalled. Her instincts yelled to get out, but leaving wouldn't be simple; she couldn't slip away without raising suspicion.

The words rang in her mind once more, louder, *A Killing at Early Dawn.* The eerie promise of it clawed at her, burrowing deep into her consciousness. She couldn't ignore it, and she couldn't wait to find out if she was right.

Taking a steady breath, Lexie forced herself to her feet. She moved with careful steps, unsure if William was watching and listening. Her heart pounded in her chest and as she straightened, she caught her reflection in the mirror. She didn't recognize the woman staring back at her—a woman hardened by fear, eyes shadowed with suspicion, her jaw set with a determination she hadn't known she possessed.

The overhead lights over the kitchen counter provided a faint light as her eyes darted around the room, searching for an escape, a plan—*something*. The keys. She spotted them on the counter, her heart leaped. But no. She recognized them as the keys to William's office, not her car. She had left the car keys somewhere... *but where?*

A vision flashed. Her keys rested on the bathroom counter upstairs. Her heart raced, but instead of heading for the bathroom, her legs carried her to the sofa. *There's only darkness. You can't leave.* Cold sweat trickled down her face, her mind racing with every scenario of how he'd find her, corner her, and end this twisted game.

Her hands trembled. She grabbed her phone, the screen was dark—*dead battery.* The charger was in the bedroom... *with*

William. The last shred of security vanished. A dark calm swept over her. Her eyes drifted to the knife block, the gleam of steel reflecting the faint light. She edged toward it and pulled out a small knife. No. She slid the knife back with a shaky hand. She rifled through drawers, her hands grazed over the rough handle of the meat mallet, and she pulled it out. She lifted it high as if to strike...

Out of the corner of her eye, she caught sight of a plaque on the wall. It held a weapon her husband had once purchased as a twisted joke, the shiny *Dragon Knife*. She retrieved it. The polished blade gleamed in her hand, intricate carvings glinting under the kitchen light. She took a deep breath, grasping the meat mallet in one hand and the Dragon Knife in the other, and began her ascent, step by step, each creak of the stairs magnified in the silence.

The hallway stretched before her like a tunnel, A dark tunnel with walls pressing in and suffocating her. She pushed the bedroom door open. The room was dark and unsettling. The bed was empty, but her eyes traveled to the bathroom door that was ajar. She crept toward it, her breath shallow, heart thundering in her ears. Carefully, she used her foot to nudge it open, bracing herself for what she might find.

Inside, the faucet dripped, its rhythmic sound unnerving in the silence. She laid the meat mallet on the sink, reaching to twist the faucet off. As she straightened, her eyes froze. She squinted at the mirror, not wanting to read it again, but the message, scrawled in red lipstick, was still there, haunting her: *You broke my heart. I will kill you before I ever let you go.*

A jolt of terror shot through her as she stumbled back. Her heart raced as she edged toward the shower curtain, gripping the Dragon Knife with white-knuckled hands. She slashed through the curtain in a zigzag motion, tearing it open—*nothing*. But fear pressed down on her like a suffocating weight.

Lexie returned to the bedroom, scanning every shadow, every corner, her eyes landing on the closet. She tiptoed closer, clutching the Dragon Knife, and yanked the door open—*empty*. She dropped to the floor, peering under the bed. Nothing.

She rose, ready to turn, when she found herself face to face with William.

She lifted the Dragon Knife high, but his hand reached out before she could react, gripping her wrist in a crushing hold. They struggled, her breath coming in short, panicked bursts as he slammed her hard against the wall. With a fierce yank, he wrenched the Dragon Knife from her hand and held it to her throat, his eyes gleaming with a terrifying intensity.

"You wouldn't kill your husband, would you?" he sneered, his voice low and venomous.

"William." she gasped, her neck cold from the steel. Her pulse raced, her mind scrambling for an escape.

"Are you scared now?" he asked, his voice a chilling whisper, his hand steady.

"Put the knife away." she pleaded, her voice shaky. "Scaring me won't help."

His face twisted with anger as he shoved her to the floor, looming over her. "Scaring you? *You* tried to kill *me*. You've slept with another man, and you're having his baby. What am I missing here?"

The Dragon Knife gleamed as he raised it high, poised to strike.

Her heart pounded in her chest. Her eyes filled with terror. "William, please!" she cried. "Just let me go. Please."

Across realms, on an ancient Cosmic Chessboard illuminated by an otherworldly glow, the Devil moved His bishop, cornering God's queen. He leaned back, a smirk of victory stretching across His face, relishing the chaos He'd sown. His hand hovered over a pawn—the piece representing Lexie—His fingers tapping idly as Lexie withered under William's wrath.

God's face remained calm as He studied the board. With a slow, measured hand, He moved a knight forward, shielding His queen, positioning her on an unexpected path of escape. The Devil's smirk faded as God's move opened a way forward, a quiet strength guiding Lexie, urging her toward an unspoken resilience.

But the Devil wasn't finished. With a flick of His wrist, He advanced His rook, sealing William's fate and tightening the threads of suspicion and fury. The balance teetered on a knife's edge as the Devil leaned forward, watching with cold, calculating delight. This match was far from over, and while God's moves held grace and redemption, the Devil's grip on William's mind was fierce and relentless.

Between them, the final pieces waited, trembling in the dark, each one inching closer to a violent end, to the point where love and vengeance could no longer be separated.

FEAR NOT

L exie sat on the side of the bed. She glanced over at her husband. Peace and calm covered his face giving him vulnerability during sleep, his features softened by the light filtering in from the hallway. But she wouldn't be lulled by appearances. The words she'd read on his notepad echoed in her mind, sharp and chilling: *It must happen at early dawn.* The betrayal of trust cut deep, and with each second she stared down at him, her resolve hardened.

Lexie moved over to William's nightstand. She opened the bottom drawer, where he had placed the Dragon Knife. She picked it up and stepped closer to the bed. Lexie leaned over his sleeping form and raised the Dragon Knife, her hand steady. *I will not be his victim.*

And as her shadow fell across him, his eyes opened, a slow, almost predatory smile spreading across his face. He didn't flinch, didn't react, there was a calmness that sent a chill down her spine.

"Lexie," his voice was a low, amused whisper. "Couldn't sleep?"

The words hung between them, filled with layers of tension, of danger, of unspoken understanding. She didn't lower the knife, her eyes narrowing as she studied him, searching his face for any trace of remorse, any small hint of the man she had once known.

He glanced at the knife in her hand, his smile widening. "Planning something, my love?"

Her grip tightened. "I know about your plan, William. Early dawn? You thought I wouldn't find out?"

His smile faded, his eyes narrowing as he leaned forward, propping himself up on one elbow. "I see you've been snooping."

She took a step back, brandishing the knife. "You were going to kill me. You think I'd just sit back and let you?"

He let out a quiet laugh, "Is that what you think, Lexie? That I'm planning to kill you?"

She swallowed, refusing to let her resolve waver. "What else would I think? You've been distant, plotting something behind my back."

He rose from the bed, his movements deliberate, controlled. "Perhaps I had my reasons. Just as you had yours when you betrayed me."

She flinched, the accusation like a slap across her face, but she didn't back down. "This isn't about betrayal, William. It's about survival."

He chuckled, a dark, mocking sound as he took a step towards her. "Survival. Yes, I suppose that's exactly what it's come down to."

The Devil leaned in, a gleeful glint in His eye as He moved His queen forward, pressing God's knight into a tight corner. "They're perfectly poised for destruction," He declared, savoring every moment of their struggle.

But God moved His rook with steady hands, His voice calm yet resolute. "When the path seems hidden, there is always a way forward."

In that moment, something shifted in Lexie, a flash of clarity piercing through fear, anger, and resentment. She lowered the knife, the weight of everything left unsaid pressing down on her.

"We can end this," she whispered, her voice filled with a raw vulnerability. "We don't have to keep hurting each other."

For a brief second, his face softened. Here was the man she remembered, the man she had loved. But then he was cold as he reached out, his hand closing around her wrist, his grip tightening. The knife slipped from her fingers, clattering to the floor.

"No, Lexie, it's too late for that."

God and the Devil scrutinized their moves. The game unfolded with growing intensity, each move more crucial than the last. Their fingers poised over the board, calculating and waiting, knowing that the night's fate was tangled with each piece they moved.

The Devil's eyes gleamed as He reached out, sliding His queen with a quick, decisive motion, pinning one of God's knights with sadistic satisfaction. He leaned back, His eyes never leaving Lexie. "Fear... such a magnificent weapon," He mused, the corner of His mouth curling into a dark smile. "It drives her to the edge, pushing her to embrace the sinful part of herself. The part that seeks revenge."

God's expression was somber, His gaze steady as He studied the board, unperturbed by the Devil's maneuver. His hand drifted to His bishop, maneuvering it closer to His queen, creating a protective barrier. "Fear may drive her," He said, His voice filled with understanding. "But it is courage that keeps her moving. Even through the darkness, there remains a light."

The Devil's fingers lingered over His next piece, His eyes dancing with malice as He glanced back at the board. "Hope, light, courage... such fragile concepts. Look at her," He said, gesturing toward Lexie. "She is beyond the reach of hope now, consumed by the bitterness you think she can overcome."

But God's *White-Gloved Hand* moved with quiet purpose as He slid His rook into place, blocking the Devil's queen and protecting His knight from capture. His voice was steady, filled with a gentle assurance. "It is in her bleakest moment, Fallen Angel, that she will find her strength. Sometimes, the journey through the shadows is the only way to reach the light."

Lexie's heart pounded, her voice low and steady. "Just what are you planning to do at early dawn Or perhaps I already know."

He raised an eyebrow, his smile widening as he leaned back. "Oh, do you now?" he questioned, his voice laced with a dark satisfaction that sent a chill through her.

The Devil leaned closer to the board, delight flickering in His eyes as the interaction unfolded. His hand hovered over His knight, preparing to advance in a relentless pursuit. "She's in the palm of her own fear, crushed by the weight of her desperation," He whispered, His voice dripping with glee. "Look at how easily the heart twists, how fear drives her to the brink."

But God's *White-Gloved Hand* remained calm as He moved His queen into a protective stance, shielding Lexie and giving her strength. "Even at the brink, a choice remains," He said, His voice filled with quiet determination. "In every moment, there is the chance to turn away, to seek peace, even as the darkness threatens to consume her."

Lexie took a breath, her eyes fixed on William, her thoughts racing, tangled with fear and resolve. The tension between them, building from moment to moment. His eyes revealed a glint of satisfaction, as though he was savoring her fear, thriving on it.

"I'm not afraid of you, William," she said, her voice steady even as the weight of her decision pressed down on her. "I won't let you control me anymore."

His smile faded, his expression shifting as he stared at her, a flash of something dangerous in his eyes. But she held her ground, standing on the edge, the darkness pulling at her, yet a sliver of light glimmered within.

In that fragile moment, the room held its breath, the choice poised. The door closed, sealing them in the room together, the outcome left unwritten.

⸻◆⸻

In the bathroom, Lexie's heart raced, each breath coming in shallow, controlled bursts as she scanned the room. The silence was thick, heavy, pressing down on her, amplifying every small sound, every shift of the shadows.

Her mind whirred, calculating, piecing together his whispering phone calls and his furtive glances. Her fingers brushed against the cool tile of the sink. Her muscles were tense, her entire body ready to spring at the faintest movement.

Something shifted behind her. She whirled around, her heart leaping to her throat, only to be met with emptiness. She steadied herself, exhaling as she turned back toward the sink, her mind racing with images of the plans she'd uncovered, the notepad, the life insurance, the words *early dawn* etched in red letters across her mind like a warning. It was her or him now; a clarity that left no room for hesitation.

And yet, as she stood there, a thought crept into her mind—a glimmer of doubt, a whisper of what this final act would mean. Could she really go through with it? Was she capable of meeting him at his level, of stepping into the darkness that had taken over their lives?

The Devil leaned closer to the Cosmic Chessboard, His fingers tracing the edges of His queen as He slid it forward, trapping one of God's rooks in a cunning, ruthless move. He studied Lexie with a wicked gleam in His eye, savoring her struggle, her fear, the rage that simmered beneath her resolve.

"She's almost there," He said, His voice low, brimming with dark anticipation. "One step closer, and she's mine. Anger is a beautiful thing, don't you think? It blinds, it consumes, and in the end, it destroys."

But God stilled, he was filled with a delicate kindness as He moved His bishop, creating a powerful defense. His voice was a soft whisper as He replied, "Even in darkness, Lexie will choose the right path; anger will not triumph."

Back in the bedroom, Lexie held her breath, she turned sweeping over every dark corner, every shadow. *Where is he? Where did he go?* The silence weighed heavily, each second stretching into an eternity.

Without warning, a hand shot out from the shadows behind the door, gripping her wrist with a vice-like force. She gasped, her body twisting as she pulled away, her heart pounding as she met his eyes.

William's face was calm as he stared at her, his demeanor hard as steel. His mouth curled into a faint smile, but his eyes were cold, calculating, a look that sent a chill through her veins.

"Hello, sweetheart," he said, his voice low, mocking, as though he'd been expecting her all along.

In the shadowy recesses above, the Devil smiled as He nudged His queen forward, blocking God's rook with a slow, purposeful move. "Fear's a masterpiece, isn't it?" He whispered; His eyes never leave the game. "It seizes, it paralyzes, and in that moment of terror, it owns the soul."

God observed Lexie in the mirror. Compassion etched into His face as He responded by shifting His knight to protect her. "Fear needn't imprison her," He replied, His voice soft but steady. "I do not need her to see Me—only to keep moving toward what she cannot yet name."

The Devil, as persistent as he could be, never wavered, a dark satisfaction filling Him as He slid His queen further, the pieces closing in on their mark. "You can feel it, can't you?" He said, His tone savoring each moment. "She's seconds from surrendering to the terror that has her cornered. One more step... and she's mine."

But God advanced His bishop, standing resolute in the Devil's path, He watched Lexie. "The decision is hers," He said with unwavering calm. "Though fear may press in, it is courage that lights her way."

A glimmer of irritation crossed the Devil's face as Lexie's fear ebbed. But His eyes lingered on the game board, His lips curling into a slow, dark smile as He slid His knight forward, the pieces closing in. "It isn't over yet, she may think she's safe, but fear, once ignited, always finds its way back."

God wanted to protect Lexie as much as this game would allow. His finger rested on His rook, His voice a soft murmur of assurance. "Fear not, Lexie, I will stay with you in the dark." He whispered. "You may not feel My presence, but I have never turned away."

⸺◦○◦⸺

The silence in the room thickened, heavy and oppressive, broken by Lexie's ragged breathing. Her eyes remained fixed on William, the Dragon Knife now clutched in his hand. Her mind spun, frantic, every instinct telling her to bolt, to run, but she stayed rooted to the spot, her body tense. The way he held the Dragon Knife—a mixture of desperation and control, his knuckles white, and the way he glared at her with an intensity that sent a chill down her spine.

"Sit down." William's voice cut through the silence, his tone sharp, the words a strict order as he pointed to the edge of the bed. Lexie's legs trembled, but she held her ground, her pulse a steady throb as she weighed her options. She wouldn't test him now, not with the tension radiating from him like a taut wire ready to snap. She sank onto the bed and searched his face for a trace of the man who existed beneath the hard, unyielding mask he wore. *But he no longer existed.*

Above, the Devil leaned forward, His eyes glinting with satisfaction as He slid His bishop forward, trapping God's knight in a deadly pincer. "It's all unraveling beautifully," He exclaimed with dark evil delight. "This is the moment when fear consumes, when love turns to hate, and trust corrodes into betrayal."

But God's expression remained calm, He moved His queen into a defensive position, blocking the Devil's next advance. "Even in the shadows, a path can be found," He said, His gaze resting on Lexie with quiet compassion. "Where decisions remain, hope endures, and a way forward is always possible."

In the bedroom, William's grip on the Dragon Knife tightened, his hand shaking, as he stared down at her, his face a mixture of fury and something deeper, something unspoken. Lexie's pulse pounded in her throat, a steady, relentless beat that echoed in the quiet of the room.

"What am I supposed to do?" William's voice was low, strained, each word laced with bitterness. "You slept with another man and now you carry his child... you betrayed me." His voice broke, his eyes flickering with a pain that almost made her falter.

Lexie swallowed. "This baby... it just happened."

William laughed, a hollow, bitter sound that filled the room. "I don't believe you." He leaned closer, the blade glinting between them, his face inches from hers. "You did what you needed to do. You wanted a baby, and you made damn sure you got one."

Her eyes darted to the knife, her voice steady. "We don't have to do this. This isn't us... it's the anger, the fear. It's turning us into people we're not."

But William shook his head, a strange, almost resigned smile flickering across his face. "Maybe this is who we've always been," he whispered, his tone laced with an eerie calm. He lowered the Dragon Knife for a moment to provide Lexie with a spark of relief, only for him to lift it again. "But you're right about one thing, Lexie. I'm scared. Terrified. Of losing control, of losing you... of losing myself."

Her voice trembled. "William... please. Let's just walk away from this."

But his face hardened, and his grip on the knife tightened. "It's too late for that. If you want out, you'll have to take it. You'll have to fight for it." He paused, his voice dropping to a whisper. "Show me how much you want it. Because I'm not letting go."

The Devil's eyes gleamed as He moved His knight into place, trapping God's bishop, His voice filled with quiet triumph. "She's lost. Caught in a web of her own making, and he's sinking with her. They're both cornered now."

But God's *White-Gloved Hand* moved with passion as He slid His queen forward, protecting His bishop. "There is always another way," He replied, His voice calm yet filled with a gentle assurance. "When storms rage within, they can still choose serenity."

Lexie stared at William. She reached out, her hand trembling as it touched the edge of the knife he held, her voice soft but steady. "If you want to keep me here, you'll have to let go of the past. You'll have to accept this baby."

The stark pain in his eyes softened for a moment and his fingers loosened on the knife a fraction, his grip faltering as he searched her face, as if looking for something he'd long lost.

With a hard resolve, he tightened his grip again, his face hardening. "I can't," he muttered to himself. "I can't accept another man's baby, and I can't just let you walk away. Not now."

The Devil's hand hovered over His next piece, savoring the tension and despair that rippled through the room. "See? Even when given a choice, they cling to the darkness. They're already mine."

But God remained steady, His hand poised over the board as He peered down with a gentle patience that remained unbroken. "Even in fear, even in pain, they are not beyond redemption. Love, in its truest form, can still heal. And if they choose it... there will be light."

Lexie whispered, "Then let me go. Or I'll go alone."

For the briefest of moments, his face softened, the knife lowering as her words sank in. But the struggle remained, the choice dangling between them, suspended in the fragile silence that held them both in its grip.

Lexie held her breath as she kept her eyes fixed on the door, desperate to put distance between herself and the glinting Dragon Knife in William's hand. Her stomach twisted, every nerve screaming for her to get out, to leave the suffocating confines of the room. She clutched her abdomen, the weight of life inside her fragile and defenseless, bound up in a moment that could shatter at any second.

William's voice, low and calm, broke through the tense silence. "Going somewhere?" His eyes locked on Lexie with an intensity that made her falter, one hand twitching as though he might lunge at her at any moment. His grip on the knife remained firm.

Lexie swallowed. *Is he reading my mind?* Her hand clutched the door frame. Whatever you're doing, whatever you think this will accomplish—it won't bring us back."

But his smile was cold, devoid of any warmth or understanding. He tilted the Dragon Knife in his hand, letting the steel catch the faint light filtering into the room, a chilling reminder of how close she was to danger.

"Back?" he echoed, his tone mocking. "You think there's a possibility of us, after what you've done?"

He rose, each movement deliberate as he took a step toward her. Lexie's heart pounded, her fingers digging into the door frame as she weighed her options, knowing there was no way to escape without facing him. She stood her ground, her voice steady but low. "This is all because of you."

He scoffed, shaking his head with a bitter laugh. "And you're blameless, right? Always innocent, never the one at fault." He moved closer, his face inches from hers. "So, tell me, Lexie, how would you fix this? How would you make everything right again?"

Lexie eyed him, a surge of strength rising within her, her voice calm despite the fear coursing through her veins. "Let me go. That's the only way this ends."

A dark shadow crossed his face, and he clenched his jaw, his grip tightening on the Dragon Knife. "That's not a solution, that's an excuse to walk away. To pretend none of this ever happened."

The Devil's eyes gleamed as He observed William's face, His hand lingering over His queen, waiting for the exact moment to make His next move. "Look at him, anger, betrayal—he's a perfect instrument of vengeance, ready to destroy all that opposes him, all that threatens his fragile pride."

Laughing, the Devil leaned back with dark amusement. "Freedom isn't what he seeks. It's revenge. It's the thrill of making her suffer as he suffers. That is what he thinks will set him free."

God remained silent. His hand moved a knight forward in quiet defiance. "Even in his pain, he can find redemption. If he releases this hatred, he can yet be free. Redemption is never precious. It is costly. And yet, still worth offering."

FORGIVENESS

L exie took a small, steadying breath in the bedroom, her eyes steady as she watched William—a glimmer of the man she once loved buried beneath layers of rage and resentment. Her voice, filled with quiet strength, cut through the tension between them. "Let me go, William before you lose whatever's left of us, of who we are. This bitterness will destroy you."

Something shifted in his expression—a trace of recognition, of understanding. But it disappeared, replaced by the same hardened stare. He stepped closer, the Dragon Knife raised, his voice a hoarse whisper. "Maybe I don't care about what's left. All I care about is making sure you suffer, just like I have."

Her fingers tightened on the doorframe. But he was beyond reason, beyond words. She forced herself not to flinch, her voice unwavering. "Then do it. But it won't change anything. And you'll be left with nothing but your hatred."

He hesitated, his grip faltering as though her words had cracked the armor around his anger. But he didn't lower the knife. His face twisted with turmoil, his eyes unreadable.

The Devil's lips curled into a slow, satisfied smile. His fingers moved His queen forward with ruthless precision, positioning it for a final blow. "See how close they are to falling apart? This is when it happens—when the heart is too broken to heal. When love rots and leaves nothing but bitterness."

But God's *White-Gloved Hand* moved with purpose, placing His bishop between the Devil's queen and His own king. The gesture was firm, unwavering. His eyes remained calm, filled with tranquil determination. "When shadows surround them, I will shield them. Redemption is not so easily lost, for it is not earned by perfection but by faith and the courage to rise after every fall. Their struggles and pain are the fires through which their souls are refined. And even now, in the face of despair, I see the light within them—small but steadfast."

⸻ ◆ ⸻

Lexie took another slow breath. William's grip on the knife trembled, his face distorted by inner conflict. She didn't move or turn away, refusing to back down as she whispered, "Please, let it go. This path leads to nothing but ruin."

For one breathless moment, something inside him broke. His hand loosened, the knife dipping as her words settled in his chest. The fury in his face melted into something quieter—regret, perhaps, or recognition of how far he'd fallen.

Without a word, he lowered the Dragon Knife. His shoulders sagged as he stepped back, his eyes dropping to the floor. The strength left him in an instant, leaving behind at best, a hollow outline of the man who had once been her husband.

———◆———

A look of calm victory crossed God's face as he moved His bishop forward, frustrating the Devil. "You can't protect them forever," the Devil sneered, His fingers lingering over His next piece, poised to strike again.

But God's voice was quiet, filled with unwavering resolve. "I don't need forever. Just a single moment of grace."

———◆———

Within seconds, controlled by an unknown force, William once again lifted the knife, his eyes gleaming with strange evilness as he held the Dragon Knife steady at her throat, pressing into her flesh and drawing a thin line of blood that trailed down her chest in a vivid red streak. Lexie's breath caught, her body rigid, the cold steel against her skin made her heart hammer so loudly it drowned out all other sounds.

Lexie struggled to find her voice.

"William," she whispered, hoping to reach any remaining shred of humanity within him. She couldn't look away, couldn't dare to blink as he stared at her with eyes both empty and raging, a look that chilled her to her core.

His grip tightened, and his voice was low, edged with something dark and hollow. "You created this mess, Lexie. All of it. But I'm going to clean it up. I'll fix this—make it like it was before." His words were sharp, each one cutting into her with the weight of his resentment, his anger wrapped around him like armor.

She fought to control her breathing, her body tense, every instinct screaming to flee, to get away from the glinting blade pressed against her skin. But any sudden move could end it all. With a calmness she forced upon herself, she whispered, "By doing what? By killing my baby? So now you know how to do an abortion?"

The words slipped out in a desperate attempt to shock him, to shake him from this madness. But instead, he smiled, a chilling, humorless twist of his lips. "I'll google it," he replied, his tone devoid of any humor he may have intended, the threat hanging heavy between them.

Above, the Devil's fingers hovered over His bishop, a triumphant glint in His eyes as He prepared His next move. He leaned closer to the board. His smile widened as he delighted in the rage that had overtaken William, the blind anger that made him deaf to anything else or anyone else.

"There's no redemption here, just the ruin of two lives entwined by bitterness and betrayal," He stated, His voice filled with dark satisfaction. "Every moment, he becomes more mine."

God, His countenance calm yet touched with a profound sorrow, moved His knight into position, shielding His king with deliberate grace. His voice, steady and resonant, carried an unfathomable depth of mercy. "When anger clouds the heart, it does not extinguish the light I have placed within. Even in the storm, there exists a way forward—a way that does not demand perfection but asks only for the courage to take one step toward healing."

Lexie's body trembled. The knife dug deeper, the edge sharp and unrelenting, the blood dripping down her neck a constant reminder of how close she was to the brink. She forced herself to speak, to reach out to whatever was left of the man she had once known. "William... look at what you're doing. This isn't you. It's anger, it's the pain. But this won't bring us back. It won't change anything."

William wavered, his expression twitching for a moment, a crack in the mask of rage and resentment he wore. Buried somewhere beneath the layers of hurt and betrayal stood the man she once loved. The next second, his face hardened, his grip on the knife tightening as he leaned closer, his eyes narrowing.

"You don't get to talk your way out of this," he said, his voice low, venomous. "You brought this on yourself. You made the choice to ruin us. Now you can live with the consequences." He pressed the blade harder to remind her of its presence, of the line he was ready to cross.

The Devil sparkled, satisfied with Lexie's dilemma. His fingers guiding His rook forward in a decisive move, trapping God's bishop in a fatal formation. "She has nowhere left to turn," He purred, savoring the tension on the board and in the room. "Fear and anger—they will consume her, as they do him. They'll feed on each other's hate until there's nothing left."

But God's *White-Gloved Hand* remained steady, filled with silent determination as He moved His bishop to safety, protecting His pieces with an unending resilience. "Anger may cloud the heart, but it cannot destroy it," He replied, His voice floated in the air, strong and reverent. "Where there is love, there is always hope."

<hr />

In the bedroom, Lexie's voice softened, a thread of desperation woven into her words. "You don't have to do this," she whispered, her voice filled with a quiet plea. "You have a choice. We both do."

For a moment, the knife trembled in his hand as he stared at her, his grip unsteady, as if caught between two opposing forces. Something flashed across his face—hesitation, doubt, a fleeting glimpse of vulnerability—only to be swallowed by the returning tension hardening his features. Whatever softness that appeared vanished, replaced by the sharp edge of unspoken fury. A fury she knew she caused.

"Don't," he spat, his voice a hoarse whisper. "Don't pretend this is salvageable. Don't pretend you didn't destroy us the second you let him—"

Lexie squeezed her eyes shut, the pain of his words cutting as deeply as the knife. But she forced herself to stay calm, to keep speaking. "I still care about you, William. Enough to say... let's stop this before it's too late."

He stared at her, fury carved into his features—but beneath it, something raw and fractured trembled just beneath the surface. His grip loosened, his breath heavy and labored, as if scrutinizing her facial expression for something that might pull him back from the edge.

------◀◆▶------

The Devil's eyes narrowed, and frustration cut across His face the moment William hesitated. Still, He moved His queen forward with purpose, His voice a low, dangerous whisper. "Her pleas mean nothing. I will make him believe she's betrayed him. I will twist this into an empty ploy; another lie meant to escape consequences."

God said nothing at first. His attention stayed on Lexie, a quiet intensity radiating from Him—as though he not only witnessed her current desperation but the whole of her story: every scar, every silent ache, every fragile spark of hope still burning inside her. His hand hovered above the board, the motion deliberate, weighted with consequence, as though this move might echo through eternity.

When He finally spoke, His voice was soft but unshakable, resonating with clarity that cut through the swell of despair.

"It is not anger that will save them," He said, words flowing like water carving through stone. "But the forgiveness they choose to offer—silent, costly, and undeserved. Forgiveness that heals beneath the surface, where wounds linger unseen. It's not the absence of pain but the willingness to cradle another's brokenness... and still choose love. That is where salvation begins."

———◆◇◆———

In the stillness, Lexie reached out, her fingers brushing his hand. "Please... let's walk away from this. For both our sakes. I'll leave if that's what you need... but don't let this hatred finish what little good we still have."

William's face slackened, the rigidness in his features starting to break apart, as if—for the first time—he truly registered the person in front of him. He released a trembling breath. The fury that once consumed him now sagged beneath the weight of sheer exhaustion.

For a moment, a fragile stillness settled over them. Not peace, but something quieter. The darkness lifted just enough for something else to emerge. Not trust. Not love. But maybe... a start.

———◆◇◆———

God shifted His king to safety, the move simple and unhurried. A quiet knowing remained in His expression. "In forgiveness, they find freedom," He noted, surveying the board. "And in freedom, they may yet find love."

Lexie's body trembled. She watched William closely, sensing a change rippling through him—a dangerous charge beneath his skin, a reclaiming of control that made her throat tighten.

He reached for her slowly, his hand gliding up and down her arm. The touch was not gentle. It wasn't comfort—it was power, calculated, and quiet. Each stroke warned her of what still lingered inside him, of what might return if she wasn't careful.

"Baby is that fear I see?" he asked, his voice low, taunting. "Or are you just cold?" He smirked, fingers drifting over her skin, savoring her vulnerability as though she were the most intoxicating elixir he'd ever known.

She forced herself to speak, her voice a brittle thread. "William... please. Put the knife away."

But he laughed, a hollow, almost gleeful sound as he took a step back, bouncing on his feet like a boxer warming up, the Dragon Knife still glinting in his hand. His eyes were bright, feverish with energy. "I've never felt this type of power before, It feels good. For the first time, I feel like I can make you listen. Like I can make you stay."

Lexie's heartbeat thundered in her chest, each pulse a warning as she kept her eyes locked on him, searching for any trace of the man she'd once loved. "You can't make me stay," she said, her voice shaking. "Whatever you think you're doing—it won't work. Not like this."

He stopped bouncing, his face darkening, the mocking smile twisting into something more menacing. "You're wrong," he said, his tone calm. "I can make you stay, Lexie. I can keep you right here." His hand touched her abdomen, a shadow of anger passing through his eyes. "One way or another."

The Devil leaned over the chessboard, His eyes gleaming with satisfaction as He moved His queen forward, trapping God's bishop. "He's inches away, inches from becoming mine," He insisted, His voice dripping with dark delight. "He's tasted control, and now it's all he craves. Nothing will satisfy him but breaking her, holding her in his grasp forever."

God observed the board, His hand hovering over His remaining pieces, His expression filled with sorrow but unwavering. "He is in the throes of rage, but he has not yet lost his soul. Even now, he can choose peace," He replied, moving His knight to shield His king. "Hope remains, even in this shadow."

Lexie took a deep breath, her own resolve hardening. She won't let him harm her unborn child. *That's not going to happen.* "I don't belong to you," she said, each word deliberate. "You don't get to keep me like I'm your personal possession or punish me for choices you think I've made. That's not love. That's control."

His face twisted with anger, his grip on the knife tightening as he glared at her.

"Is that what you think? That I don't love you?" He took a step closer, the knife trembling in his hand.

Lexie forced herself to stay steady, to show no fear. "Yes, that's what I think," she whispered. "If you loved me, you wouldn't need to try to force me to stay. You would listen to me; You would try to accept this baby. I'm sorry I deceived you," Lexie exclaimed with all her soul. She grabbed William's shoulders. "But let's stop this before it reaches a point we can never recover from."

The room held its breath, the heavy and suffocating silence pressing down on them. William's expression of blind anger softened. Replaced by a flash of doubt and confusion, Lexie couldn't tell but his grip on the knife loosened. He scanned her face, unnerving her.

The Devil's eyes narrowed, His fingers hovering over His rook as He scrutinized William's hesitation with growing frustration. "She's slipping from him," He remarked, His tone edged with irritation. "One word, one gesture, and he could hold her forever... but he hesitates."

Within God, a quiet calm filled with hope as He moved His queen to shield His knight. "Love is stronger than anger," He replied. "It's in love and trust that true strength lies."

———————◆◆◆———————

William let out a shaky breath. "I... I don't know what to believe anymore," he admitted. "I don't know—"

Lexie reached out and placed her fingers to his lips, quieting him. "Then stop. Right here, right now. Just... let this go. You don't need the knife. Let's work through this, now... tonight."

He let out a breath, his grip on the knife loosening, his hand trembling as he released it, the blade clattering to the floor with a hollow sound.

———————◆◆◆———————

The Devil's face contorted with fury as the knife fell, His fingers curling into a fist as He moved His rook forward, His voice filled with frustration. "She was within my grasp, a moment from surrendering to fear. He's slipping... one more word, and he's lost to me."

But God moved His queen with purpose, the elegance of the motion reflecting a wisdom that transcended the mortal struggles playing out before Him. His presence, unwavering and full of quiet assurance, softened as it rested on Lexie's weary heart. "Fallen Angel, you have caused so much damage here, but I have faith that Lexie and William will weather this storm. Their love will endure through their deepest sorrows and their deepest wounds. Love is not a passive force; it has the power to rebuild what's shattered and mend what seems beyond repair. This is the path before them—the courage to love without condition, without fear, even when it hurts. It is this that frees them both, not from struggle, but from the chains of despair."

A glimmer of relief broke through the fear as Lexie softened. She reached for his hand, guiding him to sit beside her, the tension dissolving as they sat in silence. William's face was etched with regret.

"I didn't mean for it to get this far, Lexie. I... I just wanted to feel like I had something left."

Lexie's eyes filled with a mixture of compassion and sadness.

"I know," she whispered, her voice gentle, filled with the quiet strength of forgiveness. "But this isn't how we find ourselves. Not like this."

In the silence that followed, they sat together, their wounds raw but open, the remnants of their bitterness beginning to unravel as they faced the choice that lay before them.

Above, God moved His king to safety, His voice filled with peace. "In forgiveness, they find redemption."

The Devil glared at the board, His face twisted in fury, but He said nothing.

The game was not over, but at this moment, love had won.

ANGER

William sat on the edge of the bed. He held his head in his hands, grappling with the overwhelming sense that everything was spiraling beyond his control. Moments before, a sliver of resolve, a spark of the love that had once drawn him to Lexie, urged him to let go of the anger, to make things right. They could fix this, they could salvage the remnants of their marriage. But an evil whisper slipped into his thoughts, faint but insistent, feeding his doubts, twisting his regret into something ugly. *She betrayed you,* the voice hissed. *She's hiding something. She thinks she can outsmart you, make you a fool.*

As if a shadow had settled over his heart, William's chest tightened, his mind clouding with a simmering rage that grew with every second. His love twisted into resentment, the whisper winding through his mind like a serpent, stoking his need for control, for revenge. On the floor, the steel of Dragon Knife's glinted in the light, it had become a chapter in his own life. How ironic? A dark thrill ran through him. No, he thought, his resolve hardening. I'll make her see she belongs to me.

With a renewed sense of purpose, he rose, his eyes gleaming with a determination that bordered on cruelty. He turned toward the door, his expression hardening, the evil whisper in his mind now a steady, relentless force. He no longer wanted to make things right—he wanted her obedience, her submission. And he was ready to take it, no matter the cost, no matter the blood dripping down her chest—it didn't deter him.

"Take your robe off." he insisted.

She gawked at William, but she obeyed.

His eyes swept over her body, lingering on her breast, her mound, and her thighs. *I will take what belongs to me.*

He roared. "Get in bed."

Lexie got under the covers. She peeked at the cold steel of the Dragon Knife on the floor.

He shuffled through the top nightstand drawer. Nothing. He opened the bottom drawer. Bingo. He pulled out the treasure. She *stared* at the handcuffs. She gasped. "No."

"Yes, Lexie. Fun and games," he taunted.

He lowered his head and kissed her. She recoiled.

"Don't worry my dear. We've played this game before."

"Not with a knife between us."

"Indeed. But what's a little fear between a husband and wife?"

"I'll forget about leaving you, I'll give the baby up for adoption. Don't do this."

"Spoken under the threat of death. How can I believe you?" He stroked her arm.

He snapped the cuff onto her left wrist with the casual finality of someone sealing a box. Not rushed. Not angry. Just... decided.

She jerked. "William—what are you doing?"

He said nothing. Walked around the bed.

The second cuff locked around her right wrist with a sharp click. He didn't even glance at her face—just made sure the metal held. Like securing furniture to the floor before a storm.

He ran a hand up her arm slowly. Too slowly. The stroke once meant comfort. Now, it's clinical. Dissecting.

"You always needed me to take the lead," he growled. "You begged me to fight for us. I'm fighting now, Lexie."

He stepped away.

Her breath caught as he opened the closet. He pulled out a white sheet with quiet precision, as if choosing an outfit. Then, with the same calm detachment, he stooped down and picked the Dragon Knife off the floor.

Lexie's body recoiled as far as the cuffs would allow. "William don't—please. What are you doing?"

He turned toward her, and his familiar expression—was hollow.

"Patience, grasshopper," he said.

He laid the knife on the bed beside her like a final course at a dinner party. Then he began to rip the sheet. Each tear sounded like bone splintering.

"Spread your legs," he said, not with lust, not with love—but with control. Pure and practiced.

Lexie froze.

William's mouth twitched. "Don't make this ugly, Lex."

She didn't move. He grabbed her ankle and yanked.

She cried out, "Ow!"

"See?" he muttered, shaking his head like a disappointed parent. "You always push too far."

He cuffed her ankle to the lower bedpost, then walked to the other side. Fastened the second. All with the same eerie quiet.

Then he stood back, arms crossed, admiring the scene.

"There," he whispered. "Finally, still."

Lexie trembled, chained at all four corners, the knife lying mere inches from her skin.

"You want honesty?" he said, leaning in. "This is the most honest we've ever been. No more hiding. No more pretending you're the victim."

He lowered his voice, his lips near her ear. "You'll stay here until you remember who you belong to."

"William!" Lexie screamed.

"Best not to move too much."

"I hope you are enjoying yourself."

"I would enjoy it more if you would shut the fuck up."

Lexie gaped at her husband.

His robe fell to the floor.

The weight of the Dragon Knife in his grip anchored him, the cool steel pressing against his palm, grounding him in a storm of emotions he didn't understand. His breath came in heavy bursts, chest rising and falling with each surge of adrenaline that pulsed through his veins.

William climbed onto the bed, his body hovering over hers. The knife lingered near her head, not touching, but close enough to remind them both of its presence. A tool of precision. A weapon.

A symbol of control.

Control. The thing he was always supposed to have, the thing that slipped through his fingers like sand whenever it came to her.

His hips moved with forceful determination, each thrust driven by something deeper than just lust—anger, betrayal, desperation. A need to possess her, to make her understand, to remind her who she belonged to. The bed creaked beneath them, the rhythm of his body colliding against hers drowning out everything else. Holding the Dragon Knife near her head, he pumped into her over and over again. Hard pumps of frustration and desire.

Her tears slid down her cheeks, shining in the low light. Her body trembled beneath him, but something in his mind—some primal, frenzied part—kept him moving. The frustration coiled inside him, deep and unrelenting, like a beast clawing at the walls of his sanity.

William slammed his manhood into her... again and again.

"Why?" Lexie moaned.

He slammed into her again. His jaw clenched. The question slashed through him, cutting deeper than he expected.

Why?

Because she lied. Because she had cheated. Because she had created this monster.

With a low growl, he drove into her again, harder this time, as if the force alone could silence the war raging inside his head.

"Not another word," he ordered, his voice sharp and breathless.

His body shuddered in an exploding climax, pleasure and fury twisting together in a sickening blend that left him shaking. His hand still clasped over her mouth, relaxing as he rolled off her... but he kept a tight grip on the Dragon Knife.

Silence stretched between them, thick and suffocating.

William turned to her and caught her staring at him, unblinking, her eyes wide and glossy. There was no anger in them, no retaliation—only something worse. A hollow kind of acceptance.

His stomach turned, the weight of what he had just done slamming into him like a wrecking ball.

What have I done?

A lump rose in his throat. His free hand hesitated before reaching for her, fingertips grazing her damp cheek. She flinched. A small reaction, but it sent a jolt through his chest like a bullet.

"I don't know what came over me. I—hey," William murmured, his voice hoarse, uncertain. "I'm sorry."

She said nothing.

He sat up, the Dragon Knife still clutched in his grip. The blade caught the faintest glint of light, a stark contrast against the darkness pooling inside him. He should put it down. He wanted to put it down. But his fingers refused to release it, as if part of him believed that without it, he would lose whatever thread of control he had left.

She remained still, her chest rising and falling in shallow, measured breaths. She didn't move away, didn't fight back. That should have reassured him. Instead, it filled him with something worse than guilt.

Dread.

William swallowed hard, the silence in the room closing in around him. The air thickened, pressing against his chest, choking off breath.

They were supposed to be perfect. She was supposed to love him.

So why did it feel like he had just lost her completely?

———◆———

Above them, in realms untouched by mortal eyes, the Devil smiled. His hand moved His knight closer to God's queen, positioning his pieces to trap and torment. His voice purred with satisfaction. "Yes, that's it. Let him feel the thrill of power—the addictive rush of control." His smirk grew wider as William's cruelty seeped further into his actions.

God's *White-Gloved Hand*, steady and sure, moved a bishop forward, blocking the Devil's knight. "True power lies in love," He said, His voice filled with empathy. "Control is a prison built from fear, and in that prison, he will only lose himself."

But the Devil chuckled, savoring the struggle below. "Then let him lose himself, let him fall. He'll be mine in the end."

Confusing thoughts trampled through his brain. *What kind of man rapes his own wife? What's wrong with me? I love Lexie with all my heart, but I... I can't handle what she's done. I can't—*

"I won't stay in a prison you've built for me," she whispered. "You can't force me to love you."

William didn't flinch or soften as his shadow moved against the far wall.

"You won't have another man's child. Not ever. I won't allow it."

"Uncuff me!" she screamed.

He turned, a grin creeping across his face. "So, you can kill me? And your other weapon of choice? *A meat mallet?* Lexie, really?"

"I wouldn't kill you; you know that."

His gaze darkened. "And if I cut that seed from your belly, would you kill me?"

"Several times past your death."

"Damn baby, I can only die once."

"What can I say? I'd be the most passionate killer." Lexie snapped.

"There are much better ways to use that passion... how about grabbing me in the middle of the night and passionately fucking my brains out?"

"Can't. Handcuffed to the bed."

"Okay, grasshopper, be nice."

He moved closer and the fact that she was recoiling from his touch as he unlocked the restraints didn't matter to him. He leaned in and whispered. "If you run, I'll kill you."

Lexie picked up her robe from the floor. She wrapped it around her like armor. "I hate you."

"Sweetheart, after that? After what we just shared?"

"You raped me."

"You're my wife, I didn't rape you."

"It's still rape."

William stood over Lexie, watching her cower in fear, and he was ashamed. *The woman I love.* For a second, he hesitated, then something in him hardened. *But she betrayed you with another man.* "Again, you're my wife. I'm sorry I took you that way, but you're not going anywhere."

Lexie's voice sharpened like glass. "Stop threatening me, you can't make me love you."

"But I can make you stay. Eventually, you'll come around."

"Eventually, I'll kill you."

"I don't think you will." he declared, his voice too confident for a man who had just violated everything sacred.

Lexie stomps to the dresser, she opens the drawer and yanks out a pair of uninviting pajamas and slips them on.

"Your plan for me will never work."

He turned toward her, brows narrowing. "What are you talking about?"

She stood there bracing herself against the dresser. "Like I said before, I was in your office."

A pause. His jaw tensed. "I thought I'd locked the door. So careless of me."

"At least I know where I stand, and I'm not afraid of you."

He plopped onto the edge of the bed. "You know nothing."

"Million-dollar insurance... ways to kill your spouse."

William jumped to his feet. He crossed the space between them and grabbed Lexie by the shoulders so hard she cried out. His face was contorted with anger. "You have no right to enter my cave. You don't trust me."

"Trust?" Lexie snapped. "Why not kill me now and get it over with? Do it. No Lexie and no baby."

"I must say, it's tempting." Disgusted, he shoved her away.

Lexie stumbled backward, bumping against the dresser. "You want me to beg for my life and my baby's life—"

"—There's no baby."

"There will be," Lexie said through clenched teeth.

"No, Lexie, you won't have a baby."

Lexie gasped. "Why? Will I be dead? I cheated on you. I didn't know why it was taking so long for me to get pregnant. I thought to myself, is he not a man?"

William SLAPPED her hard. Her head snapped sideways, and the world tilted. She hit the floor hard, a sharp cry breaking from her lips. She rubbed her cheek, it was hot.

"You're such a bitch." William shouted.

"Then let this bitch go. I don't want to be here with you, not like this." Lexie's voice had cracked open, raw and wounded. She pushed herself up, staggering toward the door with a hand pressed to her face.

He dashed to close it. He struggled with hating and loving her all in the same minute. "You're not going anywhere."

God's White-Gloved Hands gripped the Cosmic Chessboard. But he remained calm. "You whispered rape in his ear?"

The Devil leaned forward, a gleam of satisfaction in His eyes as William asserted his dominance, taking pleasure in the tension and fear filling the room. "I did, see how control warps the soul," the Devil sneered. He moved His queen closer to God's bishop. "What's your move, Holy One?"

But God's *White-Gloved Hand* moved with quiet resilience, shielding His pieces with patience. "You won't destroy him, his heart is good," He replied, a soft certainty in His voice. "Love is not about control. He cannot force her to stay, but he can choose to love her well."

A tear slipped down Lexie's cheek. She whispered, "You won't break me, William. You might have me here, in this room, but you'll never control my spirit."

For a fleeting moment, there was a glimpse of the love that once bound them. A love that tried to hold on as her words floated through the haze of anger and dominance that clouded his mind. But the Devil's influence was strong, his whispers of power intoxicating, and that glimmer of remorse vanished. William's face hardened once more.

———◆◯◆———

The Devil's *Red-Gloved Hand* moved His bishop to press God's queen into a trap, a smirk spreading across His face as a low laugh rumbled through the ether. His fingers hovered over His next piece, ready to close in.

But God, calm and resolute, moved His rook, protecting Lexie with unwavering patience. "The long night yields in time," He whispered, His voice soft yet filled with unyielding hope. "Even in the coldest moments, warmth returns."

The Devil sneered. His laughter echoed as He tightened His hold on William's spirit. The sinister allure of power pulled him deeper into the abyss, threatening to close around him—and Lexie—forever.

———◆◯◆———

William's hand trembled as he tightened his grip on the Dragon Knife, the cold steel a reflection of the distance that had grown between them. Lexie presented a silent challenge that pierced through the thick haze of anger clouding his mind. Her words lingered in the air, as though they had the power to unravel everything he had built up in his mind—the resentments, the control, and the twisted satisfaction just moments before.

His voice, low and strained, broke the silence. "You talk as if you know me. But I don't think you know a damn thing about me anymore." William clutched the Dragon Knife as if he couldn't believe what he was holding, and he lowered it, his hand hanging limp at his side.

Lexie let out a slow, measured breath. "Maybe I don't know who you are now," she said, her tone gentle, cautious. "But I know who you were. I know there's a part of you that doesn't want this, that wants to be free from this anger."

A brief flash of recognition persisted, a vulnerability he'd buried beneath layers of resentment. He took a shaky step back, his grip loosening on the Dragon Knife as though he were waking from a trance. "Free?" he scoffed, his voice breaking. "Free from what, Lexie? The mess you made. The lies?"

But his words lacked the previous venom, and the armor he'd built around himself was cracking. Lexie took a tentative step toward him, her voice unwavering.

"Free yourself from this need to control—this anger—it's eating you alive."

The hardness in his eyes softened, replaced by a mixture of confusion and regret, a dawning realization of the darkness he'd allowed to take root in his heart. He released the Dragon Knife, letting it fall to the floor with a hollow thud that echoed through the tense silence.

The Devil's eyes narrowed. His hand hovered over His queen as He observed William's hesitation. "He wavers, after all this, and he's still tethered to the hope she offers. This weakness will ruin him."

But God's *White-Gloved Hand* moved His bishop into a protective formation, shielding His pieces from the Devil's advance. "It is not weakness," He replied. "It is strength—the strength to choose love over fear, to find redemption even when all light seems lost."

In the room below, William took a step back, his hands trembling, the weight of what he had done settling over him like a shroud.

Lexie's eyes remained on him.

"You don't have to fight me. We don't have to be enemies."

"I don't know how to stop," he admitted, his voice breaking. "All this anger... it's the only thing I've felt for so long. It's all I know."

Lexie reached out and placed a hand on his arm, her soft touch grounding him. "Just let it go, William," she whispered. "Let go of this anger. We can't change the past, but we don't have to keep destroying each other."

William's face twisted, and his eyes glistened as the weight of her words pressed down on him. He nodded, the anger melting away, leaving a fragile vulnerability that he had buried deep within himself.

The Devil scowled, His hand tightening around His rook as the connection between them rekindled, the dark hold He had over William slipping. "Fool," He muttered, seething with frustration. "You had her—she was yours to break, and now you throw it all away for a glimpse of forgiveness?"

But God's face softened, a gentle smile playing at His lips as He moved His queen to safety, protecting His pieces with a quiet resilience. "Forgiveness is the path to freedom," He said, His voice filled with hope. "In forgiving each other, they free themselves from the chains of anger and control."

William's shoulders sagged, the tension draining from his body, a sense of calm settling over him, the fury that had consumed him, subsiding. He reached out, his hand hesitating before resting on hers, his eyes filled with remorse.

"I'm sorry," he whispered. "For everything. I... I didn't mean for it to go this far."

Lexie's hand squeezed his, a small, forgiving smile breaking through the weariness in her expression. "Then let's end it here, let's find a way forward, without all of this... without the hurt, the anger."

Together, they sat in silence, the remnants of their bitterness melting away as they faced the choice that lay before them.

They remained on the bed, trying to work through their challenges. They were not aware that their thoughts and actions were being controlled and manipulated by beings they could never imagine. Every evil word, every loving glance, beyond their control. They remained puppets in a never-ending game of chess. How will their lives be changed? Will they survive?

Above, God moved His king to safety, with quiet satisfaction as He studied the board. The game was not over, but in that fragile moment, love and forgiveness had won.

A low rumble shook the room, the vibrations intensifying as the Devil's *Red-Gloved Hand* moved a piece across the Cosmic Chessboard, a triumphant glint in His eyes as William asserted his hold. "She's slipping further, losing her footing with each passing moment," He leaned in with a gleeful smile. "He's sealed her fate with fear."

God's face remained somber, but His hand remained steady as He moved His rook to shield a threatened piece. "Love turned to fear is a twisted weapon," He replied. "But her heart remains untouched; there is strength yet within her."

William wanted nothing more than to wipe everything away that had happened over the last few months.

"Lexie, it's just you and me. It makes sense to give the baby up for adoption. It'll be a constant reminder of your betrayal. Our love won't survive this."

"What love?" Lexie asked. "If you think this is love, you're more lost than I thought." Her words were sharp, cutting through the haze of control with an intensity that rattled him.

A hint of doubt passed across William's face before, but he masked it. "Love doesn't look like it did years ago. It has changed, we have grown."

"Love isn't control," Lexie whispered, her voice calm, cutting through his justifications. "It never was."

The silence that followed pressed down on them, heavier than before. He reached down and retrieved the Dragon Knife from the floor. His fingers traced the hilt as he considered what to do next. It had become obvious to him that Lexie was trying to hide her fear.

In the quiet of the room, his control, though hard-won, seemed fragile in the face of Lexie's unbroken spirit, her quiet strength cutting through the tension, making him doubt his next move.

He turned away, an expression of frustration smeared across his face. She must not see his confusion and regret. He had to stay strong and focused. Lexie couldn't know that he wanted nothing more than to go back, even a few months, when things were good between them. Everything is slipping away now, but he can't lose her. *What happened to us?*

The Devil moved His queen forward, His face filled with chilling satisfaction. "See how deeply control consumes? He thinks he has won."

But God moved His knight in a protective maneuver, a quiet assurance in His eyes. "Her strength lies in what he cannot take. And that is something he will never own."

STRENGTH

Lexie paced the room, her pulse racing with each step as her eyes darted around, landing on every shadow, every corner, every faint glint of light that sharpened her sense of unease. An oppressive quiet tension wrapped around her like a cold shroud. She paused, her hand moving to her belly, a reminder of what was at stake, of the life she intended to protect at all costs.

Her eyes drifted to the nightstand on William's side of the bed, where the Dragon Knife lay in stark contrast to the faint bedroom light. The blade's edge captured every reflection, every shadow, throwing it back with a menacing glint that made her shiver. The weapon sat there, cold and still, a silent reminder of the danger hovering over her. Lexie leaped to the nightstand, grabbed the Dragon Knife, and placed it under her bed.

A rumble reverberated through the room—a low, unsettling vibration that spread like a warning from somewhere beyond. Above, in an unseen realm, the Devil's *Red-Gloved Hand* moved His bishop forward, the piece casting a long shadow across the

Cosmic Chessboard. "She's near the breaking point," He said with satisfaction. "One nudge, and she'll reach for it. Fear is a potent force, after all."

But God's steady hand moved His knight in a defensive stance, blocking the Devil's advance. His voice was calm, resolute. "Fear may control for a moment, but love will guide her path in the end," He replied as He held the pieces with a gentle determination. "She must hold onto her purpose, or she'll lose more than she can bear."

In the room below, Lexie shook her head, forcing herself to turn away from the Dragon Knife, fighting the temptation it held. But the idea gnawed at the edges of her resolve. Her fingers itched for the knife. She needed something secure, something that could shift the power back into her hands, if only for a moment. She breathed, steadying herself, her mind whispering her need for calm.

The soft creak of a floorboard outside the room startled her, snapping her out of her trance. She tensed, listening to the faint sounds of William's footsteps as he moved down the hallway toward the kitchen. Her heartbeat thundered in her ears, and her mind raced. He made one promise. At early dawn, he will let her go. But did he mean it? *Could she really trust him to keep that promise?* The memory of him raping her and the veiled threats lingered on her mind, casting dark shadows over her hope.

A low laugh drifted through the silence, although far away, it pierced like a knife. The Devil leaned back, a smile curving at the corners of His lips as Lexie's turmoil unfolded. "See how the seed of fear grows?" His eyes gleamed with triumph. "She feels the weight of control tightening around her, and soon, she'll reach for what she believes will free her."

God leaned forward. He moved His rook in a protective arc, His voice a soft rumble that carried the weight of eternity. "You underestimate the resilience of love and the strength of grace. They are not pieces to be moved at your whim, but hearts that I have shaped, capable of finding their way back to Me, no matter how far they stray. Your queen may strike, your game may scheme, but my purpose endures, and it is greater than your cunning. Hope is a delicate light, but it endures," He countered. "Her strength will hold, even in the face of darkness."

William's footsteps grew louder, breaking the stillness. Lexie's fingers twitched as she cast one last glance at the Dragon Knife, its dark steel gleaming with an ominous promise. She took a breath, willing herself to focus on her resolve.

William entered, carrying two steaming cups of tea, his face a mask of satisfaction as he approached her. "Tea, the kind you like," he said, his tone light but with an edge of something darker beneath.

Lexie's face curved into a smile as she accepted the cup he offered, its warmth radiating through the porcelain. Her fingers tightened around it, and she forced herself to meet his gaze, striving for a calm demeanor that belied her inner turmoil.

"One more night," she reminded him, her voice steady. "And... you'll let me go."

William smiled. But his eyes gleamed with a strange intensity. "Of course, grasshopper," he said, his tone smooth, almost soothing. But there was something in his eyes that made her blood run cold, a flicker of something possessive, something unyielding.

Lexie placed her cup on the nightstand, the faint clink of ceramic against wood seeming louder in the charged silence. She took a slow breath, steadying herself.

"You meant what you said, didn't you, William?" she asked, her voice carrying a delicate balance of defiance and vulnerability. "You'll let me go in the morning?"

William's smile widened, but it didn't reach his eyes. Instead, that unsettling gleam remained, a hint of something dark and inscrutable lurking beneath the surface. "I always keep my promises," he replied, his tone smooth, too smooth. He leaned forward, resting his elbows on his knees as he studied her with an intensity that made her chest tighten. "But you know, Lexie, promises can be... flexible. Don't you think?"

Her throat constricted, but she forced herself to remain calm, her fingers tightening around the rim of her cup. "Promises are promises," she said, her voice firmer now. "And you gave me your word."

"I did," he acknowledged, his voice quiet but loaded. "And yet, here we are, sitting together like we always have. You, sipping your tea, me, admiring the way the moonlight catches in your hair." He reached out and brushed a stray strand from her face. The gesture was almost tender.

"Why does it have to change, Lexie? Why does it have to end?"

"It's not working anymore," she replied, her voice trembling despite her best efforts to steady it. "You know that as well as I do."

His hand hovered for a moment longer before he withdrew it, his expression darkening.

"You're trying to throw away everything we've built. Everything I've sacrificed for you."

"You don't understand—"

"Oh, I understand, grasshopper," he said, leaning back in his chair, his eyes narrowing. "I understand perfectly. Do you think you'll find freedom out there? Peace? You think walking out that door at dawn will erase everything that's happened between us?"

"It's not about erasing anything," she said. "It's about starting over. For both of us."

"Starting over," he echoed, his tone laced with bitterness. He shook his head, the shadow of a smirk playing on his lips. "Do you really think it's that simple? That you can just leave, and all the broken pieces will somehow fit back together on their own?"

She hesitated, the weight of his words settling over her like a shroud. "I don't know," she admitted. "But I can't stay here. Not like this." *And you can't leave. You've been warned. There's a black void outside the door.*

The silence that followed was deafening. He studied her, his expression unreadable, and for a moment, a glint of pain resided in his eyes. Moments later it was gone, replaced by the cold, calculated look she'd come to dread.

"You think I'm the reason you're unhappy," he said, his voice low, dangerous. "But have you ever stopped to wonder if the problem is you? Could you be running from yourself?"

Her breath caught, the accusation hitting her like a blow. "That's not fair," she whispered.

"Fair?" He let out another bitter laugh. "You're talking about fair while you're planning to walk away from everything we've built— from me? After everything I've done to hold us together. And now you want to leave our marriage and have another man's child?"

"You haven't held us together," she said, her voice trembling with emotion. "You've held me here. There's a difference."

"You're here on your own free will, I didn't force you. And now that you're pregnant, you want to leave."

His jaw tightened, and for a moment, she thought he might lash out.

"You're right about one thing, it will be dawn soon. And with it, your chance to leave. But I wonder..."

He turned to face her, his expression unreadable. "Do you really have the strength to go through with it?"

Lexie's heart pounded in her chest, her pulse a steady drumbeat of fear and resolve. "I do," she said, forcing the words out despite the lump in her throat. "I have to."

He took a step closer, his presence almost suffocating as he loomed over her. "We'll see." His voice is soft but menacing. "We'll see if dawn brings the freedom you think it will—or if it brings something else entirely."

Lexie refused to back down despite the fear coiling in her stomach. "I'm leaving, William," she said. "No matter what." *If I can.*

His smile returned, but it was colder now, devoid of warmth. "I guess we'll both find out what the morning has in store, won't we?"

Lexie nodded, her hand clutching the cup like a lifeline. As he turned and walked away, disappearing into the shadows of the hallway, a chill swept over her, the weight of his words pressing down on her chest.

She closed her eyes and took a deep, shuddering breath. Dawn couldn't come soon enough.

EARLY DAWN

The figure before her was a man she didn't recognize. One she feared. *How could she get through to him? Could she make him see how evil he had become, willing to do anything, even murder, to get what he wanted? Murder—He wouldn't kill me.*

"Are you okay?" His voice broke through her thoughts.

She swallowed, her voice low. "Fine. I'm fine."

The weight of his control pressed down on Lexie, but she didn't protest. Instead, she sank down to the edge of the bed, hoping he couldn't see the panic rising within her.

"William?"

He raised his cup, his eyes never leaving hers. "Let's toast," he said, his tone almost cheerful. "To early dawn. Cheers."

The words struck her like a warning, but with a defeated sigh, she raised her own cup, mirroring his gesture. "Cheers."

"Shall we go to bed?" he asked, his gaze penetrating. "I know you're as anxious as I am for dawn."

"I'm... I'm not in a rush," she replied, fighting the tremor in her voice.

A low chuckle escaped him. "I look forward to it."

His calm certainty was unnerving. She glanced at him, her pulse quickening. "You've been planning for—?"

He cut her off with a cool smile. "For well over a year. But now... everything has changed."

"Why?"

"Your deception has caused an abrupt change in direction," he said, as if savoring the admission.

A shiver ran through her as she managed to ask, "What are you planning?"

"Come, dear, let's go to bed," he replied.

She hesitated. "Uh... I'm not exactly sleepy."

He moved closer, his smile widening.

"Come lie with me. I promise not to bite... unless you ask me to."

Lexie forced a smile, though dread curled in her stomach. "How will you wake up at early dawn?"

"Silly grasshopper, I set my alarm. No worries."

They climbed into bed, each movement surreal. Lexie lay motionless, staring at the ceiling as William spooned her, his arm heavy around her waist. Her eyes stayed wide open, her mind racing, each tick of the clock an unbearable reminder that dawn was inevitable.

Above, the Devil leaned over the Cosmic Chessboard, His hand poised, a glimmer of satisfaction in His gaze as He slid His rook forward. "See how she folds under his power? She's tethered in every sense, and by dawn, she'll have nowhere left to hide."

God studied the board in silence, His face filled with a mixture of sorrow and resolve. Moving His bishop, He countered the Devil's advance. "Even in the silence of her suffering, hope will anchor her." His tone was calm, yet resolute. "The final move is not Yours to make, Fallen Angel."

Lexie's mind whirled. She held her breath, waiting for William's breathing to show that he had indeed drifted to sleep. She couldn't afford to waste a single second; every instinct told her that dawn would bring something she couldn't escape.

She attempted to ease her body away from him, trying to slip out from under his arm, but as soon as she moved, his grip tightened, pulling her close against him, his whisper slicing through the darkness, sharp as a knife.

"Going somewhere, grasshopper?"

Lexie froze, his breath warm against her neck, her body taut with terror. No escape waited, only the sense of being ensnared, trapped in a game whose stakes she didn't comprehend.

As the hours passed, the first light of dawn began to creep through the windows, casting faint shadows across the walls. Neither of them moved, caught in the liminal space between the darkness of their fears and the faint promises of a new day.

The alarm's harsh ring shattered the stillness of the room, its sharp, grating sound echoing through the quiet dawn. Pale morning light filtered through the blinds, casting muted beams across the bed where Lexie lay unmoving, her eyes wide and unblinking, as if she hadn't slept a single moment.

William reached over, turning off the alarm with a satisfied grin. "Wake up, my dear. It's early dawn." His voice was cheery, too cheery, a dark thrill underlining his words. He leaned over, pressing a kiss to Lexie's cheeks, the affectionate gesture almost sinister under the circumstances.

Lexie didn't respond, her body tense, her gaze fixed on a distant point across the room, her mind filled with nothing but an impending sense of dread. Her heart pounded, heavy and irregular, as she listened to the sounds of William moving around.

As he headed to the bathroom, whistling, Lexie's mind raced. The promise of early dawn, the cryptic notes she'd found, the veiled threats, it all culminated in the hollow ache in her chest, the certainty that whatever he had planned was about to unfold.

———◦———

A Red-Gloved Hand hovered over the Cosmic Chessboard, fingers tapping lightly against the rook, considering the move. The Devil's lips curled into a wicked smile as He slid His rook forward, its path obstructing any escape. "Doomsday." The Devil's voice, a seductive whisper that reverberated like dark silk.

God hovered over the board with His expression resolute and calm but weighted with sorrow. His *White-Gloved Hand* lifted His knight, placing it beside the rook, a subtle but powerful defense. "Sometimes the faintest hope is all that's needed to withstand the greatest darkness," He whispered, His tone unwavering.

In the bedroom, Lexie clenched her fists under the covers, forcing herself to focus as the seconds ticked by. She had to leave; there would be no mercy in waiting. Lexie jumped out of bed and dashed to the door. She turned the doorknob and attempted to open the door. She pulled and pulled. The door didn't bulge, not an inch. Something or someone held it closed.

Lexie backed away from the door. Beads of sweat ran down her entire body as she stumbled back to the bed. *This is a nightmare.*

William stepped toward the toilet, but before he reached it, he caught sight of the mirror and gasped. Glancing at the mirror, staring back at him were those slashing words scrawled in red lipstick: *"You broke my heart. I will kill you before I ever let you go."*

The message sent a chill down his spine, a harsh and unbidden reminder that cut through his carefully crafted plans. His face contorted as he absorbed the message.

William's heart stirred with words he didn't hear but somehow surfaced within him.

"Remember the vow you made, to love for better or for worse? This child is innocent, your love can provide healing for you and Lexie and a future for one of My children."

But it's not my child.

"No, it's My child, a child of God. If you love me, you will love all my children and provide for all my children. You are not lost William, you know my word."

William's expression shifted from resentment to acceptance. He shook his head, grabbing a towel, his movements stiff and deliberate as he wiped away the incriminating words smeared across the glass in jagged streaks.

When the last remnants of the words faded, he exhaled, the tension in his shoulders unwinding. A slow smile crept onto his face as he let the towel drop to the floor. A strange peace settled over him.

———◆———

In the stillness, a *White-Gloved Hand* descended upon the Cosmic Chessboard, gliding with divine precision. The white bishop moved forward, landing with a decisive clack, bolstering the defense around Lexie's queen. The room trembled under the weight of the move, a bold sacrificial act in the silent battle.

A low, dark chuckle echoed across the other side of the board. The Devil's fingers lingered over his own pieces, savoring the pressure mounting in the game. He leaned forward, eyes glinting with a feral gleam, and inched his rook forward, edging dangerously close to the white king.

William pressed his hands against the edge of the sink, his reflection wavering in the mirror as the morning light filtered in. The thought clawed at him, relentless and raw: *the child couldn't be his, could it?* It was a jagged truth, one that scraped against his pride and everything he thought he could bear. But beneath the bitterness, something else stirred—something quieter, harder to name.

Could he let this baby define their future? Could he punish an innocent life for circumstances it didn't choose? The ache in his chest deepened as he thought of Lexie, her fragile hope radiating through every glance, every word she'd spoken. She carried more than a child. She carried their future, fragile and uncertain, waiting for him to decide if he was strong enough to shoulder it.

On the other side of the door, his wife lay waiting, steady and patient. This wasn't how he imagined life would unfold. It wasn't the clean, clear path he'd once envisioned. But that's the point, he thought, his fingers relaxing their grip on the sink. *This child may not be mine in blood, but it will be mine in every way that matters.* The resolve emerged, like the first cracks of light across a dark horizon. His heart was now heavy with the weight of purpose, with the weight of choosing to stand when every instinct told him to run. As the first rays of sunlight stretched farther into the room, illuminating the door like an invitation, his decision no longer centered on Lexie or the child. It centered on the man he chose to become.

———◆———

Lexie lay trembling, her mind a storm of memories and sinister words twisting her sense of reality into a dark, inescapable knot.

You broke my heart. I will kill you before I ever let you go. seared into her memory as if it had been written in blood instead of lipstick.

The notepad on his desk, with its sickening message:

Order the book "100 Ways to Kill Your Spouse.

The scrawled note on the nightstand, chilling in its intent:

A Killing at Early Dawn.

Lexie's breath came in shallow gasps.

William's words replayed in her mind, each one a jagged cut to the fragile hope she clung to.

I have a wife who's a whore.

No, Lexie, you won't have a baby.

Her hand reached beneath the bed, fingers searching until they closed around the cold, unforgiving steel of the Dragon Knife. Holding it reminded her that even in her most helpless moments, she still had a way to protect herself. With a trembling hand, she tucked it under her pillow, its weight a small, cold comfort.

Till death do us part.

No, Lexie, you won't have a baby.

As if summoned by her deepest fears, William returned to the bedroom, his every step measured. He carried a quiet intensity that made Lexie's heart pound, her eyes darting toward the knife hidden beneath her pillow. She had to stay calm, stay in control, even though her body wanted to leap up, to run, to scream. To defend herself, she had to be careful.

William crossed the threshold, and for a moment, his eyes were unreadable. His mouth curved into a smile. *Was he enjoying this, enjoying what he was about to do to her?*

"So, you're awake," he glanced at Lexie, a cold chill ran up and down her spine. His tone was soft but heavy and alive with the undercurrent of a menace she had become accustomed to. He tilted his head, studying her like a puzzle he had yet to solve. "It's early dawn, Lexie. The time we talked about."

Her throat tightened, and she forced herself to nod, hoping he couldn't see the fear flashing in her eyes. She needed to play the game, to keep her posture calm and her voice even, anything to prevent him from seeing how dangerously close she drifted to the edge. One crack in her composure, one misstep, and he might glimpse the panic clawing just beneath her skin.

He took another tentative step toward her, his eyes narrowing, shifting to the pillow where Lexie had hidden the Dragon Knife—drawn there as if something dark throbbed beneath the fabric, calling to him.

Across an invisible plane, the Devil leaned back with a satisfied smile, His fingers hovering over the Cosmic Chessboard, savoring the tension as He prepared His next move. He shifted his attention toward God, whose posture remained steady and resolute, a hint of sorrow resting behind the stillness of His expression, even as He studied the pieces.

The Devil's *Red-Gloved Hand* moved a black rook forward with gleeful precision, His voice dripping with delight. "No piece can outrun its destiny," He purred, His hand lingering over His queen. "She's boxed in, nowhere left to turn."

God turned to Him, unmoved. His *White-Gloved Hand* glided to the board, reinforcing a line of defense around the queen, protecting her even while she was in her most vulnerable position.

"True strength is shown in the face of fear," He said, "in the willingness to endure even when the end seems inevitable," His focus remained fixed on the board, His features softening as He made His move.

In the bedroom, Lexie braced herself, gripping the edge of the pillow, waiting for the right moment, her heart hammering like a trapped bird as the early dawn light filled the room.

As William leaned in, his expression unreadable, Lexie's instincts flared, every nerve in her body alert to his subtle, almost practiced movements. A chill ran through her as his eyes fixed on hers with an unsettling intensity, and a sense of dread spread through her as he came closer. In a flash, her hand slipped under the pillow, fingers closing around the cold hilt of the Dragon Knife.

Without fully processing the movement, Lexie's body reacted. She lifted the knife up in one swift motion, her breath held as the blade connected with William's chest. A sickening gasp escaped him as his eyes, wide and filled with disbelief, met hers. For a brief, horrific moment, they stared at one another, locked in a silent exchange of shock and betrayal; the realization of what had happened settled over both like a heavy fog.

The first splatter of blood hit her gown, warm and shocking against her skin, breaking the trance. William's face twisted in pain as he staggered backward, clutching his chest. His body slumped, falling from the bed to the floor with a heavy thud that echoed in the stillness of the room.

Lexie's hand, still wrapped around the knife, trembled. The Dragon Knife—slick with his blood—rested in her grip like something foreign, alien, as if it belonged to someone else entirely. She stared at it, unable to connect the weapon to her own will. The sharp, metallic tang of blood flooded her senses, curling into her nose, coating the back of her throat. Her vision tightened, the edges closing in, while her mind scrambled to make sense of the moment, of the unthinkable choice she just made.

The Dragon Knife slipped from her fingers, clattering to the floor beside him. She stared, horrified, as crimson spread in a widening pool around William, staining the carpet. His body convulsed, the life within him struggling, rebelling against the inevitable, his limbs twitching in sporadic, involuntary jerks.

"William..." Her voice trembled with disbelief. She dropped to her knees beside him, hands hovering over his body as though she could pull him back from the edge. Her fingers traced his face, cold and lifeless now, his once intense gaze replaced with a vacant, glassy stare that shot straight through her.

"William!" The name fell from her lips like a plea, a desperate prayer that wouldn't be answered. She gripped his shoulders, shaking him as though he were asleep, as though she could wake him from this nightmare. But his body was limp, lifeless, his blood pooling beneath him, soaking into the fibers of the carpet with a dreadful finality.

A *Red-Gloved Hand reached* for the Cosmic Chessboard, sliding a dark queen across the board with a satisfied smirk. The Devil's eyes gleamed with cruel amusement, His fingers drumming against the polished wood. "A well-executed end," he drawled, his voice a low, dangerous whisper. "Nothing more thrilling than a desperate act." He leaned back, satisfied with His move, His attention focused entirely on God, who sat opposite him with an unreadable expression.

God's *White-Gloved Hand* lingered over the board, His mind fixed not on the pieces but beyond, as if seeing through the confines of the game. He moved a pawn forward, reinforcing a delicate, protective barrier around the last remnants of hope. "Fallen Angel, even in darkness, there is a chance for light." His voice was calm and steady—a quiet power that refused to yield.

Lexie cradled William's face in her hands, her heart pounding with the sickening realization of what had happened, what she had done. She hadn't wanted it to end this way, hadn't wanted to resort to violence, but she was trapped, cornered by his threats, by his unrelenting hold over her life. Violence never belonged in her vision of love, yet here she knelt, fingers pressed to the face of the man she once trusted and loved. She couldn't escape. His threats backed her into a corner, his control tightening around every part of her life until the walls closed in.

She told herself she tried. That she pleaded, reasoned, waited. But when no mercy came from him, when her fear screamed louder than her guilt, she moved. Not out of hate. Out of survival.

As the dawn light crept further into the room, warm air brushed against her skin, a bitter reminder of the life she'd fought so hard to protect. Her fingers slipped from William's face, her hands falling to her sides, numb and heavy. The weight of the silence pressed down on her, filling the room with a suffocating stillness that mocked her.

William's blood drowned the once pristine blade of the Dragon Knife, now only a brutal symbol of the choice she'd been forced to make. She took a shaky breath, the enormity of her actions settling over her, threatening to crush her beneath its weight.

A small movement outside the window caught her attention, drawing her to the early morning light spilling into the garden. The world outside continued as if nothing had changed, as if her life hadn't been shattered. The birds chirped, the breeze stirred the trees, the world indifferent to the tragedy that had unfolded within these walls.

She pulled herself to her feet, her legs unsteady beneath her, the blood from William's lifeless body soaking into the hem of her gown. she couldn't stay here, couldn't face the life they had built together, now tainted beyond repair. She took a final, lingering look at his face, her heart heavy, filled with sorrow that words could never express.

The first rays of dawn washed over her as she stepped away from the bed, leaving behind the shattered pieces of her life.

As she lowered his head to the floor, Lexie's hands shook, her mind a storm of confusion and horror. She stared at her bloodied fingers, her breath coming in ragged, panicked bursts. The realization crashed over her like a wave, its weight forcing her to her knees beside him.

"Oh my God!" she whispered, the words catching in her throat. "What have I done?"

William's fixed, vacant eyes stared at Lexie with an emptiness that penetrated her soul. She couldn't look away, her mind reeling with the gravity of what lay before her. The faint dawn light, once promising hope, now cast a sickly pallor over everything it touched.

A loud rumble filled the air, and the entire room vibrated. A *Red-Gloved Hand* moved a rook across the large, ornate Cosmic Chessboard, its calculated slide ending with a sinister finality. The Devil's laughter echoed through the silence, a sound so menacing it seeped into the room's walls, reverberating through the air.

God's eyes followed the Devil's move with unyielding calm, His *White-Gloved Hand* resting on the Cosmic Chessboard as though pausing to consider the consequences of every square, every piece. "Free will can be a fragile gift," He said scrutinizing Lexie, as His fingers brushed over a single, solitary pawn on the board. "And yet, she still has a choice."

But the Devil leaned forward, His eyes gleaming with satisfaction. "Choices made in the shadows often reveal the truest nature," He sneered, fingers drumming along the edge of the Cosmic Chessboard. He reveled in Lexie's despair.

Lexie's entire body shook, her hands still holding William's head as if her touch alone could breathe life back into him. The laughter echoed through her mind, mocking her and drowning out her desperate thoughts. She released him, pulling her hands back, cradling them as though they belonged to someone else, someone capable of such violence. The weight of her guilt pressed against her, cold and relentless, an inescapable reality she could no longer deny.

The dawn broke through the window, casting long shadows across the room as if mocking her with its peaceful light. The full extent of what she had done hit her with unrelenting force. The Dragon Knife lying near William's head in a dark pool of blood sent chills through her body. She pressed her trembling hands to her face, her breath catching as silent sobs wracked her body.

A single tear traced down her cheek, leaving a faint track on her skin, and in that moment, something stirred within her, a faint whisper, a glimmer of strength. She could still choose her next move and could still take control of whatever life was left in her fractured world.

God made a small, deliberate move on the Cosmic Chessboard. His *White-Gloved Hand* settled over a single pawn, guiding it forward in defiance of the Devil's ruthless advance. He remained calm and unshaken as the Devil sneered.

"You underestimate her," He whispered, His voice kind but unwavering. "Even now, in her despair, she has strength you cannot comprehend."

The Devil leaned back, a twisted grin spreading across His face as He regarded the piece God had chosen. "Strength or weakness?" He taunted. "The line between them is thinner than you think. Let's see if she falls—or if she rises."

"She might fall. But even if she does, that is not where her story ends."

THE EARLY DAWN GIFT

T he doorbell rang, echoing through the quiet house. Lexie's entire body jolted as if the sound itself had struck her. She rose from the floor, her blood-drenched nightgown heavy, clinging to her skin, the damp fabric reminding her of the brutal reality of what she had done.

Lexie took quick, shallow breaths as she staggered back, her vision blurring as her hand reached for the wall behind her. She leaned into it, gripping the edge as though its solidness could anchor her unraveling mind. Could she make it through the bedroom, through the long hallway, to the front door without collapsing? The insistent, jarring doorbell rang a second time. A rush of terror filled her veins. *Who would be here this early? Did they know? Did they suspect?*

Her body moved independently, each step slow and disjointed as she stumbled toward the bathroom. She glanced down at her hands, still slick with William's blood, then back to the empty doorway where his lifeless body lay twisted and contorted as if trapped in some grotesque dance.

Inside the bathroom, Lexie flipped on the light, her pale face staring back at her in the mirror. Her eyes were wide and panicked and almost foreign, as if they belonged to someone else, a stranger forced into the brutal aftermath of violence. The words William had erased from the mirror earlier bled back into her memory: *You broke my heart. I will kill you before I ever let you go.*

Her shaking hands grasped the edge of the sink as she leaned forward, her breaths coming out in uneven shudders. She scrubbed her hands raw in hot water.

The water turned pink as it mixed with the remnants of William's blood. Panic clawed at her chest, every heartbeat a painful reminder of the events she couldn't take back.

Lexie stood there, trembling.

Outside the bathroom, the doorbell chimed again. She gripped the sink tighter, the sound twisting her insides with fear. Could it be the police? Or worse, someone who knew? She didn't have a plan and didn't know if there was any way to explain the tragic scene in the bedroom.

⚜

The Devil leaned in over the Cosmic Chessboard, a gleeful glint in His eyes as His *Red-Gloved Hand* moved His queen. The piece slid forward in one swift motion, its move calculated, designed to close in. "She's on the edge, wouldn't you agree?" He taunted, glancing across the board with a crooked smile. "One more move, and she'll topple."

God exuded tranquility. His *White-Gloved Hand* hovered over a knight, moving it in a protective stance between the queen and the remaining pieces, creating a barrier. "Where you see vulnerability, I see strength. Where you lay traps, I build a way forward.

You may plot and strike, but you cannot overcome the grace I have bestowed. Lexie will find her strength," He replied. His eyes were steady as He peered at Lexie as if seeing beyond her immediate panic to something deeper, something she had yet to discover within herself.

———◆———

Lexie splashed water onto her face, each droplet chilling her as she struggled to shake off the dread that clung to her. She lifted her head, staring once more into the mirror. She couldn't run from what had happened, and now, whoever was at the door would demand an answer she wasn't ready to give. Lexie removed her blood-stained gown. She pulled a robe from the bathroom hook and threw it over her naked body.

The doorbell sounded again, tingling her head like a migraine. A strange calm settled over her. She took a breath, steadying herself, knowing there was no escaping what lay on the other side of the bathroom door—both the nightmare she had created and the uncharted course that lay ahead.

Lexie's steps were slow, each one heavy with the weight of the devastating horror she had left behind. She edged past William's body, avoiding the blood pooling beneath him and the lifeless eyes that stared at her accusingly, trapping her in a silent, eternal confrontation.

What have I done?

The pale morning light filtered in through the windows, casting a haunting glow over everything it touched, illuminating the red streaks she left in her wake. Lexie's mind buzzed, each thought a fragment of confusion and shock, swirling in a dizzying fog. The hallway stretched before her, pulling her forward against her will.

The doorbell rang again, and she flinched at the sound, her eyes widening as the vibrations rippled through her, echoing up the hallway walls and piercing her fragile composure. *It's just a sound.* She forced her feet to move one step at a time, and every step brought her closer to the front door and to whoever—or whatever—awaited her on the other side.

———————— ◆ ————————

A *Red-Gloved Hand* gripped a knight on the ethereal Cosmic Chessboard sliding it forward with measured patience. The Devil, his dark eyes gleaming, leaned back with anticipation. "She's moving like a pawn in a trap," he said, his voice dripping with satisfaction. "Her fear has already paralyzed her."

God's White-Gloved *Hand* moved a bishop in quiet defiance, shielding Lexie's piece from the onslaught. "Her path is not defined by fear alone," He replied, "In these moments, she is discovering herself, and sometimes, courage takes its first breath amid terror."

———————— ◆ ————————

In the hallway, Lexie's trembling fingers brushed the wall for balance. The sounds of her own shallow breathing filled her ears, drowning out everything else. She pressed her hand against her stomach, a reminder of the life she still protected within her, and with it came a surge of strength. No longer drifting through her own nightmares, she now fought for the child growing inside her, the fragile thread that tied her to the future.

She drifted forward, inch by inch, until the front door loomed before her, the weight of every memory and mistake pressing down on her. Her hand hovered over the doorknob, hesitating, as the silence settled once again.

The doorbell rang one final time, and this time, it carried more than sound—it delivered a summons.

Lexie's hand shook as she gripped the doorknob, her breath catching as she opened the creaky door. It cut through the silence like a blade. The fresh morning air mingled with the stale dread that clung to her like a second skin. The hideous black void was gone. The sky, the trees, the neighborhood, everything had returned to normal. But not for Lexie. She would never be the same again.

There, in perfect contrast to the nightmare unfolding inside, stood Carol James—a vision of calm elegance in a crisp executive suit and towering heels, her polished smile frozen in polite expectation. Her eyes held a glimmer of curiosity as she took in Lexie's disheveled appearance, but Carol's professional demeanor remained intact, every detail of her look meticulously composed. She held a gift-wrapped box with its red bow vivid and unnervingly cheerful.

"Mrs. Grant, I'm Carol James, your husband is expecting me," Carol began, her voice smooth as velvet. "I hope I'm not intruding.

William asked me to be here specifically at early dawn for this occasion."

Lexie's eyes darted to the box, and her mind raced. The words surreal, out of place—a piece of some twisted puzzle she couldn't quite fit together. Her pulse thundered in her ears; the memory of William's lifeless eyes burned into her vision. "*For this occasion*," Carol had said, as if this morning was like any other. She forced herself to respond, her voice faint and strained.

"N-no... it's fine. I...wasn't expecting anyone."

Carol's smile never wavered, but Lexie's wide-eyed stare prompted her to peek toward the house's interior.

———— ◆◦◆ ————

High above, the Devil's *Red-Gloved Hand* gripped the rook, sliding it forward with a smooth, relentless motion. The Cosmic Chessboard rattled, a faint tremor running through the room as the Devil leaned in, his eyes gleaming with amusement. "She's unraveling with every move," he drawled, watching Lexie's pale face through the shimmer of his twisted vision. "That, my friend, is how you corner a queen."

God's steady, *White-Gloved Hand* lingered over the board, considering his next move. He remained solemn, unflinching. "Not every queen is vanquished. Sometimes, they're only tested." His voice was calm, a subtle resolve woven through His words as He shifted His knight, creating a path for the embattled piece to maneuver.

———❖———

Facing Carol, Lexie wanted to scream, to retreat, to run and leave it all behind. But instead, she forced her expression to mask the terror still churning within. She had to remain calm.

"William... he's not ... he's not here right now," Lexie said.

"Not here? But he must be," Carol said, a hint of something unreadable flickering in her eyes, a quiet confidence that sent a chill down Lexie's spine. "He wouldn't miss this...for anything."

Lexie's eyes traveled over Carol with a cold, assessing stare. Everything about Carol—her white hat with a matching white tailored suit and polished heels, her blond coiffed hair without a strand dangling—clashed hard against the nightmare Lexie had endured. Without doubt, a perfect picture of composure.

Behind Carol, across the street, her neighbor Jane pretended to garden, her eyes trained on Lexie's doorway like a hawk. *That bitch is so damn nosy.* Every movement, every gesture will be stored, and ready for the gossip mill.

"This isn't a good time," Lexie said, her voice tightening. "I have to call the police." She moved to the counter and picked up her cell phone, her hand trembling. Dead battery. With a surge of frustration, she plugged it in and turned back to Carol, who, without invitation, had stepped inside the house.

"The police?" Carol asked, a polite mask of concern settling over her face. "Is something wrong?"

Lexie faced her, the chill in her eyes sharpening. "Why are you here, in my house? What do you want?"

Carol met her stare unflinching. "It was your husband's idea."

The words struck Lexie like a punch, and her chest tightened. "Were you sleeping with my husband?" she asked.

Carol remained calm. "No, of course not. We—"

"—you need to leave my house." Lexie's voice cracked, the words slicing through the tense silence between them.

Carol's expression shifted, her eyes sweeping around the room as if searching for William. "Where's William?" she asked, louder now, the edges of her voice fraying with something akin to impatience.

Before Lexie could respond, Carol took another step forward, calling out into the house. "William! William!"

Lexie's heart pounded, each echo of his name a bitter reminder of what lay beyond in the bedroom. She crossed the room, her face a mask of fury and fear.

"He can't hear you," she said, her voice thick with suppressed rage. Her eyes fell to the package Carol held, and she snatched the gift-wrapped box from her hands.

"What's this?" Lexie demanded, her fingers digging into the wrapping paper, already unraveling at the edges.

"William insisted I bring this to you...at early dawn," Carol replied, her voice softening, almost wistful, as if she were reliving an intimate moment.

"Early dawn? Lexie repeated, a bitter laugh slipping through her lips. *So, this is the early dawn gift.* The weight of it was strange and ominous in her hands, but it was the most beautiful, gift-wrapped box she had ever seen.

"Why you?" she demanded, her fingers tearing into the paper, ripping it open as her frustration bled through.

"So, you <u>were</u> sleeping with my husband," she muttered, more a statement than a question.

Carol shook her head. "I—I"

"Do you deny—"

"What?"

"—you do understand English?" Lexie hissed. Her words were sharp as a blade.

Carol was flustered; her voice wavered. "Yes... Ah... No, I wasn't sleeping with your husband. We've been working closely together for over a year... shouldn't we wait for William?"

Carol yelled in the direction of the stairs. "William! William!"

Lexie's eyes held an unsettling mixture of sorrow and rage as she repeated in a hollow voice, "Like I said, he can't hear you." With a forced calm, she scanned the contents of the box, then Carol's anxious face and back to the box.

Lexie's mouth fell open. "I don't understand."

"I'm his editor," Carol said, her voice shaky but firm.

"What... his editor?" Lexie's voice trembled as she spoke, her fingers moving with rigid precision as she pulled a small, tucked card from the box.

Lexie opened the card, her heart pounding as her eyes scanned the words in William's familiar handwriting. His voice echoed in her mind, each word slicing through her.

To my beautiful wife, my greatest inspiration, and the love of my life. Thanks for encouraging me to write... again. You made this happen. You. I'm forever grateful and forever in love with you, my little grasshopper.

Lexie's hands trembled as she laid the card aside, her vision blurring as she pulled out a book from the box and read:

A Killing at Early Dawn
A Murder Mystery by William Grant

The title loomed up at her in bold, ominous print. Beneath the title, a familiar, haunting image—a *Bloody Dragon Knife*, its blade dripping blood.

Oh my god, William was writing a book! The two-million-dollar life insurance policy, the book "100 Ways to Kill Your Spouse. It was all research. Oh my god, Oh my god.

Lexie now grasped what it all meant and what she had done to the man she loved who had only supported and loved her the best way he could.

A cold, strangled scream escaped Lexie's throat. She collapsed to the floor, the book clutched against her chest as if it could shield her from the weight of her actions, her sobs breaking through in uncontrollable waves. Her mind raced, fragments of memory, words, and emotions spinning together until they became indistinguishable.

Lexie clung to the book, hoping to undo the horror she'd unleashed. Her sobs were deep and broken, each one wracking her body until she couldn't breathe. Carol knelt beside her and touched her shoulder.

"Lexie...what's wrong?" Carol whispered, but her words were hollow, lost in the tremors of Lexie's grief. "William wanted to surprise you. Where is he and why are you crying?"

Lexie struggled to pull herself together. A strange calm settled over her, the weight of her actions still present but softened, her mind no longer spiraling with dread. She stared at the book in her hands, its title *A Killing at Early Dawn*, and the bloody Dragon Knife on the cover, glinting in the early morning light, all made sense to her now, and for a moment, her sobs stilled, replaced by a quiet spiritual resolve.

Carol observed, her face pale with uncertainty. She whispered, "Lexie, what happened?"

Lexie swallowed hard, wiping her face. "I... I don't know. I can't explain it. But whatever it is, it's not over. Not yet."

A subtle warmth filled the room, the despair lifting as if graced by an unseen hand. This was her move to make, and this couldn't be her future.

⸺◆⸺

God's *White-Gloved Hand* paused, hovering over a solitary piece. He remained solemn as he settled on the board, yet His voice held a gentle strength. "This game was always hers to play."

The Cosmic Chessboard rattled, the Devil's *Red-Gloved Hand* moved a piece forward, with a victorious, final laugh that echoed like thunder.

The Devil leaned back; His dark, mocking laughter grew louder and louder.

"Checkmate." The voice, dripping with malice, rang out as the laughter reached a fever pitch.

God's *White-Gloved Hand* lingered, fingers extended with gentle precision. He blew upon the board with a soft breath, a mere whisper of divine intervention. The *black queen* shimmered, its surface rippling and fading until it transformed into a gleaming *white queen.*

"Not so fast," God's voice, steady and calm, cut through the thick despair, resonating with a quiet power.

The Cosmic Chessboard trembled again, the echoes of the devilish laughter fading, its grip loosening as if caught by an invisible wind.

THE SERPENT

L exie's steps were slow and heavy with the weight of her
actions, as she ascended the staircase. Each step upward
stretched into eternity. Memories and emotions swirled around
her, yet a fierce, newfound sense of resolve rose to meet them.
She reached the top, stopping at the doorway where William lay
still, his figure outlined by the light filtering through the cracked
bedroom window.

A surge of strength that she couldn't fully explain rose within
her. She knelt beside him, her fingers trembling as they brushed
against his cold, still face. Her heart thundered, yet there was a
calm clarity in her soul—a presence that guided her. She closed her
eyes, tears streaming as she lifted her face and prayed to God, her
heart breaking under the weight of desperation. She whispered,
her voice, raw and wavering:

"Lord, I come before You, broken and pleading. I know I've
been a stranger to your word. I've never believed in your existence.
But I want to believe. I need to believe. If you are there, if you will
be so kind, dear Lord, please, hear me. I know I've doubted, I've
feared, and I've strayed, but I'm here now, asking for mercy that I
don't deserve. William... he's my everything, even when I've been
too blind to see it. Even when we've hurt each other, he's still the

man You brought into my life, the one I vowed to love through every storm.

"Father, I know we've failed You, and I know I've let anger and doubt lead my heart. But, Lord, I can't lose him. Please, I beg You to reach down and restore his life. Breathe Your spirit into him, heal what is broken, and bring him back to me—not for my sake, but for the love we've shared and for the future we can still build together.

"I don't understand Your plan, and I know I don't deserve to ask anything of You, but You are the God of miracles, the One who restores what seems lost. If there is still hope, Lord, let it be in this moment. Let William wake, let him live, and let us find our way back to You, together.

"I surrender it all to You, God—my fears, my anger, my pain. If it is Your will, I ask You to restore William's life, even if it means sacrificing my own. If You bring him back, I promise to trust You, to follow You, and to love him the way You've called me to. Please, Lord, forgive me for breaking the sixth commandment, *Thou shalt not kill,* I am truly devastated by what I've done. Don't take him from me. Cleanse me of my sins, Lord, and hear the cry of my heart. I ask for forgiveness in the name of Jesus Christ, my Savior. Amen."

Her voice broke on the final word as she bowed her head, tears pooling with the blood on the floor beneath her. In the quiet that followed, the room held its breath, and she waited, her heart clinging to the faintest glimmer of hope.

Lexie held her hand over his chest, but not even the faintest hint of a heartbeat stirred beneath her palm. This leap of faith—daring and delicate—left no room for hesitation. Her fingers pressed into the fabric of his blood-soaked shirt, as she surrendered completely, casting aside the resentment, the hurt, and the doubts. Instead, she let her love and compassion for William surge forth, offering it up as her plea for redemption.

She didn't know what would happen next. Lexie waited, her breath suspended, her heart steady as she opened her eyes and took in the stillness around her.

A shift in the air, subtle at first, like the entire world stopped to listen. The shadows along the walls lengthened, curling at the edges, moving in ways they shouldn't.

A voice. Deep. Resonant. Final.

"You and William have listened to the Devil and done his bidding. You've committed unspeakable sins, and your vicious words to each other have dripped with the snake's venom. And now you pray for forgiveness. The Devil's influence is powerful, yet you must resist temptation. If you and William want to walk side by side with Me, and have My grace, you are required to be steadfast in your commitment to My word. I am the Lord."

Lexie's entire body froze. The voice echoed everywhere and nowhere, filling the space around her, inside her. A presence so vast, its weight pressed against the edges of her soul. Tears streamed down her face. "Who—" But she knew. The presence did not belong to the Devil. God had made his move.

At first, there was this deafening silence. But a shift—a faint, subtle stirring within the room, and the air grew dense, thick, heavy with energy she could almost touch. A whisper of wind brushed past her, growing stronger, until it escalated into a powerful whirlwind that spun through the room, making her hair whip around her face, tugging at her clothes as if some invisible force had descended upon them both.

A blend of coldness and warmth, the supernatural gale seeped into her bones. Lexie's eyes widened, and her pulse raced. Something stirred, something vast. This wind held no place in the natural world. It defied reason, defied understanding. She held onto her faith, her heart swelling with awe.

The whirlwind reached William, brushing over his still form and filling his lungs with an unearthly chill. Lexie's heart raced as his chest rose and fell in shallow breaths. His hand twitched, his fingers curling, as though the grip of death had been loosened, its hold on him slipping.

"William..." Her voice trembled, his eyelids blinked and opened. His eyes were unfocused, disoriented, but she could see life in them, a spark that hadn't been there. He glanced around the room as if emerging from a dream, struggling to make sense of his surroundings.

He pushed himself up with sluggish movements, his shirt still soaked in the blood that clung to him like shadows. Lexie held her breath, watching in stunned silence as he struggled to his feet, each motion laced with a kind of raw, unfamiliar weakness, like a man reborn yet still bearing the marks of death. She stayed kneeling, eyes fixed on him, waiting for him to fully awaken, hoping that what was coming back to life wasn't the man she had fought against, but the man she had once loved.

Lexie leaned forward; her voice gentle yet commanding. "William," she said, "you're here. You're alive."

William blinked at Lexie, his expression a mix of confusion and surprise as the cold, blood-stained shirt clung to his skin. His fingers brushed over the fabric, touching the dried blood as if unable to comprehend its meaning. Yet, even in his dazed state, he sensed something profound had changed—something he couldn't yet grasp.

"Lexie... what happened?" he rasped, his voice hoarse and weak.

Lexie did not move. She couldn't. Her pulse roared in her ears. This defied reality. It made no sense. But William breathed—alive. Staring straight at her. And he knew.

He knew she had killed him.

Her entire world tilted as William pushed himself up onto his elbows, his expression unreadable. Lexie's chest tightened. He looked different now. Not just alive—transformed.

In a quiet voice, he finally spoke.

"A huge chessboard..."

Lexie blinked. "A chessboard?"

His jaw clenched and his eyes darkened. "The one *they* were playing on."

A chill wrapped around her spine and her pulse pounded. "Who?"

"We were pawns on this gigantic chessboard. Moved and manipulated at will by God and the Devil. All the bad things, it wasn't us, it's not who we are—we would never be that cruel to each other."

"We were pawns?" Lexie asked.

"God showed me." William said, his voice hoarse, disbelieving. "The Devil moved a chess piece, and God moved a chess piece."

Lexie grimaced, her face flushed a bright red. She had played right into it. She had killed him because she believed she had no other choice, because the Devil wanted her to, forced her to. And yet—God had changed the rules.

William inhaled, pressing a hand to his chest, feeling for the life that had been given back to him. "I was dead, Lexie. I felt it. I was...gone." His voice dropped to a whisper. "And He brought me back."

Lexie swallowed hard, her entire body trembling. "Why?"

"I don't know why."

Lexie nodded. "I think I do," Lexie whispered. "God answered my prayers. He sent you back to me."

William smiled, and her heart surged with fierce protectiveness, a conviction that steadied her. This was her moment to take control, to be the one who chose mercy over vengeance, faith over despair. She rose to her feet, offering him her hand, her eyes fierce with purpose.

"You have been given a second chance," she said, her tone unwavering. "We both have."

A shiver ran through her as the invisible presence lifted, like a gentle release, leaving them in the quiet aftermath. It was done; the prayer had been answered, and a new path had been carved from the ashes of their mistakes. God had intervened, but it was her plea, her faith, which had turned the tides.

William took her hand, his grip weak yet steady. Together, they made their way out of the room, each step like a cleansing rebirth. For the first time, the pieces on the Cosmic Chessboard had shifted in her favor, as if a checkmate that had once been inevitable had dissolved into a new beginning.

The silent promise of divine intervention hung in the air, a reminder that even in their darkest hour, there had been light.

As Lexie and William descended the stairs, the stillness of the house wrapped around them, broken only by their quiet footsteps. Lexie's hand remained entwined with William's; their fingers laced together in a silent acknowledgment of the miracle that had taken place. Her heart was steady, but her thoughts raced, filled with the echoes of their past—the mistakes, the heartbreak, the moments that had driven them apart. But at this moment, there was a profound sense of calm.

As they reached the living room, William's eyes widened, and Lexie turned and witnessed the transformation. She gasped. Before them stood Carol, but not as she remembered. This was a vision, an ethereal transformation that left Lexie comforted in her presence.

Carol's figure stood bathed in a bright white light, her familiar white hat was no longer an accessory but a halo that crowned her in a gentle, divine glow. Her clothing shifted before their eyes, transforming into a white gown that shimmered like the surface of a tranquil lake under the morning sun. The light, warm and enveloping, reached out and filled the room, touching every corner and every shadow.

Lexie's eyes were fixed on Carol with both awe and a strange sense of peace as if she were in the presence of something far beyond human understanding. It was a breathtaking vision. The massive white wings, soft and radiant, unfurled from Carol's back. Each feather pulsed with a celestial glow, shimmering with subtle, quiet energy. The feathers stretched outward, casting their warmth over Lexie, cocooning her in a tranquility that had escaped her for years.

Carol's angelic image held something both familiar and ancient, a kindness that spoke to their heart. She spoke in a low tone; her voice layered with authority and tenderness that transcended words.

"William will be William again, and you, Lexie, will be yourself once more," she began, her voice resonating with a depth that reached past their defenses, "And yes, you will bear William's son. God's miracle is upon you. This is His will. Trust in the Lord. Have faith, and do not despair."

Lexie's hand went to her abdomen, and an indescribable warmth bloomed within her, a new life, a presence—awakening inside her, like the faintest pulse of energy. It was subtle, yet undeniable, confirmation that sent tears welling up in her eyes. William's hand tightened over her hand, his own eyes widening in amazement as he followed her gesture, realizing the weight of Carol's words.

"Lexie... you're... we're having a child?"

Lexie nodded, her emotions spilling over as she glanced at him, seeing the same astonishment and wonder mirrored in his expression.

"Yes, William," she cried. "We're going to have a son."

"What if I fail?" William asked.

"You won't fail, not with God on our side."

In that instant, everything—their fractured past, the arguments, the betrayals—faded into the background. The struggles that were once insurmountable were dwarfed by the enormity of the gift they were being given. This child, this miracle, was their chance to begin anew, to create something that was theirs alone, untouched by the darkness they had both endured.

As they stood there, Carol's wings wrapped around them like a blessing, filling Lexie with deep reassurance. Her soul, once scarred and weary, is now healed, infused with hope and strength. William's hand nudged hers. She opened her palm, and he took her hand in his. He regarded her with a vulnerability she hadn't seen in him in years. Her William had returned to her, the man she had once fallen in love with, the man who had been buried beneath layers of pain, bitterness, and manipulation.

Carol's angelic presence began to fade, the light around her dimmed as she dissolved back to her real self. Carol didn't seem to register the time gap or the change of clothes. She glanced at William and Lexie.

"I guess my work is done here."

"Thank you, Carol. Thank you... for everything," William said.

"My pleasure." Carol walked to the door and turned back. "Let me know before you start on the next book; I have some ideas for a series."

William nodded. A smile spread across his face.

But Lexie could still hear the angel's voice, a final whisper that settled into Lexie's heart like a promise. *God's miracle is upon you. Fear not, and do not despair.*

Carol was gone, leaving Lexie and William standing alone in the soft glow of the room, as if the walls had absorbed her light.

Lexie let out a shuddering breath, turning to William with tears still glistening in her eyes. "We've been given a second chance, William. For us and for him," she said, her hand resting on her abdomen, where that new life was stirring once more.

William's face softened, and he brought his hand over hers, covering it with a tenderness that caught her off guard. "Lexie," he whispered, his voice choked with emotion, "I don't deserve this. I don't deserve you."

She shook her head, lifting her other hand to cradle his face. "Neither of us is without fault, William. But we've been given grace—grace to start over, to be who we're meant to be. This... this child... is a symbol of that grace, a reminder that we don't have to be perfect. But we must be willing to change."

His eyes searched her eyes. For the first time, something broke within him, a softening, a vulnerability that he had fought to keep hidden for so long. He pressed his forehead to hers, closing his eyes as he held onto her like a lifeline.

"We can do this, Lexie. The book will sell—and even if it doesn't, we'll be okay. I'm determined to make you proud," he whispered. "I can be better—for you, for him."

"You already are." Lexie smiled.

And at that moment, Lexie's faith solidified her, grounded her, and gave her a strength she hadn't known she possessed. Her life rearranged like the shifting pieces of a Cosmic Chessboard that had once been locked in opposition now moving together, their purpose aligned in ways she hadn't thought possible.

They stood in silence, each wrapped in the other's warmth, letting the realization settle around them. A new chapter was beginning, one built on faith and hope, on a love that had weathered the fiercest storms. For the first time, William and Lexie fully grasped the weight of their journey—their prayers, their sacrifices—each step now leading them toward a future filled with the promise of healing and redemption.

Lexie looked deep into William's eyes, the man she had fallen in love with all those years ago—the man who, despite everything, still held her heart.

"I love you, William," Lexie stated.

"I love you more," he whispered, his voice raw with emotion.

And now, Lexie had her William, her king, back.

Hand in hand, they turned and walked forward, stepping into the unknown, carrying with them the memory of Carol's blessing and the quiet assurance that they were no longer bound by their past. Together, they would face whatever came next, not as adversaries or wounded souls, but as partners, as parents, and as people who had been forever changed by the miracle of God's grace.

In a realm far beyond mortal comprehension, high above the veil that shrouds human sight, the final move is made. The Cosmic Chessboard, vast and boundless, lies suspended in the dark void. Each piece glows with an inner light or smoldering darkness, representing the choices, battles, and hearts it has influenced. This board was more than a game—it was a theater of manipulation and resilience, a silent testament to the clash of souls William and Lexie have unknowingly fought for.

At one end of the board, a hand clad in a spotless *White Glove* hovered with purpose. The hand of God embodied timeless patience and unerring vision. His fingers rest over the *white queen,* a piece maneuvered across the board with the careful grace of love and forgiveness, embodying the spirit of Lexie's relentless faith, her quiet strength, and her capacity to forgive. At every turn, she resisted the lure of bitterness, the dark seed of mistrust that the Devil planted with cunning precision.

With a deliberate motion, God's *White-Gloved Hand* lifts the white queen and sets her down on the board with undeniable certainty. As the piece lands, a powerful *Boom* echoes across the heavenly plane, a sound that reverberates into eternity, sending tremors through every shadowed corner of the universe.

God's deep voice echoed through the celestial void.

"Checkmate."

"Damn! A Hail Mary!" The Devil's anguished, frustrated growl ripped through the heavens.

A low guttural snarl cuts through the silence and the darkness. It is the Devil's voice, dripping with venomous frustration, His tone filled with the bitterness of a plan unraveled. For so long, He has moved His pieces with precise skill, seeking to isolate William and Lexie, twisting their love, warping it with seeds of doubt and jealousy. Every choice, every whisper in the dark, was meant to fracture them, to corrupt their faith in each other and turn their love into a battlefield.

The last flare of a defeated mind that once took pride in his machinations. His growl fades, the bitterness of centuries dissipating into the void, as the weight of his defeat settles. His influence over them, once a dark thread binding their hearts, frays, and dissolves, leaving the pure, resilient love they have reclaimed.

Darkness consumes the scene as the chess game dissolves, the light of God's final move overtaking it, washing over the board with a quiet brilliance that obliterates every shadow of manipulation, every falsehood. The board fades from sight, leaving silence in its wake—a stillness that speaks of a conflict resolved, an enduring peace that cannot be disturbed.

The dawn edges its way into the world, casting the Grant family's home in a soft, misty glow. From heavens above, something hurtles downward, a fiery object slicing through the mist. It is the remnants of the Cosmic Chessboard, a burning symbol of the struggle that has finally ended.

With a resounding *Thud*, the board lands on the Grant's front lawn, smoldering and scorched, embedding itself into the earth with a force that shakes the ground. The grass blackens in a perfect circle around it, a mark of the dark influence that has been cast down. Beside the Cosmic Chessboard lies an enormous black serpent, its once-glossy scales now dull and lifeless. This creature—the embodiment of lies, of whispers and doubts—had once coiled around William and Lexie's minds, tightening its hold with every seed of distrust and evil deeds it sowed.

The serpent lies motionless, defeated, the twisted energy that had once animated it drained to nothing. Its form slackens, scales peeling as the remnants of its dark influence dissipate into the dawn, a reminder of the corrosive power that once threatened to break William and Lexie. This serpent had been the Devil's instrument, whispering half-truths, and fueling their fears, feeding on every moment of anger and sorrow. Now, its power is gone, leaving behind the scorched ground—a shadow that will soon fade under the morning sun.

A deep, resonant laughter rolls across the sky, breaking the silence. It is a sound rich and triumphant, full of warmth and wisdom. It is the laughter of a victor who has seen through every deception, who has outwitted every trap. This is God's laughter—a celebration of a love reclaimed, a bond renewed, a victory over the forces that sought to twist and tarnish it.

As the dawn's light spreads, casting its golden glow over the Grant's home, the remnants of the battle dissolve into the peaceful morning. The defeated serpent begins to disintegrate, its dark form lifting like mist under the warming rays. Its essence, its poison, banished from their lives, leaves a quiet serenity behind.

The fiery Cosmic Chessboard cools, the once-gleaming pieces dulled as they settle into the earth, no longer needed in this game. The dark energies that once consumed Lexie and William are now scattered, leaving a sweet and soft scent of dawn, a new beginning, free from shadows.

The light grows stronger, washing over the Grants' home with a warmth that seeps into every corner, an invisible shield of protection and peace. The burdens they have carried, the doubts they have endured, are lifted, leaving only a love that has been tested and strengthened.

The sun climbs higher, brightening the day, as victory settles over them, a promise that light has triumphed over darkness, that faith has overcome despair. The power of the Almighty rests upon their lives, unyielding and eternal, casting away the last traces of manipulation and binding them with an abundance of joy and peace that cannot be disturbed.

—◆—

Thanks For Reading! Please CLICK HERE to leave a review.
If you enjoyed this, you may also enjoy SinSation!

ABOUT THE AUTHOR

Kathryn McGrady is an accomplished author and film-maker whose creative voice spans multiple genres and for-mats. Writing both fiction and nonfiction, she explores the emotional weight of relationships, often layered with suspense, psychological depth, and spirituality. Her background in film and storytelling brings a cinematic richness to her work, inviting readers into worlds, some imaginary, some real, where boldness, tension, and transformation collide.

Beyond writing, Kathryn is a visual artist, coloring book creator, and an unapologetic lover of word games. She can often be found behind camera lens, filming, other times immersed in a marathon of gripping television dramas or locked in a fierce yet friendly game of Scrabble.

Thank you so much for taking the time to read my novel. Subscribe to my newsletter by CLICKING HERE to grab your free copy of "I Was Not Innocent".

To connect with Kathryn
Visit her website: https://www.kathrynmcgrady.com
www.amazon.com/author/kathrynmcgrady
www.instagram.com/kathrynmcgradybooks
www.tiktok.com/@visionkbooks
www.pinterest.com/visionkbooks

ALSO BY

FICTION
A Killing at Early Dawn
Redemption By Default
SinSation
Dinner With Lexie (A short story)
The Silent Syringe (A short story)
The Queen's Quest (A short story)
ALL-IN (A short story)
The Good Daughter (A short story)
Free Psychological Thriller Novella: I Was Not Innocent
You can pre-order **Sin of the Priest** on Amazon by CLICKING HERE

NONFICTION
Letting Him Go When He Cheats
The Treasured Coloring Book Collection For Toddlers